Bullets for Silverware

Jim Antonini

Pump Fake Press—Morgantown, WV
ISBN: 978-0-578-67121-5
Library of Congress Control Number: 2020907827
Title: Bullets for Silverware
Author: Jim Antonini
Digital distribution | 2020
Paperback | 2020

This is a work of fiction. The characters, names, incidents, places, and dialogue are products of the author's imagination, and are not to be construed as real.

Dedication

For Grant Hart and finding home.

Caldwell, West Virginia was nowhere. And I chose to go there. I could have moved anywhere I wanted. Sure, the pay was great for a kid in his early twenties, just days out of college. But I was leaving just as much, or even more, behind in Pittsburgh- an invitation to medical school, a talented and successful fiancée, and a comfortable, familiar way of life. And I really liked that way of life. But I needed out. I wanted to discover who I was and if I could make it on my own. I wanted a challenge. As it turned out, I got more than a challenge. I would never be the same.

Chapter 1
Sorry Somehow

Caldwell County, West Virginia.

It was a clear late September night in an unnamed hollow (pronounced 'holler' by the locals) hidden in a valley among a collection of green hills that rolled into one another. There was a coolness to the air, hinting that winter was not far behind. A tied-up pit bull barked, and a coal train whistled in the distance. The muffled sound of Johnny Dowd records played from inside a rundown rusted mobile home trailer, miles from anything that resembled civilization and a lifetime away from the real-world. The nearest stoplight was sixty-five miles away. The closest McDonald's was much further than that.

Inside the front room of the trailer, two local backwood types, Johnny Fogg and Tolly Atwater, sat at a table covered with bottles of cheap whiskey, beer, and assorted pills and drug paraphernalia. The Dowd song, *"Butcher's Son"*, blared from a record-player console cabinet filled with bullet holes and cigarette burns. Johnny smashed oxycontin tablets with the butt of a handgun. Dragging hard on a cigarette, Tolly baited a strung-out young pharmacist named Aaron Morgan, who nervously fidgeted by a broken screen door.

"Hey, pretty boy?" Tolly taunted Aaron. "I went to the drug store today. Where were you?"

"Fuck off."

"What happened? Finally get your candy-ass fired?"

Aaron didn't respond. The two glared at each other.

"Yeah, that's what I thought. They were all talkin' about it this mornin'. We wondered what took 'em so long."

Aaron had indeed been fired from the pharmacy the night before. Having lost complete control of his life due to alcohol and opiates, he no longer could make it to work on time or, on some days, even at all. He was embarrassed and frustrated- frustrated by a life that didn't turn out as it should have but even more frustrated by a life that brought his mother shame. She had always been proud of him. Haunted by demons after taking the job to work at the local pharmacy in Caldwell, Aaron fell victim to the same temptations that took his father's life at an early age. Aaron was supposed to be the lucky one who beat the odds of being raised by a single mother on welfare in a lost part of West Virginia, approximately forty-five miles south of Caldwell.

Growing up in squalor in an unpainted wooden shack without running water, he had little food, torn clothes, and no guidance. He had nothing. His toys were the rocks and strings he found around the shack, and his playground was a nearby polluted creek he tossed them into. But fortunately, because of his superior intellect, he was awarded a prestigious scholarship for the underprivileged at the state university. The goal of the program was to graduate in pharmacy and return to one's hometown to work in the local drug store. He did fine in school, maintaining perfect grades with little effort. He was, however, more legendary for mostly living on a daily diet of ninety-nine cent mini-cheeseburgers and twelve-packs of Busch beer. With the sudden boost in pay after taking the job in Caldwell, he slowly graduated from beer to whiskey- lots of whiskey, all night drinking marathons of nothing but whiskey. To help take the edge off the brutal morning hangovers in order to work (and with the easy access to every drug imaginable at the pharmacy), he quickly moved from alcohol to Xanax, then Vicodin, and eventually opiate injectables.

In a gutted backroom of the trailer, the fat local pharmacist, James Butterman, counted pills and added them to small plastic Ziploc bags. He placed the scores of plastic bags into larger paper Avon sacks, before stapling them shut. His phone rang constantly. Not once did he answer it or even check the number to see who was calling. Sweating profusely, he rushed to complete the orders as quickly as possible because he had an unusually large number of deliveries to make the next morning. He didn't like to keep anyone waiting. Some of his best customers could get desperate, and in his business, he learned a long time ago that a desperate customer was a dangerous customer. The only thing he didn't understand regarding the current bump in business was the local economy had been hurting. It had always struggled, but no one had remembered it being that depressed. Many of coal mines were shut down, and the oil and gas companies had shipped in workers from Texas and Oklahoma instead of hiring the locals. And everyone knew Butterman had the goods to escape the current reality if needed. Life in the hollow could be slow, especially if you had nothing to do and nowhere to go.

As Johnny melted crushed pill pieces with a lighter and a spoon in the front room, Tolly reached for the handgun on the table and aimed it.

"Johnny? Johnny!"

Johnny briefly glanced up to Tolly who aimed a gun at him, before looking back to the syringe.

"You'd only be doin' me a favor," Johnny replied, injecting himself with the milky-white solution he pulled from the spoon.

"Leave 'em alone, asshole!" Aaron called out.

Tolly quickly stood and turned, pointing the gun at Aaron.

"Drop the gun, if you think you're so tough."

Still aiming the gun, Tolly slowly stepped towards Aaron.

"You're not so tough."

"You think you're better than me, college boy?"

Tolly stared Aaron down, still pointing the gun at him.

"You're so fucked. Hide in this rat hole all day. Butterman had to get another druggist. Can't do the drug runs alone no more. Can't keep hours at the drug store. You're nuthin' but an overeducated, worthless piece of shit!"

A loud thud distracted Tolly as Johnny passed out, striking his head on the table, face first- the needle still in his arm. As Tolly glanced to the noise, Aaron charged. The gun dropped to the floor as Aaron lifted Tolly off his feet. The two rolled around on the floor, knocking over furniture, and banging against walls. Aaron had one of Tolly's arm pinned behind his back, pressing, and pushing his face into the worn and stained shag carpet. At the same time, Tolly yanked at a fistful of Aaron's long and greasy blonde hair. In a tight, violent embrace, they eventually struggled back to their feet scratching, pinching, gouging, and kicking at each other.

"I thought you'd be tougher than this!" Aaron grumbled, nearly out of breath- his face flushed red.

"I heard what you like!" Tolly barked, tightly wrapping his arms around Aaron neck, trying to strangle him.

"It wouldn't look so good, gettin' your ass kicked by me!" Aaron shouted.

Squatting and pushing himself far enough away, Aaron delivered a hard kick to Tolly's testicles, dropping him to the ground in obvious and extreme pain. As Aaron tried to kick him again, Tolly grabbed his leg and pulled him down to the ground, causing Aaron to strike the back of his head hard on the floor.

"You're dead man, motherfucker!" Tolly warned, quickly scanning the floor for the gun he had dropped.

The scuffling noises in the front part of the trailer had distracted Butterman who suddenly appeared in the room.

"What in the hell?" Butterman yelled.

As Tolly searched for the gun, he continued to kick Aaron who had been knocked unconscious and bleeding from the mouth and nose.

"Stop it!" Butterman shouted. "Stop it, you fucking inbred!"

Butterman spotted the gun at his feet and scooped it up. Tolly quickly stood and turned. Without hesitation, Butterman pulled the trigger.

BANG!

Pittsburgh, Pennsylvania.

A cork from a champagne bottle popped. Startled, I momentarily ducked and covered my head at the unexpected loud noise. I was at a party to celebrate my graduation from pharmacy school. Even though the party was held in my honor, I was a little uncomfortable as I knew only a few of the folks there. It was quite the festive scene with nearly one-hundred people in attendance. The party was being thrown for me by the parents of my fiancée, Meredith Stone. I was grateful to her parents for taking time out of their busy schedules to do this for me, but for all intents and purposes, the party was as much a celebration for them as it was for me. Throwing parties and entertaining were what the Stone family did extremely well. But more importantly for me, Meredith was coming home to visit for my graduation. She had been living in Houston at the time, and I couldn't wait to see her.

The party was held in a swanky gated neighborhood a mile or two outside of downtown Pittsburgh at their palatial family estate- a fifteen-room, three-story, turn-of-the-century Tudor-style house complete with swimming pool, tennis courts, maid, and gardener. Dr. Stone had done well for himself and his family. He had been a successful radiologist in Pittsburgh for over twenty years. I always felt awkward, and out of place at their home. Although technically only four miles to the south on the Allegheny River, it was a world away from the hard scrabble, working class mill town where I had grown up.

"So, you're Michael?" a blushed and swollen-faced party stranger asked.

"Yessir."

"I hear 'ol Bob Stone is talking you into radiology," he said, glancing around before whispering. "Dermatology is the way to go. Don't tell, but we never cure anyone. My patients keep coming back, and so do their itches and rashes. Allergies are a bitch, my boy."

Meredith's father, who I never connected with, mostly because of our different upbringings and backgrounds, pushed me, maybe a little too enthusiastically, to apply to medical school. I'm sure he expected his daughter and only child to marry a doctor. But I wasn't a one-hundred percent sold on continuing my education at that time. I was exhausted, and more than a little burnt out. I needed a break from the classroom. Also, I promised my grandmother that I'd not only pay the mortgage off on her current house at the time, but I'd help buy her a new house in a better neighborhood. Going to medical school would push that promise back several more years and surely sink me into even greater debt. And I knew my grandmother didn't have that much time.

"I'm not sure about medical school yet," I answered the stranger.

"Who wouldn't go to medical school if given the chance?"

I nodded and excused myself to the snack table. I kept checking the front door. Meredith was to arrive any minute. It had been many months since I had last seen her. I badly missed her. It had been a lonely two years without her.

"Your parents must be proud," said a bedazzled woman who did her best to look thirty years younger than she was, wearing a gold lame top and tight designer denim jeans. "I heard you finished number one in your class. Congratulations!"

But I never knew my parents. Not wanting to explain, I politely nodded and thanked her as she filled a tiny plate with exotic cheeses and Italian meats before disappearing into the crowd gathered in the dining room. I basically was alone at the party, having been raised by my grandmother on my mother's side. My grandmother had declined an invitation to the party. She, like myself, often felt overwhelmed or intimidated by such an event. I had lost my mother at any early age to breast cancer, and I never knew my father. He left soon after I was born. When I was a baby, my mother was never around, and I don't remember a thing about her. I was told she had to work multiple jobs to support us.

I spent most of my time with my grandmother, too young to process my father's absence or my mother's death. My grandmother took great care of me. I was well-fed, well-loved, and extremely fortunate. I wouldn't trade my childhood for anything. She treated me like a prince. But something was missing- a longing that couldn't be described unless one had grown up without parents. I could never shake the feeling I was waiting for something. But I wasn't sure for what- maybe for my father to return. Even if he never came back, I prayed each night that he remembered me and thought of me. Because I thought of him- always, although we never met. Despite the warmth, comfort, and security my grandmother provided, her house always seemed somewhat empty, and sadly, never felt like home.

My grandmother made sure I didn't miss school and always completed my school assignments on time. When I turned fourteen, she sent me to work in the neighborhood drug store, manning the cash register. On busy days, the druggist sometimes would let me help fill prescriptions orders. I guess that's where the whole drug store-pharmacist thing came from. It could have ended much worse for me. I was lucky, and I guess smart, at least good in the classroom and with exams. Through hard work, a second mortgage on my grandmother's house, some financial aid, and a partial scholarship, I was accepted to a prestigious private university in Pittsburgh to study pharmacy.

Fortunately, I breezed through pharmacy school, clinical rotations, and a community drug store internship. I graduated with a near perfect academic record. My advisor and other faculty members were pushing for me to continue my education in medical school, as was Meredith. I had met her early in my first year of pharmacy school. We had worked together on a local community outreach program. She was a junior nursing student and a couple of years older than I was. She also had done well in school, making the dean's list every semester, and graduating at the top of her nursing class. After graduation, she left for Houston, enrolling in a master's program in public health.

Obviously, I found Meredith attractive. When I first met her, I couldn't keep my eyes off her. But more than that, I was struck by her maturity, confidence, and empathy for others less fortunate than her. And she was only twenty years old. We got to know each other after working together on several community projects. It took me months before I could get up the courage to ask her out. Once I did, we started dating and enjoyed an exciting and drama-free two years together before she graduated. On the night before she left for Houston, I proposed to her. Somewhat to my surprise, she said 'yes' without hesitation.

Finally, the front door opened, and Meredith entered the foyer. She looked stunning, and different. I almost didn't recognize her. She appeared older and more cosmopolitan with a new style of hair and clothes. Glancing around, she set down her luggage. But before she could get too far inside the house, I intercepted her. We immediately hugged.

"God, you smell nice."

She softly kissed my ear and whispered, "I've missed you."

"I'm glad you're home."

She started to walk into the party.

"Hold on a minute."

"Is everything all right?"

"Can we talk in private?"

"I haven't even said 'hello' to my parents yet," she said, staring into the crowded kitchen.

"It's important."

Still scanning the kitchen, Meredith nodded as I led her down a set of hallways to a spare bedroom. We slipped into the room and closed the door behind us. I playfully started nibbling her neck. Giggling, we fell back onto the bed piled with jackets and handbags. I crawled on top of her, nearly smothering her as I ran my hands over her body.

"Michael?" she said, continuing to giggle. "Slow down."

"I've missed you so much."

She pushed me off and sat up. Looking down, she stared at me. I glanced away.

"You're not going to medical school, are you?"

I didn't immediately answer.

"I had a sense you were leaning that way."

"I'm sorry."

"My father will be disappointed."

"But it's my life."

"Our life," she said, getting up and pacing the floor.

"I want to experience the real world. I've lived my whole life in a classroom."

"We're engaged to be married."

"This doesn't change anything. I just can't go back to school- not now."

"I know, but..."

"What does it matter if I'm doctor today, tomorrow, or ten years from now. I want to set out on my own. I want to make my own way, my own name.

I want to experience something new, something totally different."

She turned to me. We briefly stared at each other. She glanced away.

"You knew I had my doubts about med school," I said, standing up from the bed and approaching her. "It'll all work out."

"I have a surprise as well."

"Yeah?" I said, wrapping my arms around her.

"I'm moving back to Pittsburgh."

"What?"

"I took a faculty position at Pitt. We can finally be together."

I pulled away from her and turned my back.

"Michael?"

"I took a job in Caldwell County, West Virginia with Super-Rite Drugs."

"West Virginia?"

"There's a shortage of pharmacists in rural West Virginia..."

"And not Pittsburgh?"

"But I didn't know you were coming back so soon."

"What's your grandmother think?"

"You're the first person I've told."

"Why West Virginia?"

"They're paying me an obscene amount of money. No one will go to Caldwell. It's only for a year."

I moved over to her, and we embraced.

"I don't like this," she said, shaking her head.

"I thought you were coming home next year."

"I wanted it to be a surprise- a graduation gift."

"You should have told me."

"I didn't think you'd get a job in another state."

"It's only a five-hour drive from here."

"What will my family think?"

"It's not forever. I'll make some money. I'll pay off my student loans. And you know, I promised to help my grandmother buy a new house."

"When do you go?"

"I have to be at work on Monday."

"This Monday?"

"I need this," I answered, nodding.

"I know, Michael, but I don't like it at all."

With a handgun stained with bloody fingerprints on the table in front of him, Johnny remained passed out in a chair. Splotches of blood dotted the front of his flannel shirt, face, and the Pabst Blue Ribbon Beer trucker hat he always wore. Tolly's lifeless body was slumped at the bottom of a wall in a pool of clotted blood. A large hole had been blown out of the middle of his head where his face used to be. A wide streak of blood ran down the wall behind him. He no long looked human but more like a prop from a horror movie.

The sun had just come up. The pit-bull in front started to bark as a Cadillac Escalade parked. Butterman entered the trailer. He slammed a bottle of bleach on the table and kicked Johnny's leg.

"Get up!"

Johnny struggled to open his eyes.

"Clean your fucking mess!"

Johnny sat up forward. Confused, he scanned the room, first noticing the blood, then the gun in front of him, and last, Tolly's body.

"No! No! Tolly?"

"You got to get off the dope, Johnny. It's killing you and your friends."

"Tolly!" he shrieked, shaking his head, and staring at the gun, before glancing up to Butterman.

"You just doubled your deliveries this morning. And there's a lot of 'em."

"What?" Johnny continued to shake his head.

"Now get up and get rid of the body before someone finds it!"

Not moving from the chair, Johnny shook his head in disbelief, staring at the body.

"I said, get up!" Butterman shouted, throwing a mop at Johnny who ducked out of the way. "Get up, goddammit!"

Butterman charged Johnny and violently grabbed the front of his shirt, dragging him from the chair and slamming him to the ground into the puddle of blood next to Tolly's dead body. Butterman picked up the mopped and again threw it at Johnny.

"Why'd you do it, Johnny? Why'd you kill your best friend?"

"I didn't kill no one," he said, shaking his head.

"Don't lie to me, Johnny!"

Still looking confused, Johnny shook his head. Butterman kicked a bucket at Johnny. The mucky water splashed all over him.

"The deliveries are ready to go. They're in the back room. You got a busy day today. I better not see a speck of blood in this place when I get back. You hear me?"

Johnny nervously nodded and stared at Butterman who pulled out an envelope with cash and tossed it at him.

"Just because you killed your partner, and there's only one of you now, don't think I increased your pay."

As Johnny reached for the envelope, Butterman left the trailer with a slam of the door.

It was just after daybreak on the Sunday morning I would leave for Caldwell. My car was loaded and ready to go. As my departure time neared, I felt more nervous than ever. I was having second thoughts about the decision. I had spent a tearful night before eating dinner with my grandmother to say goodbye. She certainly didn't want me to go, and because she was in her eighties and lived alone, it made leaving even harder. In addition, I hadn't seen Meredith or barely heard from her since the graduation party. We hadn't been calling or texting much. It seemed easier that way for both of us. I felt somewhat guilty for leaving, and even sorry somehow. I wished I had known she was coming home for good. Both of our lives certainly would have turned out differently.

As I pulled out my phone to try and call her one last time before I left, her dad's luxury pick-up truck pulled into the driveway. Meredith got out and approached slowly.

"I was just going call…"

Before I could finish, she wrapped her arms around me and held me tightly.

"It's not forever," I whispered.

"I know. But it still hurts the same."

"The time will go fast. You'll see."

"Please stay in Pittsburgh and get a pharmacist job here."

"I already signed the contract."

She pulled away from me.

"I'll only be a few hours away."

"What about your medical school slot?"

"I'd have to re-apply next year. They can't save it for me."

Both of us wiped tears from our eyes.

"I better go. I'm supposed to meet the other pharmacist there at the store later this afternoon."

"It seems we're always saying goodbye."

"We'll talk all the time. I promise."

"But still..."

"I'll be working nearly every day. I'll save some money, then go back to school, and we'll get married."

She nodded and tried to smile as I got into the car. She studied me as I started the engine. Before I could put the car in gear, she leaned into the driver's side window. We gently kissed. Trying my hardest to keep it together, I slowly pulled out of the driveway and briefly glanced into the rear-view mirror. She waved goodbye as I drove away from a contented way of living, hoping it wasn't a mistake.

Under a mostly sunny sky, I easily navigated the sleepy Sunday morning streets of downtown Pittsburgh. Like never before, all the traffic lights were green. I was mostly alone on the road, zipping in and out of the early morning shadows cast by the tall city buildings. I passed eateries and watering holes I enjoyed with friends and Meredith. Merging onto a highway bypass, I circled around Heinz Field and PNC Park, the palaces of worships for the many local sport fans in the area. I crossed a series of bridges over the Allegheny and Monongahela rivers, two of the three rivers which come together at a point where the city started. At the end of a bridge, I slid my sunglasses up on my forehead as the car disappeared into the blackness of the Fort Pitt Tunnel. The music from the radio gradually went silent as I moved deeper into the tunnel, replaced only by the hum of the car's engine as I left the city behind.

In the distance, the pinpoint light at the tunnel's end slowly grew. Exiting the tunnel, I slid the sunglasses back over my eyes, nearly blinded by the bright light from the morning sun. As I drove away from the city, the surrounding landscape gradually transitioned from concrete and steel to miles of hillsides and meadows in different shades of green. Wildflowers of violet, yellow, and orange grew in the median of the highway that separated the northern and southern routes. Traffic was light, and the scenery didn't change much for the next seventy miles or so. Approaching the West Virginia state line, I was greeted by a sign that read- 'Welcome to Wild, Wonderful West Virginia'. Speeding into West Virginia, the landscape again changed, becoming more rugged but just as beautiful. The open fields along the way were replaced by tree-covered hillsides and vivid green mountains in the distance. The straightaways were fewer, and the flat sections of the road gradually disappeared behind me. As I drove further into the state, the roads turned and curved more and rose in elevation.

On an isolated hillside that overlooked the valley, a constant westerly wind howled. Johnny stood alone, staring into the deep, black void of a forgotten mine shaft. Few people knew about the shaft. Its opening was marked only by a circular row of stone stacked three blocks high around the shaft's perimeter. The shaft was believed to be several hundred feet deep and had been used years ago to ventilate one of the many mine passages that ran underground throughout the county. Alongside Johnny, there was a wheelbarrow that held Tolly's rigid, dead body and a kid's red wagon filled with most of everything he owned.

Johnny pulled the wagon to the edge of the shaft and dumped a collection of worn clothes, winter coats, and other gear that had belonged to Tolly into the hole. He pulled out Tolly's wallet. The outline of the state of West Virginia with the word 'HOME' had been ingrained into the leather. He checked the money pocket in the wallet. It contained a twenty and four one-dollar bills that he stuck in his back pocket. Johnny shuffled through the few items inside the wallet- a frayed and yellowed social security card, a driver's license, a United Mine Workers of American union card, a Sam's Club membership card, and a black and white photo of an older woman, perhaps Tolly's mother. Johnny tossed the cards, one-by-one, into the shaft, followed by the wallet.

Turning to the wheelbarrow, Johnny studied Tolly's lifeless body for a few moments. Like Johnny,

Tolly was an only son, probably an accident between two people who never should have been together. Even though Tolly and Johnny constantly battled and competed with one another, they were like brothers who genuinely loved each other. Unable to hold back a flood of tears that had been welling up in his eyes all afternoon, Johnny pushed the wheelbarrow to the stone perimeter of the shaft. Tolly would be the fourth person that Butterman had ordered Johnny to make 'go away'. But this one would be the hardest. Johnny didn't really know the other three. He tried to justify it all. Tolly likely wouldn't be missed- he tried to reason. He had little family. If someone did miss him, they'd probably associate his disappearance with a drug overdose in some sad, lost place with no one else around.

After wiping his eyes with the sleeve of his flannel shirt stained with blood, Johnny took a deep breath and lifted the handles of the wheelbarrow. Tolly's body shifted and slightly slid forward. With another deep breath, but this time with a grunt and groan, Johnny raised the wheelbarrow higher with a turn and a shake. Tolly's body quickly slid off and disappeared into the black hole without a sound. Crying like a baby, Johnny immediately dropped the wheelbarrow and fell to his knees, not to move from the spot for most of the morning. He wasn't cut out for that kind of work. That wasn't who he was. He knew it. And everyone in the area knew it. Because Johnny had a heart. He cared about the others in his life, always helping them out if he could, even when he was young. Unfortunately, he needed the money and was controlled by a drug habit that had spiraled out of control. He had to quit doing Butterman's dirty work as soon as possible. Even though he never made it past the sixth grade, he was smart enough to know that one day he might be the body in the wheelbarrow about to join the others at the bottom of the shaft.

Chapter 2
Don't Want to Know if you're Lonely

As I continued the drive to Caldwell, I finally took an exit off the interstate and followed a quiet, scenic route that wound its way through the valley of the Little Tug River. I passed through a handful of unincorporated and mostly unpopulated towns that were nothing but a post office or a service station-convenience store. The cars on the roadway were few, however the trucks were many. They headed to natural gas wells set up in clearings along the river or fracking well pads that were mostly hidden in the dense patches of trees that covered the rolling and winding hillsides in the distance. The posted speed limit was fifty miles an hour, but most of the trucks seemed to be moving much faster than that.

I reached the edge of Caldwell and drove into town. It was a clear, spectacular day with the bluest of skies. Caldwell was isolated in a valley below a series of rock-faced ridges and green slopes framed against a big open sky. Never had I been to a place so naturally beautiful. I immediately noticed that nearly all the cars were parked and not stuck in traffic like I was used to in Pittsburgh. I eased my car into a parking space on a curb of Main Street and got out. The town was much quieter than I was accustomed to, almost too quiet. I could hear bells from a local church softly ring in the distance. I heard the squealing, happy voices of children, echoing off the hillsides. The soothing and constant sound of singing birds and chirping crickets provided the chorus.

There wasn't much to downtown Caldwell- a bank, an eight-room motel with a diner, a small hardware store and pawn shop, a florist, the Super-Rite, a courthouse with a post office, and even a video rental store. It must have been the last one in America. There wasn't a single stoplight, only one stop sign at a three-way stop in the middle of town. I walked down the street towards the Super-Rite. The diner was full. A delicious-looking treasure of homemade cakes and pies were displayed in the window. A long line waited outside. Everyone was dressed in their 'Sunday-best'. The clothes and hair styles were outdated as if time had taken a giant leap backwards. The 21st Century had not yet caught up with Caldwell. I stood in the middle of 'small-town nirvana', but a 1990's version. As I reached for the front door of the Super-Rite drug store, it suddenly felt as if a large rabble of fluttering butterflies entered my gut.

The drug store was quite busy and especially lively, even for a Sunday afternoon I thought. But it was church day- a day when a good number of folks in the county come out of the hollows. I walked to the pharmacy at the back of the store. A long line of customers stood at the cash register, waiting for prescriptions. A charming-looking and plump, middle-aged woman, Tammy, waited on customers. Behind a glass partition, the pharmacist, James Butterman, mostly kept his bald head down as he filled the many prescription orders lined up in front of

22

him. I had only spoken to Butterman a couple of times on the phone. He did not look at all as I expected. His phone voice could be soft and sweet. He was heavier and more imposing in person than I imagined. And knowing about his long service time in Caldwell, I expected him to look much older.

"Can I help you?" Tammy asked as I reached the pharmacy counter.

"Uh, yeah. I'm Michael Young, the new pharmacist."

An awkward quiet quickly followed as everyone in the pharmacy area turned and looked. Butterman stopped working and glanced up. We stared at each other a moment. No one said a word. I was gawked at as if a freak in a circus side show. Sensing I was uncomfortable with the sudden attention, Butterman walked to a locked door near the counter, opened it, and waved to me to join him in the pharmacy.

"Michael. Michael. Come on back. Welcome. Welcome."

I glanced around the cluttered and unorganized pharmacy. Pill bottles, soda cans, opened bags of potato chips, paperwork, and coffee cups were scattered everywhere. A half-eaten deli sandwich sat on a paper plate next to the cash register.

"Busy?" I said, scanning the pharmacy.

"No time to get bored here," he said.

"Or clean up as you can see," Tammy said.

"You don't know how bad I need a break from this place, Michael. Tammy will show you everything."

I nodded and glanced to Tammy. A frail and boney elderly lady suddenly appeared at the register and started tapping her empty prescription bottles on the counter.

"I'll be with you in a minute, Mrs. Dawson," Tammy called out as one of the two pharmacy phones began to ring.

"You'll be staying at my place after I leave, right?" Butterman asked as he went back to filling prescriptions again.

"Yes, thank you. You sure I won't owe you anything for rent."

"You're doing me a huge favor. I haven't had a vacation in over a decade."

I nodded as one of the phones continued to ring, and the line at the counter grew.

"I leave for Florida in a week. Super-Rite has set you up in a room across the street at the motel. The accommodations aren't much, but the rooms are clean and quiet."

He slapped computer labels on multiple prescription bottles and placed them in bags. The second phone started to ring along with the other one.

"Tammy?" Butterman barked.

"Okay. Okay. I'll get it," she said, cashing out patients at the register.

"You see, Michael. We can get remarkably busy."

"Do you need me to help until you get caught up?"

"No. No. We're used to this. You don't start here until morning. Go get checked in to the motel and grab a bite to eat. The food at the diner is especially delicious, particularly the baked goods."

I nodded as a doorbell loudly chimed.

"We aren't expecting any deliveries, are we?" Butterman asked.

"I'll check," Tammy said.

"I better let you go."

"Come to my house Tuesday night for dinner after your shift. We'll talk more then."

"Thanks," I said, letting myself out of the pharmacy.

"You have a visitor," Tammy informed Butterman.

As Butterman watched me leave the drug store, he turned to Tammy and finally asked, "Who is it?"

"Johnny."

Butterman stopped filling prescriptions and scanned the pharmacy area. He grabbed an aluminum baseball bat that leaned in a corner and disappeared into a backroom. He unlocked a thick, reinforced steel door and kicked it open, startling Johnny who waited for him. Butterman charged Johnny who retreated against the back-brick wall of the building.

"What do you want?"

Johnny shrugged- his eyes glued on the bat in Butterman's hand.

"You clean up your mess?"

Johnny nervously nodded and tried to say something.

"You haven't even changed!" Butterman shouted, grabbing Johnny's blood-splotched shirt, and knocking the stained ball-cap off his head.

"What is it, goddamit? I'm too busy for games!"

"I...I can't do it no more," Johnny said, leaning down and grabbing his hat. "I jus' can't, Mr. Butterman. It ain't right."

"Can't do what?"

"I...I quit. I quit workin' for you."

"You can't quit, Johnny," Butterman said, raising the bat and resting it on his shoulder. "You're not quitting. No one's quitting."

"I am. I am, sir."

"You can't. I need you. Seeing that you blasted the face off my other delivery boy, I can't let you go."

"But...Mr. Butter....," he tried to talk.

But before he could finish, Butterman grabbed Johnny's neck and rammed him against the brick wall. With his face red, Johnny struggled to breathe. Butterman then slammed the bat against the wall by Johnny's head. Johnny closed his eyes and cringed.

"You want to end up in jail?"

Johnny struggled as Butterman tightened his grip. He cringed again as Butterman slammed the bat against the wall inches from his head.

"You know, me and the sheriff are real tight."

Johnny shook his head as Butterman let him go. Johnny slid down the brick wall into a sitting position.

"Why'd you do it, Johnny? Why'd you pull the trigger?"

"I didn't do nothing!" Johnny hollered back, not looking up to Butterman.

"Why'd you kill Tolly?"

"I didn't do it!" Johnny yelled back as he stood. "It ain't in me!"

"I was there. You had the gun."

Pacing back and forth, Johnny shook his head.

"Do you want me to give the gun to the sheriff? It has your bloody prints all over it."

Johnny stopped pacing and stared at Butterman.

"I take care of you, Johnny. You know that."

Johnny shook his head as tears ran down his cheeks.

"I didn't kill no one."

"And, what about Aaron?"

"Huh?"

"He was gone after I got back."

"Gone?" Johnny asked with a puzzled look, shaking his head. "I don't remember. I don't remember Aaron."

"Come here," Butterman said, draping his heavy, fleshy arm over Johnny's shoulder. "Just help me for another few months while I'm in Florida, and I won't tell anyone what you did."

Johnny shook his head as Butterman patted his back.

"You going to help me, Johnny?"

Wiping the tears from his face, Johnny finally nodded.

I arrived at the pharmacy thirty minutes early. I had trouble sleeping the night before as I was nervous for that first day. Luckily, Tammy was already in the pharmacy when I got there, preparing for the day, and filling a few call-in prescription refills that I had to check and approve before they could be picked up by the patient. She quickly got me up to speed on the computer system and showed me where everything was and how Butterman had arranged and organized the stock drugs within the pharmacy. I was raring to go when the drug store doors were unlocked at nine o'clock. But the first couple of hours after the store had opened were terribly slow, even boring. Tammy and I stood around and fidgeted, making small talk, and learning a little about each other. I found out she had lived her whole life in the county, and she was married for over twenty years to local fellow who worked for the state roads. They had two young daughters, and they only left the state once a year during the summer- that was to go to Myrtle Beach, South Carolina for vacation. She also had plenty of questions for me.

"Why did you come here of all places? What was wrong with stayin' home?"

"Do you want the selfish or unselfish reason?" I asked.

"The unselfish."

"My grandmother needs a new house. She's lived in the same one all her life. She's in her eighties now and probably doesn't have many years left. She's always wanted a brand-new house in a better neighborhood. I want to do that for her."

"Couldn't you have done that stayin' in Pittsburgh?"

"I'm getting paid a lot more money here. And I practically have no expenses. I was thinking of staying here a year, maybe two, and saving all my money. I figured I'd have enough for down payment for a new house in a nice suburb outside of Pittsburgh."

"That's sweet."

"Yeah, but I owe her so much more. She saved me. And after she's gone, my fiancée and I could live there and start our own family."

"Fiancée?"

"Yeah, Meredith and I have been engaged for two years."

"And she didn't want to come here with you?"

"She couldn't. She just took a job at a university in Pittsburgh."

"So, no chance you'll stay here for the long term?"

"That's not the plan- no."

"Can I ask you what the unselfish reason for coming here was?"

"I've lived a sheltered life- the same friends, same neighborhood, same city, the same house even. I don't really know who I am. I want to find that out."

We had only filled five prescriptions before the shit finally hit the fan. For the next four hours, it was an all-out assault of new prescription orders, doctor phone calls, patient phone calls, patient questions about specific over-the-counter drugs, more doctor calls, and more patient calls. I didn't even have time to eat lunch. I think Tammy was impressed with how I could keep up with all that was happening at the same time.

I knew it was real when one of the first patients, an elderly man, asked, "let me speak with the man."

"I am the man," I replied.

"No. I need to speak with the man."

"I am the man," I repeated, not sure I convinced him.

It was an eventful first day. I met many of the regulars who visited the pharmacy on an almost daily basis. I chatted mostly about the weather- how the days were still warm, but the nights were getting colder. I also was met with odd stares from folks who were expecting to see Butterman. They weren't too sure about letting the new guy fill their prescriptions but seeing Tammy's familiar face assured them it would be all right. A sweet elderly woman named Evelyn Ryan bought me a coffee when she heard a new pharmacist had started. Later in the day, she brought me chocolate chip cookies from the diner that were still warm from the oven. I had a couple of thirty-something single women come in to introduce themselves. One was a nurse at the local medical clinic, Sharon Weaver. The other, Kelly Stalnaker, was a teller at the bank. I also met an eighty-seven-year-old character named Archie Atwater who always wore a yellow cowboy hat and red cowboy boots. He needed his blood pressure measured. I had to turn my head as I attached the cuff to his arm. He reeked so strong of garlic you would've thought he bathed in it. He had the blood pressure of a twenty-year-old man. He attributed his perfect blood pressure to eating an entire bulb of raw garlic every day.

"Not only is it good for my heart," he told me, "but it keeps the ghosts away."

And other things, I guessed.

"You know, in all these years," he confessed, "I never had a single girlfriend."

At five o'clock, Tammy's shift ended, and I worked the last two hours alone until closing. After that first night, I understood why she left early. Business grinded to halt sometime around five-thirty. That also was about the time the downtown Caldwell businesses closed, except for the diner and motel. The down time in the pharmacy allowed me to catch up on the daily paperwork, clean the pharmacy, and eat some dinner. The diner delivered, thank goodness, and the homemade pot roast and mashed potatoes special were on point. Before I left for the night, I made my first phone call home.

"Hey babe, I made it."

"I want to hear everything," Meredith said.

"I feel like I've entered another world."

"How's the pharmacy?

"The drug store's fine. It gets busy at times, which is good. The days will go by faster."

"How about your co-workers?"

"There's really only two I work with directly. Tammy, who's the pharmacy tech, and James, the other pharmacist and manager. Tammy's great. She makes the job much easier for me. James wasn't at all like I expected. I'm going to his house for dinner tomorrow night. I'll also be staying there over the winter during his time in Florida. Right now, they've put me up in a motel room across the street."

"His house?"

"It's out in the country, I guess- twenty or twenty-five miles from the store. I haven't been there yet. I'm sure I'll get lonely out there by myself. According to Tammy, it's pretty secluded."

"I don't want to know if you're lonely. You could've gotten a job here and stayed with me. You can always leave."

"I can't do anything about it now."

"My father has a chat with the dean of the medical school tomorrow."

I didn't respond.

"Michael?"

"I better go. I'm still at the store. It's looks like I have a patient here to pick up a prescription."

"It's good to hear your voice. I know it's only been one day. I miss you."

"I miss you, too. I promise I'll call you almost every day."

"When can I come for a visit?"

"Anytime."

"I love you, Michael."

"I love you, too."

The second day at the pharmacy was more of the same- slow morning, crazy busy afternoon, and dead at night. Archie Atwater waited for me at the front door before the drug store had opened. I could almost smell the garlic on him as I approached. I measured his blood pressure. It was the same as it was the day before. We chatted for an hour about his garden, the weather, and the local high school football team that was in the midst of another losing season.

"They got to run the ball," Archie said as I nodded, filling prescription orders. "Jus' run the ball! Too many things can go wrong when you try and pass it. They ain't got no Bart 'fuckin'' Starr on the team. Geesh! The coach thinks he's the second comin' of Bill Walsh. West Coast offense my ass. This is Caldwell Country for chrissakes. Them kids are teenagers."

Evelyn Ryan also came by the store early, dropping off coffee and doughnuts from the diner. She lived alone and offered to cook me dinner some evening.

"You got to go," Tammy insisted. "Evelyn's the best cook in the county."

Sharon from the nursing home showed up later that afternoon. I learned that she wasn't married and lived alone with her ailing mother. It was no secret to why she was stopping in to see me. There were few available men, at least one's with decent paying jobs, in the county. She didn't have to tell me she was lonely. I could see the sadness in her eyes.

"It's nice to talk with someone on the younger side," she would always say. "Most everyone around here it seems is over sixty."

As a service provided to the less fortunate in the county, Butterman offered limited prescription delivery after closing each Tuesday. Because I was going to dinner at Butterman's house that was located over twenty miles away in the northwestern part of the county, Tammy prepared a set of deliveries for me to make in that area on my way there. As we filled the orders, I checked the addresses and names of the deliveries I'd have to make later.

"What's the name on this one?" I asked, studying the label on a package that had already been prepared by Butterman. "Johnny Fogg?"

"He's one of the local characters," Tammy replied.

"The local idiot, more like it," a customer at the register spoke up.

"At Shady Fork, you'll need to get on a dirt road at a grouping of mailboxes off Route 15," Tammy informed me, "then up a holler for about three or four miles to find him."

As we continued to work on the delivery orders, I glanced up and noticed a pretty young woman with shoulder-length brown hair staring at me. She quickly looked away the moment our eyes met. I studied her briefly as she walked the store aisles, casually throwing assorted items into a shopping basket that hung from her arm. I looked back to the prescriptions in front of me and finished filling the orders. I again glanced up and scanned the store, searching for the young woman. But she was gone. Later I would come to meet her. Her name was Crystal Foley.

The gray overcast sky grew darker as nightfall approached. I had one more delivery to make before meeting Butterman at his house for dinner. The drop-off for the delivery was approximately twenty miles away from the drugstore. Speeding over the winding, rural backroads, I finally turned off the paved Route 15 onto a gravel road partially hidden by overgrown weeds. I slowly navigated the busted road, climbing in elevation for a mile or two. Thick brush and woods lined each side of the road, blocking out the light from the full moon and stars and throwing shadows over me. Eventually, the road peaked and slowly transitioned to a one-lane dirt road that was substantially more damaged than the gravel road. It was filled with deep ruts and grooves caused by previous rainfalls and heavy truck traffic to the many fracking sites in the area.

Barely reaching ten miles per hour, I bumped and bounced a few miles down to a clearing in the woods near a creek bed. As I neared the creek, I came upon a littered yard that was bordered by multiple dilapidated mobile homes and several poorly constructed cinder block and wood houses. Many of the windows in the trailers were broken or even missing. Bright floodlights lit the yard. Some rough characters waited for me. Two brothers, Whitey and Dorsey Blosser, stared as I approached. They were joined by Johnny Fogg and numerous other relatives and friends of all ages from newborn babies to elderly grandparents.

Not feeling safe or comfortable, I parked the car and got out, leaving the car headlights on. AC/DC music blared. There were jugs of homemade wine and shotguns on a picnic table. Roaming dogs of different breeds angrily barked at me. Teenagers recklessly raced back and forth through the muddy yard on all-terrain vehicles. As I shut the car door, I watched Whitey slowly fill a 10-foot long cast iron drainpipe with acetylene gas using a rubber nozzle connected to a gas cylinder. The top end of the pipe was simply covered with a paper plate, whereas the bottom end was sealed with a welded metal plate. After filling the pipe with gas, he looked over and grinned at me before igniting the gas through a small orifice in the bottom of the pipe with a lit cigarette.

KA-BOOM!

A fireball thirty-feet in diameter exploded out the end of the homemade cannon. The roar echoed through the valley. Frightened by the excessively loud noise, all the dogs scattered into the woods. The heat from the blast singed my face as I fell to me knees. I hadn't expected such a shock as the ground trembled and the mountain shook. Everyone laughed hysterically as I gathered myself and returned to my feet. A spinning and sliding, out of control all-terrain vehicle nearly struck me as I jumped out of its way.

"Where in the hell am I?" I mumbled.

Whitey continued to laugh as I approached him, wiping at the dirt on my trousers.

"Anyone named Johnny Fogg?" I asked, reaching out a bag of prescriptions.

"Who's wonderin'?" asked Whitey, the cigarette dangling from his lips.

"I have a delivery for him."

"What delivery?"

"His medicine. I'm the new pharmacist in Caldwell."

"I'm him," Johnny said, stepping forward.

Whitey glared at me as did Dorsey who held a shotgun.

"New druggist, huh?" Whitey spoke up and looked to Dorsey. "Maybe we'll stop by sometime and spook ya'."

Whitey and Dorsey laughed as Johnny snatched the bag from my hand. I didn't know what was in the bag, but Johnny was anxious to get it. We all stared at each other a moment before I started back for the car.

"Mister, wait!" Johnny called out.

I stopped as he rushed up to me.

"I need your help."

"My help?"

"I need it bad."

"What can I do?"

"Do you know about the last one?"

"What last one?"

"The last druggist, Aaron, was a young one like you. He's gone, you know. They all thinks he's dead."

"Uh, okay, but uh, I need to get going," I said, turning away and reaching for the car door.

"He's alive. I know it," he continued as I pulled open the door. "You need to listen to me."

"I really don't know what you're talking about."

"You don't want to disappear, do ya'?"

We studied each other before I got in the car and turned the key in the ignition.

"Please help me," he said, leaning in the driver-side window.

I didn't respond as he glared at me with the coldest of stares. As I put the car in reverse, he leaned back from the car. Driving away, I checked the rear-view mirror. He watched me, not taking his eyes off the car until I was out of sight.

The sheriff's car idled in the driveway of Butterman's house. Robert Walls, the county sheriff, sat behind the wheel. He was a thin, wiry and paranoid bald man who always seemed to have had one too many cups of coffee. It was an understatement to describe him as 'high-strung'. His squad car was mostly hidden by rows of tall shrubs that lined each side of the driveway. Butterman stood by the car, leaning in the passenger side window. He wore a chef's apron and had a kitchen dish rag slung over his shoulder.

"The Morgan woman's been callin'," the sheriff said.

"I'll talk to her."

"Do you know what happened to her son?"

"I really don't, Bob."

"He didn't stumble into the old mine shaft on Buntner's Ridge, did he?"

"Not that I know of."

"His disappearance may cause some problems."

"For both of us."

"Yeah, so you may want to lay low for the time being."

"That's what I was thinking. We hired another pharmacist at the drug store. I'm conveniently taking a working vacation to Florida for the winter while he fills in. I'll be gone for three months. He'll be staying here as well. Hopefully some of these little problems will be solved by the time I get back."

"Okay, good," the sheriff said, nodding. "All the investigations will have to come through me. I'll stay on it. But we still have one problem. What if he shows up?"

"I have eyes out all over the county, looking for him."

"What'd you think happened to him?"

"I don't know, but he can't get too far. His habit's too big. And there's a lot of bad junk floating around these hollers. There's a very good chance he's already gone for good."

After returning to the main road, I raced to Butterman's house for dinner. I suddenly felt different than I had earlier in the day about the pharmacy and Caldwell after my encounter with Johnny Fogg and the Blosser brothers. The job may be a great deal more challenging than I first thought. And what did Johnny mean by 'you don't want to disappear?' I had many questions for Butterman.

As I neared the entrance to the long driveway that led to his house, the Sheriff's squad car pulled out in front of my approaching car. Passing me, the sheriff slowed and studied me closely as I signaled to turn into the driveway. I found his reaction odd and wondered what the reason was for his visit with Butterman.

At the end of the driveway, Butterman's house was situated several hundred yards off the main road and was barely visible, except in the wintertime when the trees were bare of leaves. I stopped the car in front of the garage and parked. Butterman lived in a modern, three-story house built on a secluded two-acre piece of wooded property. Dark brown wood siding covered the entire house that was built into the side of a hill. Large glass picture windows that faced the road highlighted the front. Black rot iron stairs led from the driveway up the hill along the front of the house to the entrance. A large satellite dish, positioned in the middle of the yard, was aimed to the east. A customer at the store earlier in the day joked that the satellite dish was the 'county bird' as most people in Caldwell had one perched in their yard. Cable television had not yet reached that far into the countryside at the time.

I got out of the car. It was dark and eerily quiet. The wind was brisk and steady. Autumn was in the air. I glanced around the property and studied the surroundings. This would be where I would live while Butterman vacationed in Florida through winter. He was waiting for me at the front door. He enthusiastically shook my hand and even hugged me, before leading me inside the house. Little did I know, a brand-new, shiny Ford Mustang was parked across the road, partially hidden. Crystal Foley watched from the driver's seat.

The inside of the house was dimly lit. Numerous scented candles were arranged throughout the rooms of the main floor and provided the only light. I was immediately struck by an expansive great room that greeted me as I entered the house. The room was 'tricked-out' with a state-of-the-art, surround-sound audio system, an 80-inch wide-screen television, leather sectional sofa, and glass-top coffee tables. Hundreds of vintage vinyl record albums were carefully organized amongst shelves of books on a series of bookcases that warmed the room. A John Coltrane record quietly played on the turntable. A small mobile and fully stocked cocktail bar was tucked in one corner. The kitchen and adjoining dining room were located just beyond the great room. Around the corner, a hallway connected the dining room with a main bathroom and multiple bedrooms.

"I'll give you a tour of the place later," he said, leading me into the dining room. "Let's eat! I don't want the food to get cold."

The dining room table easily could have seated twelve people comfortably. On one end, it was covered with multiple bottles of different wine varietals. On the other, decorative ceramic serving bowls and plates were filled with lamb chops, loaded baked potatoes that exploded off the plate, roasted corn, green bean casserole, a mixed garden salad, as well as three different kinds of fruit pies, obviously picked up from the Caldwell diner.

"I don't get to entertain much, but when I do," Butterman said, opening his arm and motioning to the delectable-looking food.

"Did you prepare all this yourself?"

"It's always nice to have a day off," he said, nodding.

The food tasted better than it looked. I was overstuffed. Both of us had nearly eaten ourselves sick. We had finished all the lamb, potatoes, and the salad. We hadn't even touched any of the pies. All that was left were a couple ears of corn and a small helping of green beans. Butterman was an exceptional cook and host. Not since my grandmother was younger and still regularly making me dinners, did I have such a fine and tasty home-cooked meal.

By that time in the evening, we had just opened the third bottle of wine. Despite my full belly, I was rather tipsy. My face was warm and flush. My head was light and a little foggy. And as the wine flowed, our conversation became more intimate. We no longer talked about the logistics and other mundane pieces information that I needed to know about running the pharmacy. We talked about ourselves and families. I knew Butterman must have been a bit intoxicated because he had taken control of the conversation. I just peppered him with questions.

"I'll ask you what everyone's been asking me- how'd you end up in Caldwell?"

"I was running away from a bad divorce," he confessed. "Super-Rite needed an experienced pharmacist to get the store here up and running. I had done that for them at a few pharmacies in the Jacksonville, Florida area. This seemed like a good place to hide. And here I am- ten years later, still here."

He reached for a framed photograph and handed it to me.

"But I left two beautiful daughters behind."

I studied the photo.

"That's how I remember them. I never got to see them grow up."

"What about them now?"

"The older one won't speak to me. The younger one is, well, a little wild, reminds me of her mother. And God, did I love their mother."

"What happened?"

"I was young, working too many hours but obsessed with the cash flow. My wife and I slowly drifted apart, or rather she slowly drifted into the muscular arms of our health-nut neighbor- the car salesman. She left me for a goddam car salesman. Can you believe that? Still with him, I hear. And always driving a brand-new luxury car. Good for her."

Butterman looked to the ceiling and shook his head, before reaching for the bottle of wine and refilling our glasses.

"It's been mostly sixty-six-hour work weeks since I started here. I've gone months at a time without a day off. Super-Rite has never been able to find me consistent help, and they still can't."

"Do you have any regrets leaving Florida?"

"I gave up the best years of my life to come here."

"So, I take that as a 'yes'."

"Not necessarily. I've done things here that I couldn't have in Florida."

"Like what?"

"I have more control over how I run the store and live my life. And in Jacksonville, nobody knew me. There was a pharmacy on every corner. Here, everyone knows me and relies on me. I'm one of the most important people in this whole area. And, I like that feeling. I like that feeling a lot. But it can get boring here, especially in the winter."

"Do you ever get lonely? You don't seem to have any neighbors."

"Maybe a little at first but not now."

"Did you meet anyone, you know, someone special, after you got here?"

"Michael? So many questions."

"I want to know what I'm getting into here in Caldwell."

"Sure, I've had my share of fun in the ten years here, but…"

"But never met that special someone," I interrupted.

"I did fall in love one time since the divorce. But I knew from the start that it'd never work."

He immediately glanced away and raised his glass, swallowing hard on what was left of the wine in his glass. Sensing that I touched a nerve, I quickly changed the subject.

"Why's it been so hard to get pharmacists in here?"

"The store's too busy. You'll see," he said, reaching for the bottle of wine. "You'll need more help. And some of the clientele here in Caldwell can be a little difficult, especially to outsiders."

"Like Whitey Blosser."

"Yeah, like Whitey Blosser," Butterman said, nodding. "But I can assure you, he's harmless."

"I'll be the judge of that."

"And there ain't shit to do here outside of work for someone young like you," he said, raising his wine glass. "Except drink, smoke, and screw, at least, that's what the teenagers that come in the store tell me."

Grinning, he reached his glass out to me.

"But I'll warn you," he said, tapping my glass with his. "Some of the young woman around here, they can't be tamed. Don't even try. Many young guys have tried, and they've all failed."

Taking a sip of wine, he studied me closely. Uneasy in his stare, I looked away.

"But seriously," he spoke up. "There's no place I'd rather be. I've grown to love the people here. They're the kindest and friendliest people in the world- almost too friendly, sometime to the point of being painfully friendly. Many just have been dealt a bad hand of cards."

I nodded as he attempted to pry some personal information from me.

"Do you have a girlfriend or significant other?"

Before I could answer, the doorbell chimed.

"Will you excuse me?"

"Of course," I nodded as he got up and answered the door.

A cute and heavy-set woman in her middle fifties with wispy gray hair entered the house. Butterman led her into the dining room as I stood.

"Phyllis, this is Michael Young," Butterman announced as she gave me a friendly little wave. "He'll be working the store and staying here while I'm away."

"Michael, this is Phyllis Moody, our very hard-working Avon Lady, which by the way, is a damn tough way to make a living in these parts. There's no actual neighborhoods that are easily navigated around here, and thus few doorbells to ring."

Butterman handed Phyllis two large paper Avon bags stapled shut in exchange for an envelope.

"It's easier for some in the more distant areas of the county to pick up their orders at the drug store."

I nodded, sensing an awkwardness between Butterman and Phyllis. It seemed she needed to tell him something of importance but in private. She stared at him, while glancing back and forth at me.

"Bathroom?" I spoke up.

"Down the hall," Butterman said, pointing.

I started down the hallway and went to open the first door I came upon.

"No, not that room," Butterman called out. "The next one."

As I disappeared into the bathroom, Butterman turned to Phyllis.

"I have a lot of deliveries for you."

"Don't go to Florida, Jimmy," she pleaded as Butterman shook his head. "I know you don't want to hear this…"

"Phyllis, please," he interrupted.

"Let's get married."

"You know how I feel, having already failed miserably the first time I tried that."

"But that was such a long time ago. Your life's different now."

"I need you to get these deliveries made," he said, ignoring her.

"I told you I didn't want to do this anymore."

"But be careful out there. Those holler roads are tricky at night."

"Why me, tonight? Where's Tolly? Or Aaron?"

"Drop off the sheriff's and mayor's things first. Their wives have been bugging me all day, calling over here."

"But, Jimmy...," she started to say as I walked back into the room.

"Say goodbye to Michael, Phyllis," he interrupted as she showed him a disappointed gaze. "We'll talk in the morning."

"Nice to meet you, Michael," she said, gathering the Avon bags and leaving.

It had gotten late, and I had to be at the drug store early in the morning. Phyllis' visit had taken some of the steam out of the evening. Butterman was no longer in the mood to tell me more details about his life. We finished what was left of the third bottle of wine as I quizzed him, almost to the point of annoying him about the pharmacy as well as any other information that was pertinent to the people and businesses of downtown Caldwell. As he showed me the spare bedroom where I'd be sleeping that night, he motioned to the closed door he didn't want me to enter when Phyllis was there.

"That's Aaron's room."

"He lived here?"

"Ever since he took the job at Super-Rite."

"What happened to him? They were asking about him at the store today."

"He disappeared."

"Disappeared?"

"The sheriff was here earlier."

"Any leads to his whereabouts?"

"Not at this point."

"Why would he leave?"

"I think he had some issues to work out."

"Issues?"

"He was a passionate young man. He liked to live his life to the fullest, if you know what I mean."

I nodded as we studied each other.

"I love that boy."

"Should I be worried?"

"Not at all," he replied with a chuckle. "An isolated incident."

"What do you think happened to him?"

"You sure are a curious guy."

"Wouldn't you be if you were me?"

It was after two o'clock in the morning, and I was far from sleep as I tossed and turned in an unfamiliar bed. Even though I was alone in the bedroom, it eerily felt as if someone was in the room, watching me. I had felt the same when I pulled into Butterman's driveway and drove up to his house, when I stood in his front yard, and when I was by myself in the bathroom. I never felt alone in that house. As I rolled over in bed and waited for sleep, the door to the bedroom creaked open. I immediately rolled back over and looked to the door.

"James?"

The light in the hallway had been turned off, so I couldn't see him, only a shadow.

"Is that you?"

"Yes."

"Is everything all right?"

"Just checking to see if you need anything."

"No, I'm good."

"Okay," he said before a long pause. "Goodnight."

"Goodnight."

The door remained open for ten, maybe fifteen seconds, but it seemed much longer. Even though I couldn't see him, I knew he was still there. I could hear him breathing. Finally, the door closed. Never in my twenty-two years of life had I been more creeped out.

CHAPTER 3
Crystal

Trying to function on little sleep and not enough coffee, the third day on the job was unlike the first two in every possible way. It was the first day of the month- October 1st. So that meant nearly everyone in the county was in town to collect, cash, and spend their monthly check, whether it be from welfare, social security, disability, retirement, payroll, pension, or whatever. Driving into town after a restless night at Butterman's place, I was surprised to see a long line waiting at the front door of the drug store. Archie was the first in line. The store wasn't to open for another twenty-five minutes. I parked, but before leaving the car, I dialed my phone. Meredith's familiar and soothing voice came over the line.

"Michael? Is everything all right?"

"I just wanted to hear your voice this morning."

"It doesn't have to be this way. Please come home."

"You know I can't."

"My father is trying to schedule a meeting with the dean of the medical school."

"Meredith, don't."

"It's still not be too late for med school."

"I have to go. I just needed to hear your voice."

"Michael?"

"I love you, Meredith."

"I love you, too. Please come home."

"I'll call you later."

I turned off the phone and took a deep breath before getting out of the car and slipping through a backdoor of the drug store. Thank goodness, Tammy had already been there and prepped the pharmacy for what surely would be a busy day.

"The next three days will be a bear," she warned as I pulled on my pharmacist smock.

And a bear was right. At exactly nine o'clock, the front doors were unlocked, and the pharmacy quickly and completely collapsed into madness. I took Archie's blood pressure. It was normal as usual. He tried to converse with us, but we were much too busy. The two phones began to ring non-stop. Phoned in prescription refill orders started to pile up. Scores of empty prescription bottles were dropped off and lined across the pharmacy bench, waiting to be filled. Stacks of new prescriptions were being dropped off. The waiting area quickly became crowded with wait times for some people as long as an hour. Everything was flowing as best as possible until the cash register ran out of receipt paper. And that's all it took, a seemingly minor event to turn the whole system upside down. For I discovered that morning as I tried to cash out one of the patients, the register would completely shut off when it ran out of paper. It took me a few frantic minutes to discover that as I unsuccessfully pounded at the dead keys of the register.

"You need to change the roll of paper," Tammy called out as she attended to the many prescription orders in front of her.

"How?"

"Flip up that plastic piece on the top."

I found the place on the register she was talking about, opened it, and pulled out the empty cardboard roll that once held paper.

"In the drawer," she pointed, "the replacement rolls are in that drawer."

I searched through the drawer and didn't find another roll of register paper. Tammy joined me at the drawer and looked through it. I glanced up to the pharmacy counter. The line had suddenly grown and extended almost the length of the entire drug store to the front door. An older lady in the front of the line started to tap her empty prescription bottle against the counter. A long strand of thick drool hung from the mouth of an elderly gentleman, Mr. Morris, who leaned on a cane behind her. I glanced back to Tammy as she continued to dig through the drawer.

"You need to get one from up front," she said before pointing at the orders on the bench. "I'll work on these."

Before leaving the pharmacy area, Tammy handed me a napkin and motioned to Mr. Morris with drool hanging from his lip. I nodded and took the napkin before wiping his mouth for him. Holding the soiled napkin, I walked along the line of waiting customers.

"Sorry folks, we're having some technical difficulties. Please be patient. The cash register is currently not working. But it should be up shortly. Please be patient."

As I continued my way to the front of the store, I heard one of the phones in the pharmacy start to ring again. And seconds later, the other phone started to ring.

"Welcome to the first of the month," Robbie, the young store clerk, said as he unlocked a supply cabinet.

"Yeah, right," I said, watching more people continued to enter the store. "I never expected this."

"Days like this have a way of takin' your soul," he said, holding a box full of register paper rolls

"No kidding."

Back in the pharmacy, I refilled the paper in the cash register. Both phones were still ringing. I looked over to Tammy. Her hands were in the back of the prescription label printer. It seemed that a computer label had gotten stuck on one of the rollers, causing the printer to jam. Using a butter knife, she tried to scrape the glue from the label off the roller. I stood a moment and watched as both phones continued to ring. Finally, she looked up.

"Those phones aren't going to answer themselves."

As I was on one phone taking down the information for new prescription orders from the medical clinic, my cell phone started to ring. I pulled it from my pocket and glanced to the name and number on the screen. It was Meredith. I immediately shut off the ringer and continued to jot down the orders on prescription pads. I next got a text from Meredith. It read, 'call me immediately'. I ignored the message and tried my best to catch up with the many orders on the pharmacy bench as well as help some of the patients that had been waiting at the register. My phone began to ring again. As I answered it, I glanced to Tammy who glared at me.

"Meredith, I can't talk. We're busy beyond belief, and it'll be this way for hours."

"Please! It's about medical school!"

"I'll call you tonight. Goodbye."

The drug store was still active and filled with patients as Tammy stayed into the evening well past the end of her shift to help me fill the many prescriptions that lined the pharmacy counter from earlier. It had been an overwhelmingly busy day, and I was exhausted. We already had filled nearly four-hundred prescriptions. I kept checking my watch- closing time couldn't arrive soon enough. Having not slept much the night before at Butterman's house, I looked forward to some quiet time back in the motel room. And I was starving. Neither of us had eaten, except for a bite or two from some pastries that Evelyn had brought us from the diner. Sharon had shown up at some point but soon left after seeing I was far too busy to chat. I didn't even get a chance to say 'hello'.

"How has James lasted ten years here without much time off?" I asked as Tammy shook her head.

"Mr. Druggist?" a diminutive elderly gentleman called out. "Mr. Druggist?"

"I'll be with you in a moment."

"Excuse me. Excuse me, where can I find toilet paper?" another customer asked.

"Aisle 9," I replied, before looking over to Tammy. "Five years of pharmacy school for this?"

"Jus' lettin' you know," Tammy informed me. "I'm leavin' early on Saturday."

"What's goin' on here?" I wondered aloud, staring at the computer screen. "Vicodin. Xanax. Zoloft,

Percodan. Why all the pain and stress in Caldwell? Who's Dr. Valenzuela?"

I looked up and noticed Crystal, the attractive young woman, who had I seen in the store before. She quickly looked away as I caught her staring.

"Hey, who is...?" I started to ask Tammy.

I glanced back, but Crystal was gone.

"Who?"

"A young woman," I answered as Tammy scanned the busy store. "I think I'm seeing a ghost."

"You must be. There aren't many young people left in Caldwell."

"Why is that?"

"They all leave after high school for somethin' more, and most don't come back."

"What do you think happened to Aaron?" I asked, changing the subject.

She hesitated a moment before answering, not looking up from the orders she worked on.

"I don't know."

"What was his like?"

"A bit like you- young, quiet, but a little rougher around the edges."

"Nothing peculiar about him?"

"Not that I saw."

"What do you mean?"

"There were rumors."

"What rumors?"

"I don't know, Michael."

"He lived with James, right?"

"Yes, and Mr. Butterman really liked him, but..."

"But what?"

"Something happened between them."

"What?"

"I don't know, but something. Mr. Butterman didn't have him work the pharmacy when it was busy. Mostly, had him come in only on weekends. And then James had to let him go. He never told me why."

"What rumors?"

"There was talk of drug use, I guess. And he'd show up here for work hungover some mornings, and even drunk a couple times."

"Drug use?"

"I never saw it. But I liked him. I really did."

"Do you think he's still around?"

"I have no idea."

"Should I be worried?"

"Worried?"

"Am I in any kind of danger?"

Here," she said with a laugh, "in Caldwell. Nothin' ever happens in Caldwell."

A short time later I was the last to leave the drug store and locked the place up. It was an unseasonably warm autumn evening. As I turned for the motel across the street, I noticed a lone figure not far from the store entrance. Wearing a slinky summer dress and denim jacket, Crystal sat on the bumper of a shiny Ford Mustang, dragging on a cigarette, and seductively kicking her bare, crossed leg.

"Ah, the ghost is real."

"Do you need a ride?" she asked, not taking her eyes from mine.

"I'm only going to there," I answered, motioning to the motel.

"Do you WANT a ride?"

"I better not," I said, shaking my head as she stood and tossed the cigarette. "I've got a busy day tomorrow."

"This isn't tomorrow."

There was an awkward pause.

"Plus, I'm pretty tired. I've had a few long days in a row without much…"

"I'm Crystal," she interrupted, extending her hand and obviously uninterested in my excuses.

As I reached for it, she latched onto my hand and held it firmly. I expected her to quickly let go, but she didn't. I casually glanced up with a grin and bashfully looked her in the eyes. She stared back with a serious and confident gaze that caught me by surprise.

"I'm Michael," I said, trying to pull my hand away.

"I know," she said, finally releasing it.

Uneasy in her advance, I looked away and studied my watch.

"Come on, let me show you a little of the area."

I glanced to the motel, then to the Mustang, and back to Crystal.

"I'll get you back early. I promise."

I studied her then awkwardly glanced back to the motel. I knew that I should have turned in for the night and politely declined her invitation. And I normally would have, but Caldwell seemed such a strange and interesting place. I was unable to say no; I was curious about the town and the surrounding area, and certainly intrigued about the mysterious young woman, Crystal.

In no time, I was sitting next to her as we raced over the countryside in her flashy new car. The inside of the car was warm and comforting as she had the heat turned low. The Mustang smelled fresh and clean as a new car does. Crystal smelled nice as well- her hair still wet from a recent shower. The night was darker than usual as heavy clouds hung low in the sky, making it hard for me to appreciate the roadway scenery of the surrounding rugged hillsides and follow the route for which she drove. Neither of us said a word for most of the ride. I tried my hardest to come up with something witty or clever to say. I had nothing. She occasionally would look over to me and ask if I was all right. I'd politely nod. Because she drove, I had given myself up. I didn't know where we were going or how late we'd be out. She controlled the night.

Eventually we came upon a non-descript sign that simply directed, 'Church Next Right'. Crystal passed the sign and slowed the car, taking the right onto a gravel road. Tall field lights lit the sky in the distance. The muffled sounds of outdated public address speakers along with crowd noise echoed off the surrounding hillsides. We drove about a mile towards the lights, finally reaching a large, barn-like church that was blacked out and closed. The parking lot, however, was filled with thirty or forty cars. A crowd had gathered in grandstands behind the church that flanked one side of a boxing ring-type stage illuminated by the field lights.

Crystal parked the car. We got out. It was a damp, cool night. I followed her behind the church. A heavy fog hovered above the field lights. Reaching the grandstands, several of the spectators in attendance studied us and stared until we took our seats in the last row of the bleachers at the top of the stands. I couldn't believe what I saw. Pairs of young men raced around the ring, picking up live snakes, some as large as five-feet long, and tossing them in burlap bags. The crowd cheered wildly.

"What in the hell...?" I mumbled, gazing at the spectacle in amazement. "Is this even legal?"

"Only in West Virginia, I think."

"What kind of snakes are those?"

"Mostly black snakes."

"Are they poisonous?"

"No, but their bites can be very painful."

"Has anyone died from this?"

"Every once in a while. It's usually because of infection after the bite. I knew a kid who lost his right arm."

Mesmerized, I watched the competition as the enthusiastic crowd loudly cheered.

"What are they cheering for?"

"Their friend or relative. A bite. Just like in car racing, some people come for the wrecks."

"Have you ever...?"

"No," she said, shaking her head. "I don't do snakes."

"Other than bagging snakes, how does one make a living around here? There doesn't seem to be a lot of opportunities."

"You have to be creative."

A bell rang, and the snakes in the bags were counted. A winner was declared, and his hand was raised over his head to the delight of the crowd.

"All that for fifty bucks? Damn."

Two more guys entered the ring. A bell sounded, and the same set of snakes were dumped in the middle. The snakes seemed to be angrier at that point in the night.

"Do you go to college?"

She shook her head, staring at the ring.

"How about a job?"

She shrugged, not looking at me.

"Then what do you do?"

"Things," she glanced over.

"What things?"

"I don't know. I help my father with his business. What does it matter?"

"I'm just curious. How do people get by around here?"

"You've worked in the drug store a couple days now. You tell me- how do they get by?"

One of the men in the ring suddenly was bitten by a gnarly, ragged-looking, four-foot long black snake. Some in the crowd cheered and laughed. Others gasped.

"Goddam, this shit's nuts!"

Several people rushed into the ring to attend to the man who screamed in pain, violently shaking his bitten hand.

"So, what do you think?" she asked as I watched the medic tend to the bitten man.

"I'd rather go to a movie theater."

"There aren't any theaters in Caldwell."

A lone 40-watt bulb from a lamp missing its shade lit the damp, musty dressing room in the back of Frank's Supper Club. Dirty ashtrays and empty beer bottles cluttered the space. The chipped plaster ceiling was coming down. Staring at a mirror covered with numerous black and white photos that had yellowed with time, Jack Chub sat shirtless, meticulously applying eye liner, then lipstick. The James Brown song, "*It's a Man's World,*" quietly played through the static of old transistor radio. Its antenna aimed at the heavens. Capping the lipstick, he stared at his worn, tired reflection through the smoke from a long smoldering ash that clung to the end of a cigarette. A knock on the dressing room door caused him to sigh.

"Yes," he called as the door slowly pushed open, and Johnny Fogg cautiously entered.

"Johnny Fogg? What you doin' here? Now, this IS a surprise!"

Johnny reached out a small Avon bag that was stapled shut. Searching through the mess on the table in front of him, Jack found a small change purse and dug out some cash.

"No Tolly tonight?"

Johnny nervously shook his head as Jack handed him several twenty-dollar bills and took the bag.

"You doin' all right, Johnny? I ain't seen you in a LONG time."

Johnny nodded, but didn't answer, and only stared at Jack for a moment or two before leaving. As soon as the door to the room closed, Jack glanced around until spotting a mostly empty fifth of Old Crow whiskey. He poured himself a shot and took a couple of non-descript pills from the bag that Johnny had given him. He looked to the whiskey, then to the pills he cupped in his wrinkled hands, before catching his reflection in the mirror again. He had two shows to do, and it would be another long night. He swallowed hard on the pills with a shake of his head, not taking his eyes off his reflection.

Frank's Supper Club was situated along an old logging route in a secluded wooded area not visible from the main road. If you didn't know the place existed, you never would find it. The parking lot was filled with pick-ups and older model cars from the nineties, and even some from as early as the eighties. Crystal parked the Mustang under the club's flashing green and red neon entrance light. As I got out of the car, a rusted, red pick-up truck appeared from a lot behind the club. I studied the familiar truck and immediately recognized Johnny Fogg behind the wheel with his shaggy brown dog, Rufus. Johnny honked the horn.

"Hold on a minute," I called to Crystal before she entered the club.

I approached the truck. Johnny sweated profusely.

"I believe you," I said as Johnny studied me with a puzzled look. "Something's not right at the drug store."

"You got to help me. I didn't kill no one."

"Huh?"

"Someone killed Tolly."

"Tolly?"

"Someone killed Tolly."

"Did you go to the police?"

"No police! I need your help."

"I can't get involved."

"You already are."

I glanced to Crystal who waited by the club's entrance, then looked back to Johnny.

"You gotta help me," he pleaded.

"I'll help if you let me go to the sheriff."

"You can't! He's in on it!"

We stared at each other a moment, before he pulled the Pabst beer cap down low over his eyes

"You don't know it," he warned. "But you're already in deep."

He glanced away with the most serious look and rolled up the truck window before driving off into the night.

I followed Crystal into Frank's. I was somewhat concerned about Johnny's warning until I got my first look at the inside of Frank's. I stood in amazement, studying the club's odd and dated interior. The world outside may have changed through the years, but the inside of Frank's had remained the same, untouched in over five decades. The place was lit by red lights and crowded with rednecks, well-dressed blacks, cross-dressers, and hillbilly hipsters. A purple velvet curtain hung in front of a wooden stage. A spotlight illuminated a sign over the stage that read 'Jack and Jill Chub Performing Nightly'.

"I never expected this," I said before Crystal wandered to the bar to order drinks.

As I continued to study the inside of the club, the curtain to the stage slowly opened and a five-piece band, complete with guitars, drums, and horns, began a song. In drag, Jack Chub appeared, wearing a sparkling blue evening gown. He was flanked by twin, heavy-set teenage girls in green rhinestone jumpsuits who swayed to the music.

"Ladies and gentlemen!" the club's announcer spoke into a microphone, "Jill Chub!"

The crowd cheered in approval. Jack held out his arms and raised them up as a signal to cheer louder. The crowd roared as he started into the Conway Twitty song, *It's Only Make Believe.* The twins harmonized in perfect pitch.

Out of the dress and without the wig and make-up, Jack joined Crystal and I in a booth in the back of the club. With a handkerchief, he continually wiped at the heavy sweat that beaded on his forehead and ran down the back of his neck. He swirled a shot of cheap whiskey in a small cocktail glass and played with a burning cigarette with his thumb and forefingers. He told us incredible stories that I'm sure Crystal had heard before as she seemed to not to pay attention to a word he said. I occasionally would glance over- her eyes always locked on mine. At first, I quickly looked away, but as the evening progressed and the alcohol dulled my wariness, my looks and stares lingered. By the way she gazed at me, I knew I was in well over my head. Crystal was an invitation to trouble.

"I's jus' a kid," Jack reminisced. "I didn't know nothin' about myself. 'Til then my whole world was a two-hundred-acre peanut farm in Georgia."

"How did you end up in music?" I asked.

"We'd be singin' all day in the fields. The right white man heard me singin' the right song at exactly the right time- like he was sent from HEAVEN! Three weeks later I's openin' for Little Richard and James Brown."

"James Brown?"

"James 'FUCKIN" Brown, man! Elvis Presley, shit. James Brown was the REAL king! ON THE ONE! WHOAA!"

"Many celebrities have stopped here when passing through," Crystal spoke up.

"Who passes through here?"

Crystal lit a cigarette for herself and Jack.

"You'd be surprised," she said. "If you hang out long enough, you'll see the whole world pass through here."

"We played EVERYWHERE! Those honkies in the small towns had never seen anything like us," Jack continued. "It was three shows a night, six days a week, and always another white woman to fuck. Shit! I didn't know any better. I's jus' a dumb dirt boy from the south who'd never seen nothin'."

"How'd you end up in Caldwell?"

"I's tired, man. Three long years of twelve-hour bus rides, always wakin' up in another town, cocaine and bennies, bourbon at breakfast, you name it."

He took a swig of whiskey.

"My mama's family worked the peanut farm, and my papa's family migrated north for work in the coal mines. I took a vacation to come up here to see a sick aunt. Ain't never left. I jus' couldn't get back on the road. All my dreams had come TRUE! But too soon. I's all washed up at only twenty-two."

"And, now?"

"And, now?" He held out his arms and motioned to the stage. "It's been nothin' but rainbows and lollipops for the last thirty years in this dump."

Jack finished his drink and stood.

"Excuse me, I gots another set to do."

"I have to ask. Who's better- Jack or Jill Chub?"

He flashed a sneaky smile.

"That all jus' depends on what kind of mood I's in."

A waitress appeared as Jack slipped behind the door to his dressing room.

"Another drink?" Crystal asked me.

"One more then I have to go."

The waitress nodded and left for the bar.

"I'm sure every guy in this county would trade places with me right now. How'd I get so lucky?"

"Nothing ever changes around here. I like to try new things."

"I've seen you in the drug store. Did you know Aaron, the pharmacist before me?"

"I knew who he was, but I didn't really know him."

"Do you know what happened to him?"

"No."

"Do you think he may have been murdered?"

"You writing a book?"

At that moment, the front door to the club opened. Crystal glanced to the door where a muscular, jock-type young man entered.

"Oh, shit," she mumbled under her breath.

"What?"

"We need to go."

"Huh?"

I glanced to the entrance as she suddenly grabbed my hand.

"Come on!"

We dashed for the restrooms as the guy at the door spotted us and hurriedly chased. Crystal and I slipped into the Ladies' room, locking the door behind us. She urgently scanned the room and discovered a window above the toilet.

"Help me up!"

She hopped on the toilet seat, and I helped boost her up to the window. As she struggled to slide the window open, the guy chasing us pounded and shook at the door, trying to force it open.

"Crystal!" he yelled, banging the door. "Crystal!"

She worked the window open and pulled herself through.

"Come on!"

I quickly followed as the bathroom door kicked open. The guy grabbed my leg as I tried to get out the window. Desperately pulling my leg free, I violently kicked the guy in the face with my heel before slipping through the window and racing with Crystal to the car. We both quickly glanced back. No one followed. Out of breath, we jumped in, and she put the car in gear and sped away. Panting, I looked over to her, trying to catch my breath. She looked back with a grin.

"What'd you do to him?" I asked, gasping for air.

"I broke his heart."

Accelerating the Mustang, she looked away. Her grin was gone. She stared into the dark night and focused on the country road that rushed underneath us. Again, I turned and looked to the roadway behind us. No one followed.

With the engine still running, the Mustang was parked in front of the motel where I had been staying. It was late. The town was dark, deserted, and pleasantly quiet. A dense fog had rolled in, diming the downtown streetlights. Lost in the mist, we could've been the last two people on earth. From the passenger seat, I stared at Crystal. Just as she had all night, she wore a concerned, almost troubled look. She constantly checked her phone as if she was supposed to be somewhere else. After all that had happened and all that I had just seen, I was too juiced and not ready to turn in for the evening. I continued to stare at Crystal, but she wouldn't look over.

"What's your dad do?" I asked, wanting to find out more about her.

"I told you. Things."

"What about your mother?"

She finally looked over.

"Goodnight, Michael."

I continued to stare, before getting out of the car and leaning in the window.

"The guy at the bar. He won't..."

"No."

She looked away and gazed into the steering wheel.

"I don't want tonight to end," I spoke up, not sure what I was saying. I certainly was fueled by the excitement of the evening and a little too much alcohol.

"I have to be somewhere."

"At this hour?"

She didn't respond.

"Will I see you again?"

"You're like a cop," she quickly glanced to me, "so many questions."

"Well?"

"I know where to find you."

I stepped back from the car as she slowly pulled away. I watched for a minute or so until the Mustang's taillights disappeared in the darkness.

With a groan, then deep sigh, Butterman rolled his bloated, sweaty body off Gloria Morgan who was nearly smothered below him. Breathing heavy, he blankly stared at the cracked ceiling of the sparsely furnished bedroom. She looked away. Her damaged body remained still. She felt nothing. Pleasure had long left her.

"What happened to my son?"

In the darkness, Butterman searched the nightstand next to the bed, finding a pack of cigarettes. He pulled out two, placed them in his mouth, and lit them. He handed one to her.

"The sheriff's working on it," he answered, not looking at her.

With the cigarette hanging from his mouth, he dragged himself out of bed. The sun had yet to rise. Naked, he lugged his heavy body into the kitchen of the small apartment. He opened the refrigerator. It was empty except for a half-filled bottle of cheap vodka.

"We don't eat much around here," she called from the bed, sucking on the cigarette.

He studied the vodka a moment, before reaching for it. He opened the cupboard and pulled out a couple of glasses. He checked the freezer. The plastic ice cube tray was empty. He poured two full glasses of vodka and joined her in bed.

"Your son had a lot of secrets," he said, sampling the vodka with a grimace.

"Aaron told me everything," she replied, sipping the vodka. A cloud of cigarette smoke hung over her.

"Did Aaron have any girlfriends?"

"Of course, he did."

Butterman stubbed out the cigarette and moved to the edge of the bed, reaching for his clothes.

"I tried to set him up with the sweetest piece of ass in Caldwell. This gal would've done anything he wanted."

Gloria dragged hard on the cigarette as he dressed in the dark.

"But he wasn't interested."

"Just leave, please."

"After cocktails one evening at my place…"

"Just leave, I said!"

"He insisted on playing footsies with me under the table."

"Leave!"

"He sucked me off that night," Butterman recalled, standing. "And he enjoyed it."

"Get out!"

"And he did me the next night. Then the next night, too."

His cold stare sliced through her.

"You bastard!"

"I loved your boy!"

"Get the fuck out, I said!"

"So, I'm guessing he came on to the wrong redneck in the wrong part of the woods. They don't like that sort of thing in..."

Before he could finish, she flung the glass of vodka at him. Butterman ducked as the glass shattered against the wall.

"Get out!"

Butterman walked to the door but stopped before leaving.

"I'll be around for a couple more days. If you get lonely and want some company," he said, pointing to the bed. "You know where to find me."

Crying, she reached for a dirty ashtray and tossed it at him as he slipped out the door. She threw herself back onto the bed and violently punched at the pillows and mattress.

Chapter 4
I Don't Know for Sure

After a long and tiring shift at the pharmacy, I slipped out the back of the drug store and sneaked to the motel room. I couldn't wait to lock myself away for a few hours before sleep. I didn't want to see anyone. I knew morning would come soon enough, and I would have to get up and do the same thing all over again. After dealing with the public, a mostly sick and elderly public in my case, for an entire day, I just wanted some time alone.

As soon as I entered the room, I locked the door, kicked off my shoes for the first time in more than ten hours, hung up my pharmacist's smock, and threw myself on the bed. Never had a bed felt so warm and comforting. As I reached for the remote control for the television, my phone started to ring from the pocket of my smock. I'm sure it was Meredith, and I really wanted to talk with her, but I didn't know if I could pull myself out of bed. As I struggled and pushed myself up to retrieve the ringing phone, there suddenly was a knock on the motel room door. Reluctantly, I slowly opened it.

"So, the ghost returns."

"Can I come in?" Crystal asked.

"I had an interesting time the other night, but..."

"I'm in trouble," she interrupted as my phone continued to ring.

I hesitated a moment, before moving aside to let her enter, keeping the motel room door open. I knew it was a mistake, and I doubted she was in trouble. I studied her as she took a seat on the bed. I glanced to the smock as my phone stopped ringing.

"Sit with me, Michael."

"What kind of trouble?" I asked, standing by the open motel room door.

"Come here. Sit with me."

"The guy from the Supper Club?"

"What are you afraid of?"

"You're not in trouble."

She stood up from the bed and approached.

"I think it's best you go."

"That's not what you want."

"I want you to leave."

"Let me stay," she said, easing her body closer and shutting the door. "Have you thought about me?"

I looked away and didn't answer as she gently reached for my hand.

"You have thought about me," she whispered as I pulled my hand away. "You're an honest boy. You would never lie to me."

"This isn't a game," I said, shooting a glance to the smock as my phone started to ring again.

"It's all right," she purred, practically blowing the words into my ear.

I looked back to her. She inched closer. I didn't move. Again, she reached for my hand.

"I really am in trouble," she said- her warm hand tightly squeezing mine. "I need a place to hide."

"It isn't a good idea."

"Just tonight," she persisted, resting her other hand on the small of my back.

I glanced around the room. She leaned her face in close.

"It's all right."

I looked back to her. I couldn't escape her stare. My heart raced. My face blushed. I tried to play it cool, but I was fucking melting before her, and she knew it. She took my other hand and led me to the bed. We took a seat. I had trouble keeping eye contact. She smiled.

"Please," I mumbled, "you can't stay."

"Sssshhh," she whispered, easing her face close and softly brushing her lips across mine.

I instantly stood and reached for the smock to check the ringing phone, knowing it was Meredith, but Crystal didn't allow me to move, gently wrapping her arms around my waist and pulling me into her lap.

"Everything will be all right, Michael."

She reached over to the nightstand and turned off the lamp beside the bed that lit the room. The phone stopped ringing. Within seconds, she was on top of me, our bodies entangled. Our clothes half off. The next twenty or thirty minutes were but a blur as we explored each other's body in the dark, under the covers. I didn't recall much, and barely felt a thing. It all happened too fast and without warning. Our encounter was not romantic. It was more clumsy than sexy, more mess than emotion. When we finished, she rolled off and stared. I could barely make eye contact. It would be days before I could look at myself in the mirror.

"Can I stay?" she asked.

"Yes."

She pulled off her shirt that was turned sideways across her chest and unclipped her bra, before kicking off her underwear and pants that had balled up around her knees.

"You okay?" she whispered, glancing to me.

"Yes."

She turned away and backed her warm, naked body into mine. At first, I didn't know where to put my arms, before eventually resting them around her shoulders. She quickly fell asleep in my awkward embrace. I didn't move, staring at the wall for what seemed like hours, afraid to look at her, but not letting go, hypnotized by her sweet, inviting scent and the easy rhythm of her soft, repetitive breaths. At some point, I followed her lead and drifted off to sleep, a completely different person.

Rays of sunlight slipped through a crack between the heavy plastic curtains that darkened the motel room, waking me. I opened my eyes and wearily scanned the room. Initially, I wasn't exactly sure of my surroundings. I glanced next to me. Crystal was asleep at my side. With urgency, I popped up and frantically searched for a clock, before reaching for my phone.

"Shit!"

I was late. The drug store had been open for thirty minutes. I hopped out of bed and scrambled around the room, pulling on clothes, some of which I had worn the day before. Racing into the bathroom, I quickly brushed my teeth and dragged a brush through my messed-up bed hair. I rushed for the motel room door, but stopped before leaving, and glanced back to Crystal. The bare skin of her naked back shined in the morning light as she slept.

Already late, I dashed away from the motel room. The pharmacy couldn't dispense prescriptions without me. But also, I ran as if I had committed a crime, frightened of what I had done and needing to escape the scene as fast as possible. I'd never had a one-night stand. That kind of thing never happened before and didn't appeal to me. All my sexual relations, and there hadn't been many to that point in my life, involved Meredith and a couple of other young women with whom I had actively dated in the past. The night I spent with Crystal was wrong. I understood that. I didn't even know her. But it happened so fast- like an avalanche that wouldn't be stopped. I hated what I had done. I could never see Crystal again after that, which would be difficult in a town as small as Caldwell. I needed to talk with Meredith. I had to confess everything, hoping she'd forgive me.

With a deep breath, I pushed opened the front door of the drug store and brushed at the messy mop of hair on top of my head. I could hear the phones in the pharmacy ringing. Archie waited for me at the pharmacy counter. Pulling on my pharmacist's smock, I hustled to the back after entering. A long line of frustrated patients waited at the pharmacy counter as Tammy frantically filled prescriptions. Both pharmacy phones continued to ring. Several completed prescription orders awaited my approval. By law, they couldn't be dispensed to the patients until checked and approved by a registered pharmacist.

"Sorry."

Not looking up, Tammy pointed to the filled orders.

"You need to check those."

I started going through the orders.

"Some people have been waitin' more than a half-hour."

"It won't happen again."

"Archie's been here the longest. Better take care of him first."

I joined him in the waiting area. I practically had to hold my nose as I secured the blood pressure cuff over his arm. The garlic smell was especially strong and overwhelming that morning. I nearly vomited.

"You like eggplant?" he asked, pulling a eight-inch long eggplant from a paper bag.

"Huh?"

"You like eggplant?"

"Yeah, I guess so."

"Here," he said, reaching it out me. "I got 'em comin' out my ass. It's been a good year for eggplant."

"I really don't have the...," I started to say, shaking my head.

"How 'bout turnips?" he interrupted, pulling out a handful of turnips from his bag.

"Michael!" Tammy called. "I need help here."

The pharmacy had been extremely busy that morning. For the first time since I had started working there, I was having trouble keeping pace. The wait time for prescriptions were over an hour. We even took the phones off the hook for a short period of time to give ourselves a chance to catch up. As Tammy waited on a patient, she turned and tossed me a prescription bottle that I had filled earlier.

"You put that in the wrong bag."

Flustered, I studied the bottle and shook my head, trying to figure out the order to which it belonged.

"That was a drop off."

"What?"

"Mr. Myers dropped it off. He'll be back for it later. It must've got mixed in with another order."

Tammy and I switched places. I began to ring up and cash out several of the patients who'd been waiting for their orders. She started to fill some of the many call-in orders from Dr. Valenzuela's office that were lined up across the pharmacy counter. Studying the first one, she shook her head and called me over.

"Who's this one for?"

"Huh?" I asked, checking the prescription order.

"There's no name. You didn't write down the name."

"What?" I continued to study the order, realizing that I had indeed forgot to record the patient's name.

"You all right? You're not yourself this mornin'. You look as if you've seen a ghost."

"More than seen one," I mumbled, shaking my head. "I'll call Dr. V's office back and get the name."

"No, I'll call. Take a break."

"Huh?"

"Five minutes. Clear your head. Get one of those coffees Evelyn jus' dropped off."

I took Tammy's advice and headed for the storage room in back. The patients who waited in line at the cash register watched as I left the pharmacy area.

Staring into the motel room mirror, Crystal sat on the dresser, applying fresh lipstick. She wore only lace panties and a revealing white tank top. After applying the lipstick, she studied her reflection for a moment, brushing at the bangs of her hair. Her phone started to ring. She momentarily blinked, but didn't answer it, not once looking away from the mirror. The ringing stopped. Spinning herself around on the dresser, she reached for a bottle of toenail polish, pulled her long slender legs against her chest, and meticulously began to apply the polish in slow, short strokes. The phone started to ring again. She stared a moment, before reaching for it. First, she checked the number then answered the phone. A man's voice came over the line.

"Well?"

"I'm in the motel room now. This'll be a piece of cake."

I retreated to the storage room in the back of the store and took a seat alone on a stack of wooden shipping crates. I pulled out my phone and stared at it a moment. I had to call Meredith. But even with the door shut to the room, I could hear the phones in the pharmacy ringing. I could hear prescription labels being printed. I could hear Tammy chatting with patients as the cash register hummed. As I dialed my phone, I hadn't quite figured out how I'd deal with the fact that I had just been unfaithful to my fiancée.

"Why didn't you answer my calls?" Meredith asked before I could say a word

"I'm sorry for everything."

"Sorry? You sound different."

"I need to tell you something."

"Is everything all right?"

There was a long pause, but I cowardly chickened out in confessing my deceit.

"I really didn't know what I was getting into coming here."

"Michael, just quit. Come home. Go back to school."

"I can't now. I'm sorry. I know this is not what you planned when you moved back to Pittsburgh."

"This is crazy."

"I wish I could talk more, but we're so busy this morning."

"Michael?"

"The first day that I get off, which may not be for another week or so, I'll come home to visit. I promise. We'll talk."

"About what?"

"Everything. But not over the phone."

"Michael. Are you're all right?'

"I'll call you tonight."

"Please, wait. Don't hang up."

I turned off the phone and stared at the floor for many minutes, until scrambling to the small employees' bathroom in back with a sick feeling in my stomach. Within seconds, I violently vomited into a sink. Glancing up, I quickly looked away from my reflection in the bathroom mirror before rinsing out my mouth and wetting my face with cold water. I needed to call Meredith back, but I couldn't. I was a coward.

As the day progressed, I couldn't stop from dwelling on what I had done the night before. I felt awful about myself and how I had cheated on Meredith. Nobody deserved that kind of treatment, especially her. I had never known anyone more faithful or honest. I knew I had to tell her what I had done. But I couldn't do it over the phone. It had to be in-person, face-to-face. She deserved that much. I considered driving to Pittsburgh after work that night to see her, knowing that I'd have to turn around almost immediately after I got there and come straight back. I couldn't be late for my shift the next day. But I had to do it to save my relationship.

I had trouble focusing in the pharmacy the entire day. At one point, I kept dropping hearing aid batteries as I tried to help Mr. Morris replace the dead ones in his hearing aids. The batteries were tiny, and as I would take them out of the package, they would slip from my fingers, bounce off the pharmacy counter, and roll around on the floor. Most times I wouldn't find them and need to open another package. After finally securing two new batteries, I first had to wipe off the grease, grime, and ear wax that had collected on each of the hearing aids. Then I had to pry out the old batteries from the devices and insert the new ones. Because of the constant tremor in his hands from early stages of Parkinson's disease, I physically had to insert the hearing aids directly back into his ears. And as I discovered, this was not an easy task. As I nestled poor Mr. Morris' head between my arm and chest, Butterman appeared with a smile.

"Getting intimate with the customers, I see," he joked, then looked to Tammy. "Looks like we got a keeper here."

"He's a good one. A little shaky this morning, but maybe a bit shell-shocked after the crazy day we had yesterday."

The hearing aids were finally inserted in Mr. Morris' ears. He smiled and continually shook my hand. I rubbed his back as he pulled out his wallet to get cash to pay for the batteries. He wanted to tip me, but I wouldn't let him.

"Yeah," Butterman responded, studying my interaction with the elderly man. "The first of the month has a way of separating the men from the boys."

After cashing out Mr. Morris, Butterman handed me a key. I studied the key a moment before putting it in my pocket. At that point, all I wanted to do was to go home to Pittsburgh. Maybe coming to Caldwell was the worst decision I could've ever made. I might lose a fiancée that I truly adored over it.

"That key goes to the front door of my house. I leave for Florida this afternoon. You have the place all to yourself for the next several months. I've stocked the pantry with plenty of food, beer, and other snacks. And please help yourself to the cocktail bar."

"Thank you," I said, nodding.

"You don't know what a huge favor you're doing for me. Also, Super-Rite has reserved your room at the motel until I come back, so if you're tired or the weather's bad, especially when it snows, you can stay there. But you got to be here at the store every morning on the days you're schedule to work no matter what. And you know, we can't open the pharmacy without a pharmacist. Also, Super-Rite has arranged for a fill-in pharmacist to come here two or three days a month and over Christmas to give you some time off."

I continued to nod.

"So, you got it?" he asked, motioning to Tammy. "And Tammy will be here with you. If you need anything, you can always call her anytime, right?"

"Right," she answered.

"And remember, as I already explained, you'll get three large quarterly checks sometime late November, early December. One from the nursing home, one from Dr. V's office, and one from rehab hospital. Do not, I repeat do not, put those checks in the regular store deposit. They go into the Super-Rite outside vendor account at the bank that I told you about earlier."

I continued to nod as Butterman smiled.

"I can't get out of here fast enough," he beamed. "I'll see you two in the springtime."

"Have fun," I said.

"Don't worry about that. I don't want to think about this place for any reason. So, please don't call me unless, of course, my house is burning down or someone's died."

As the end of my shift neared, I decided I would head home to Pittsburgh and spill my guts to Meredith about the encounter with Crystal. Because I wouldn't have much time for the visit, I planned to rush to Butterman's house after closing and grab a few things I may need for the drive- something to snack on, coffee, a jacket, and a change of clothes for my shift the next day. If I left as soon as I could after I got off from work, I figured that I would get to Pittsburgh at about one-thirty in the morning. I would then need to leave by about four o'clock, so I would be back in time to open the pharmacy the next morning. That then would give me a couple of hours to spend with Meredith. The plan seemed crazy and perhaps not feasible, but it something I had to do it. I needed to save our relationship, and I knew the only way would be to confess to her face-to-face.

It was supposed to be my first night in Butterman's house. Unlike the easy two-minute walk to the motel, I had a good thirty-minute drive on unfamiliar, winding backroads to get there before I could travel to Pittsburgh. And I was tired enough. After entering the darkened and strangely quiet house, I found some lights, started a pot of coffee, and scrambled around the place, getting the things I needed for the drive. Suddenly, there was a knock at the front door.

"Who in the hell?"

The knocking continued as I eventually opened the door.

"What are you doing here?" I asked, surprised to see Crystal.

"I wanted to see you again."

"How'd you know I was here?"

"You weren't at the motel. And Caldwell's a small town. Everyone knows that Mr. Butterman left today."

She studied me. I remained in the doorway, not moving. I checked my watch, knowing I had to leave soon.

"Can I come in?"

"No."

"No?"

"I can't, Crystal."

"I want to apologize."

"Apologize?"

"I'm sorry about last night. I didn't mean for that to happen."

"Please, you must leave. I'm sorry. I have to be somewhere."

"I need a friend, Michael. That's it. Nothing more."

"I'm sorry, but...," I hesitated, and she again interrupted.

"Are you sure I can't come in? I'll only stay a short time."

"Not tonight. I'm going somewhere."

"Where?" she asked, but I didn't answer, again checking my watch. "Another time, then?"

"No, Crystal," I said, glancing away and trying my best to avoid her probing eyes. "Not tonight. Not ever."

I couldn't look back at her. I mostly kept my head down and talked to the ground. She could sense I was breaking.

"You don't mean that."

"Yes, yes, I do."

"I know you want to see me again."

"I have to go," I said finally looking up and staring in her eyes. "I'm sorry."

I stepped back inside the house and slowly shut the door. As I locked the deadbolt, I peeked out the door's window. Crystal still stood there. I took a deep breath and walked into the kitchen and poured some coffee in a thermos. Before grabbing the other items, I planned to take on the drive back to Pittsburgh, I peered out the picture window. Crystal's Mustang was still parked in the driveway. I walked back to the front door and opened it. Crystal hadn't moved. I stared at her a moment. I didn't take my eyes from hers. Eventually, I pushed the door open wider, and she stepped into the house.

"Nice gig," she said, checking out the entrance to Butterman's house. "How'd you pull this off?"

"You can't stay long."

"You giving me a tour?"

"Do you want a coffee?" I asked as I followed her into the kitchen.

"Sure."

I poured her a cup of coffee and handed it to her, checking the clock on the wall. I still tried to avoid eye contact. I led her into the living room, and we took a seat on different ends of the couch. She continued to stare at me. I wouldn't look back.

"I don't want you to get the wrong impression of me," she said. "But I understand if you do..."

"That wasn't me last night," I interrupted.

"I know."

"And that wasn't me the first night we met. I tend to be more guarded. Moving here, that first night on my own...," I paused, finally looking over. "I've been hating myself all day."

"You're a good guy, Michael," she said, sliding next to me on the couch. "I could tell that the moment I met you. That's why I had to meet you. Most of the guys I've dated here never gave a shit about me. It was all about the party. I want something more."

"A good guy wouldn't have done what I did last night."

"Who are you hurting?"

"I can't get involved, Crystal."

"I need a friend," she pressed, sliding her body closer to mine on the couch. "That's all."

"I'm here to work hard, make some money, pay off some debt," I said, standing from the couch. "I want to be left alone."

"That's likely impossible here."

"I'm politely asking you to leave," I said, holding out my hand and helping her from the couch.

"Of course, Michael," she said, taking my hand and following me to the door. "I'll be around if you need someone hang out with. I'll come see you at the store."

I nodded, not looking at her, and opened the front the door.

"You sure I can't stay?"

"I'm sorry," I said, motioning for her to leave.

"I'm sorry about last night. I never intended to come on so strong."

We again stared a moment before she started to walk away. She suddenly stopped and turned as I began to shut the door.

"I wanted to give you another chance."

"Another chance?"

"Nobody turns me down for a second chance."

"Second chance?"

I wasn't quite sure what she meant. Was she referring to my performance, or lack of performance, in bed or something else? We studied each other, before she turned and disappeared into the night. I stepped back inside the house and watched from the window as her Mustang slowly pulled away. I leaned back against the closed front door and slid down into a sitting position, knowing that I wouldn't be going to Pittsburgh that night. I promised myself I'd go the next night. Even though I was so very tired from all that had happened since I'd arrived in Caldwell, I don't believe I slept a single minute that night unable to reconcile my behavior and restore faith in myself.

It was another tiring ten-hour day at the drug store, not much different from the previous one. Again, I was exhausted and wanted to rest. On the long drive to Butterman's house, I decided I would confess to Meredith about Crystal. I couldn't wait any longer. As soon as I had opened the front door to Butterman's house, I dialed the phone. I was ready to tell her everything.

"Hey, babe. What's up?"

"I just got to the house."

"How you doing?"

"You know how yesterday I said I needed to tell you..."

"I got good news, Michael. My father spoke with the dean of the medical school today," she enthusiastically interrupted me. "You need to come home immediately. He got you an interview tomorrow."

"You know I can't get off work. I can't pick up and leave at this point."

"But Michael, we could be together."

"Meredith…," I started to say before being distracted by a noise outside as if someone had entered the garage. "I think someone's here."

"What?"

"Someone's here."

"In the house?"

"I don't know."

"Who'd be there at this time of night?"

"Maybe a neighbor, a friend of Butterman. I don't know."

"They know where you're staying?"

"Everyone knows I'm staying at Butterman's. It's a small town, and it's not a secret. I'm not hiding from anyone."

"Do you want me to call someone? 911?"

"I better get off of here."

"Michael!"

"Goodbye, Meredith. I'll call you back."

"Don't hang up! What do you want me to tell my father about tomorrow?"

I hung up the phone and heard the noise again. It was coming from the garage. I slowly crept to the door leading to a set of stairs down to the garage, pulling it open. Crystal suddenly appeared, startling me as I stumbled back into the kitchen.

"Jesus Christ! What are you doing here?"

"I thought you'd be more excited to see me."

"How did you get in here?"

"I took this the other night," she said, holding out a key and motioning to a small key rack hanging on the wall by the refrigerator in the kitchen. "I wanted to surprise you."

"Give me the key."

"Really?"

"The key."

She stared at me a moment before finally dropping it in my hand.

"I don't have to be anywhere for a little while, so I don't suppose you'd want to..."

"Leave, Crystal."

"You're serious?"

"I'm serious. Please leave."

"I guess I'll never know," she said, turning away from me.

"Never know what?" I asked, following her as she reached the front door and stepped outside.

She didn't turn to me or answer as she rushed down the stairs at the front of the house that led to the driveway. I chased after her. She still wouldn't turn to me, pulling car keys from her purse.

"Never know what?"

I grabbed her arm as she reached for the door handle of the Mustang. She aggressively yanked her arm away from me.

"Don't touch me like that ever again. You got that!"

"Never know what?"

"If you keep rejecting me..."

"Never know what?"

She threw her purse into the car, slid into the driver's seat, and pulled the car door shut with a slam as I stepped away from the car. The Mustang's powerful engine roared to life as she turned the key in the ignition. I waited for her to look to me, but she didn't. Instead, she glanced over her shoulder, put the car in reverse, and whipped it around. I took a step towards the car before she hit the gas, peeling out of the driveway, and squealing away into the night.

Feeling deflated, I retreated to the house and went directly into the kitchen. I took the house key that Crystal had stolen and hung it back on the rack by the refrigerator. I returned to the living room, threw myself on the couch, and surfed through hundreds of television channels repeatedly for hours, unable to sleep. During that time, Meredith had called back to check on me. I assured her everything was fine. But I don't think she believed me. And I still didn't tell her about Crystal.

It was a quiet Sunday in the drug store. My first week as a pharmacist was ending, and the week had been a challenge in more ways than one. I was very tired, almost to the point of collapse. I was running on fumes. I hadn't slept much. The non-stop activity within the pharmacy at the first of the month was a nearly overwhelming. My feet and back ached from standing for ten hours a day. I had just found out from Super-Rite management that they couldn't get me a fill-in pharmacist for another six days to allow me a day-off. But more importantly, I felt horrible about what I had done to Meredith. I couldn't figure out when I'd be able to go home and talk with her.

Fortunately, Tammy had come in on her off day that Sunday to help me re-stock the depleted pharmacy and catch up on some end-of-the-week paperwork. As I filled the few prescriptions orders that we did have that day, I repeatedly glanced up and scanned the mostly empty drug store. I hadn't seen Crystal in days. And since I last saw her, I kept catching myself searching the store for her. Each night at closing, I slowly would walk the dark and empty downtown streets, looking for any sign of her or the Mustang. Maybe she was gone forever I thought, and I'd never see her again. But I doubted that. Caldwell was too small. Tammy caught me with a blank stare on my face, gazing into nothing.

"Are you all right?"

At first, I didn't respond.

"Michael?"

"Huh?" I mumbled, looking over to her.

"Are you all right?"

"Yeah, yeah."

"I hope we're not losin' you. You're jus' gettin' started here. You haven't been yourself the last couple days."

"No. No. I'm just tired."

"You better get used it. You got another week of this before a day off."

"Explain to me again how Butterman's survived ten years of this."

The drug store closed early on Sunday, so I took advantage of Butterman's well-equipped kitchen and fully stocked cupboard and made a home-cooked meal. Because of the long hectic days at the pharmacy, I haven't eaten very well since I'd arrived in Caldwell. Finding jars of garden tomato sauce and green bean preserves that were gifted to Butterman by a regular at the pharmacy, I started a large pot of pasta on the stove and placed a loaf of bread coated with butter and garlic in the oven. As I waited for the pasta to cooked, I noticed something peculiar. The house key that I took from Crystal and hung on the key rack was missing. I searched around the counter and floor below the rack. I couldn't find the key anywhere.

As I tried my best to enjoy the meal, I couldn't stop thinking about what may have happened to the key. I knew I had hung it on the empty hook in the rack. Despite the nice meal I had prepared for myself, I couldn't eat much. I was worried that someone may have been in the house while I was at work. I searched the house and garage more than once. Nobody seemed to be in the house with me, and nothing appeared to have been taken. I doubled checked that all the doors and windows were locked, before eventually settling on the couch and flipping through scores of television channels for an hour or so. Eventually, overwhelmed by exhaustion after the sixty-six-hour work week, I drifted off and slept for ten straight, uninterrupted hours on the couch. Upon waking the next morning, I immediately glanced to the key rack, hoping it was all a dream. But the key was still gone.

It had been a mostly uneventful day at the pharmacy. It was near closing time, and I was wrapping up the end-of the-day paperwork and prepping the pharmacy for the next day. The only other person in the store at that time was Robbie, the teenager who ran the cashier at the front of the store after school. Glancing up, I noticed the front door to the store open, and two gentlemen entered. Usually at that time, folks came in for a last-minute pack of cigarettes or six-pack of beer. However, these two fellows headed directly to the pharmacy. I moved to the cash register to wait on them as they approached. The men were Whitey and Dorsey Blosser. Both were intoxicated and appeared to be under the influence of more than just alcohol. Their faces were flushed, and their eyes were bloodshot. With messed, wild dirty blonde hair, Whitey had one lazy eye and wore a black leather motorcycle jacket. He openly smoked a cigarette. Missing a front tooth, Dorsey sported a grease-stained work shirt with his name on a patch on the front and wore a filthy Chevrolet baseball cap that was pushed back high on top of his head.

Glaring at me and grinning, Whitey closely walked by the pharmacy counter and purposely stuck out his elbow, knocking down a display of brochures detailing specific health care information. The brochures scattered over the counter and floor.

"Sorry."

"No smoking in here," I warned him.

Whitey dropped the cigarette on the tiled floor and pressed it out with his boot. I looked to Dorsey who stood at an end-case of an aisle that displayed assorted bottles of discounted pain relievers. Not taking his eyes from mine, he began to open the bottles one-by-one and dumped the tablets from each onto the floor. He then stomped on the tablets, crushing them into pieces. I held my ground, having been taught not to confront an aggressive or dangerous customer in the store, especially one that was inebriated. I glanced to Robbie in front who held a phone to his ear and motioned to me if he should call the sheriff. I shook my head as Whitey violently pushed over a large plastic display tower that held an assortment of different-sized batteries. The packages of batteries scattered all over the floor. Whitey then angrily booted the display tower several times, putting large holes in the side of it.

"That'll be enough! I got the message."

Dorsey suddenly swiped his arm across each shelf that displayed the pain relievers and knocked all the bottles that were left to floor.

"We'll be back," Whitey warned.

"I know," I responded, trying my best to not look intimidated, when actually I was scared shitless.

As they left the store, the two dragged their arms across an entire aisle on their way out, knocking boxes of toothpaste, toothbrushes, cold medicines, and eye solutions all over the floor. Once they were gone, I rushed to the front of the store and quickly locked the door. Then over the next hour, Robbie and I cleaned up their mess and re-stocked the shelves. Although only a short distance, it was a spooky walk in the dark to my car in the parking lot after I finally left the store that night. The whole time I kept checking over my shoulder and behind my back. For I knew, without any doubt, I'd see the Blosser brothers again.

Driving to Butterman's house after the unsettling, and somewhat frightening, encounter with Whitey and Dorsey Blosser, I was more than a little on edge. And I couldn't stop think about the missing key. As I eased the car into the driveway, I parked, shut off the engine, and studied the blacked-out house for several minutes. Until that evening, I had always entered through the front door by way of the stairs along the front side of the house. On that night, I entered through the garage using the electronic door opener. Before proceeding upstairs into the house, I searched around for protection, finding an old set of dusty golf clubs. Taking the two-iron, I lightly stepped up the stairs that led into the kitchen. Without turning on the lights, I slowly crept through the house, checking every single room, holding the golf club out in front of me. Thankfully, the house was empty.

After turning on several lights in the house, I returned to the kitchen and again studied the empty hook on the rack where I had hung the missing key. I then closely examined the other hanging keys. Ever since I'd been in the house, I was curious about what was behind the locked door to Aaron's room. My imagination began to run wild. Maybe someone else, I thought, also was interested in what was in that room as well. Maybe that interested person or persons took the key. Leaning the golf club that I held against the kitchen table, I grabbed the handful of keys from the rack.

As I headed for Aaron's room, my heart nearly jumped out of my chest as there was unexpected pounding at the front door. I rushed back into the kitchen and grabbed the golf club, before slowly shuffling to the front door. I tried to peek out the small window at the side of the door to see who was there. I couldn't see anyone. I looked to the driveway. A car was parked there. I couldn't tell what type of the car in the dark. I had yet to turn on the outside lights. The pounding continued as I tightly clenched the two-iron behind my back and yanked the door open. I took a deep sigh and relaxed my grip on the golf club. It was Crystal. She spied the golf club I held and was ready with a snarky remark.

"Working on your golf game at this time of night?"

"The key's missing."

"What key?"

"The key you had. It's gone. Someone's been in here."

"No one's been in here. Relax."

Sensing my vulnerable and distracted state of mind, she slid by me and entered the house without an invitation.

"Where'd you put it? Let's look."

"On that rack," I said, motioning towards the kitchen. "By the refrigerator. Someone's been in here."

"Calm down. I'm sure you just misplaced it."

"No. It's not here. I looked everywhere."

She searched around the refrigerator, then kneeled and checked the floor. I suspiciously studied Crystal. She glanced over her shoulder up to me and stared back at my accusing eyes.

"What? You think I took it?" You saw me put it there. Why would I give it to you just to take it back?"

"I don't know, Crystal" I said, shaking my head. "I don't like this. This place scares the hell out of me. I'm thinking of moving back to the motel."

"What are you doing with all those other keys?" she asked, motioning to my hand.

"Something's not right in here, and the answer may be in there," I said, pointing to a locked door. "Aaron's room."

"You're not going in there, are you?"

Ignoring her, I began to try some of the keys in the lock as she moved close behind me. The first two didn't fit. The third key fit in the lock but wouldn't turn it.

"This isn't a good idea," she said.

The fourth key slipped into the lock like a knife through butter, and the lock easily opened. I looked back to Crystal and showed her a cautious grin while slowly pushing open the door. She reluctantly followed me into the room. It hadn't seemed as if anyone had been in there for quite some time. The air was stale and musty-smelling, and a thin layer of dust coated the furniture- a nightstand, dresser, and bookshelf. Immediately, I was struck by how organized and tidy the room was. The room was almost too neat. Without hesitation, I kneeled by the nightstand and grabbed the knob of the top drawer.

"Wait," she said, pulling the long sleeve of her shirt over her right hand and wiping off the knob I had just touched. "You don't want anyone to know you'd been in here."

Still using her sleeve and careful not to touch the knob with her fingertips, she carefully pulled the drawer open for me. Several bottles of liquid morphine were perfectly arranged in the drawer with multiple unopened packs of different sizes of needles and syringes. I reached for one of the bottles of morphine.

"Don't touch it," she said.

I nodded and motioned for her to open the middle drawer of the nightstand. It contained what looked like a stack of gay pornographic magazines. She closed the drawer as I motioned to the bottom one.

"Holy shit," I mumbled.

The drawer contained only one item- a stained handgun. Again, I reached in the drawer to pick it up.

"Is that blood?"

"Leave it be," Crystal said.

"What happened to Aaron?" I asked, intensively studying the gun in my hand.

"Let's get out of here."

"What happened to Aaron? Come on, tell me. I'm sure you know."

"I told you before. I didn't know the dude."

I studied her. She stared back, not once taking her eyes from mine.

"You better be careful," she advised. "Someone may be watching us. I wouldn't put it past Mr. Butterman to have cameras all over this place."

"No shit. I feel like he's watching my every move."

"Let's get out of here."

I returned the gun to the drawer and, we slipped out of the room and locked the door behind us. Crystal wiped the doorknob and lock clean with her sleeve.

"Somebody wants that gun."

"Why?"

"It may have to do with Aaron's disappearance."

"And you think Mr. Butterman may be involved?"

"I'm not sure. But I know someone who may be able to tell me."

"So, what's the next move, Sherlock?"

"This place creeps me out. I don't feel like staying here tonight."

"We can always go back to the motel."

"We?"

"You can go back to the motel."

"I don't have the energy to drive back to town at this hour."

"I'll keep you company."

"I don't think so."

"That's not what you want."

"How do you know what I want?"

"Come on."

"It isn't."

"I can see in your eyes, your body language. You light up when I'm around."

"Like now?"

"Yeah, like right now."

"But you have to go. I'm serious."

"What are you afraid of?"

"I'm not afraid of anything," I confidently responded, before a short pause. "But it's best you leave."

"I'm not leaving this time."

We studied each other a moment. Her stare pierced my soul. She could see right through me. I tried to look away, but she wouldn't let me. And she was right about everything. I was excited when she was around. I was thinking of her more, almost constantly, and less of Meredith. I was scared to death of her and afraid of where she was leading me. Crystal was poison, and I knew if I took one drink of her, I was finished.

"Please, Michael," she whispered. "Please, let me in."

"Crystal…"

"Can I? Can I, Michael? Can I stay?"

I didn't say no. I couldn't say no. After a very brief pause, she suddenly pressed me against the wall and started to nibble my neck, running her hands over my chest and back. I dropped the keys and quickly took her hand, leading her to the door of a spare bedroom where I had been sleeping. She blocked us from going in and instead dragged me down the hall to the main bedroom where Butterman slept, kissing and groping me the whole way. She kicked open the door that had always been closed. Not letting go, she pulled me with her down onto the bed and quickly climbed on top, kissing my lips, face, and neck. She abruptly stopped and sat up, glancing around the room that I had entered for the first time.

"You okay?" I asked.

Then, I noticed what had caught her attention. Not only did mirrors cover most of the walls of the room, but they also covered much of the ceiling as well. The sheets on the bed were made of red satin. The carpet was a heavy shag in deep purple. Funky, outdated light fixtures decorated the room.

"Mr. Butterman, I hardly knew you," she said, mesmerized by the bedroom's odd and raunchy décor.

With Crystal distracted, I glanced up and caught a reflection of myself in the mirror over the bed. I didn't recognize myself or the young woman on top of me. We were basically strangers in some mostly unknown place hidden from the outside world. I was hundreds of miles from anything familiar or that was

100

one time comfortable. I continued to stare at the reflection of a suddenly lost soul glaring back. Unable to reconcile what I was seeing, I reached over and turned off a lamp to darken the room, wanting the image to disappear and the real world to go away.

In the darkness, I aggressively grabbed Crystal's arms and pulled her off me, rolling her body underneath mine. Surprised and excited by my sudden boldness, she grinned and tried to move under the weight of my body. I wouldn't let her, pinning her against the mattress with both my legs and arms. Unlike the first time we were together, I was in control. At least, that's what I thought.

"You're not allowed to move."

"What?" she asked, staring back at me- her smile widened.

"The rule is- you can't move until I say you can. No matter what I do," I explained, slowly sliding my hand under her shirt and tickling her belly, "you have to stay perfectly still."

She giggled and squirmed, trying to kick her legs as I sat on her waist.

"Hey, what'd I'd say?"

Still grinning, she tried to remain still as I gently ran my hand over her warm, flat stomach up her chest and breasts to the top of her bra. Closing her eyes, she softly sighed and dug her body into the bed as I gently ran my fingers in and out of the bra, caressing her silky breasts. I leaned my face within inches of hers and slid my other hand down the front of her jeans. She sighed louder and bucked her pelvis into my hand, trying her hardest not to squirm.

"You can't move," I whispered.

Not taking her eyes from mine, she lifted her head slightly, searching for a kiss. I edged my face closer and touched my lips against hers. Before I could pull away, she softly bit my lower lip and held on to it for a moment.

"Uh, uh, no moving."

She let go of my lip. We continued to stare as I dug my hand deeper between her thighs. She turned her head away and sighed again, slightly rolling her body and grinding her hips into me. Easing my body off her, I lowered my face and gently moved my lips across her neck and over her ear. She turned. We studied each other a moment. Finally, I accepted her lips, and she kissed me liked I've never been kissed before for what seemed like hours. The hair on my arms and the back of my neck stood on end. I pulled my lips away and turned, not looking at her. I could feel her warm breath in my ear.

"Can I move?" she whispered.

"Yes."

"I'm so turned on, Michael," she purred.

Spent, naked, and vulnerable, I fell back onto the bed, trying to catch my breath. The ends of my fingers and toes tingled. Sweat dripped from my hair and rolled across my face onto the pillow under my head. Breathing heavy as well, Crystal was stretched out beside me, still locked in my embrace. I searched for her face, longing for eye contact. She briefly glanced over to me, before quickly looking away. Without much expression or reaction, she unexpectedly spun out of my arms.

"What are you doing?"

She rummaged through the sheets and covers of the bed and on the floor for her clothes, not looking at me.

"I have to be somewhere."

"At this hour?"

"I have to go. I'm sorry."

"Even after that?"

"You expected me to stay?"

"I thought that's what you wanted."

She started to put her clothes on but still didn't look at me.

"Did you enjoy any of this?" I asked, naively believing that I had rocked her world, moved the earth under her, and changed her life.

"Yeah, it was fun," she glibly answered, glancing at herself in the mirror and checking her appearance in the darkened room.

"Will I see you again?"

She shrugged without answering, before returning to the edge of the bed and giving me a quick peck on the cheek. At the bedroom door, she suddenly stopped and turned.

"You all right?"

"I don't know for sure."

She nodded and disappeared from the room. With a hollowness I hoped to never experience again, I stared in the blackness of the room as she slammed the front door and left the house in a rush. Any thoughts of Pittsburgh or Meredith had faded. Crystal had me right where she wanted. I was under her spell. Hearing the Mustang rev up, I slumped back in the bed and buried myself in the cold satin sheets as she drove away. I was desperate to see her again. And she knew it.

Chapter 5
Eiffel Tower High

With my life slowly spinning out of control, I vowed to begin the new day with a different attitude. I had to make a change if I were to survive in Caldwell. I arrived at the drug store an hour earlier than the store was scheduled to open and beat Tammy to work for the first time since I had started working there. I quickly got the store prepped and ready for what would be another busy day. I mopped the floor in the pharmacy and storeroom as well as disinfected the pharmacy bench and counter. I filled serving bowls with lollipops and miniature candy bars I had purchased and set them on the counter by the register with a 'help yourself' sign. I stacked several coloring books with boxes of crayons in the waiting area for the kids. The first pot of coffee had already been brewed when Tammy arrived.

"What's this?" she asked upon entering the pharmacy area and looking around. "A good night of sleep?"

"I need you to get a hold of Johnny Fogg for me this morning."

"Johnny Fogg?" she asked, hanging her purse and jacket on a coat rack. "What'd you need him for?"

"Just do it."

"Please?"

"Sorry. Please, can you get a hold of Johnny Fogg for me? I need to see him as soon as possible."

"It may not be so easy. He's pretty much homeless and doesn't have a phone that I know of."

"He has a phone."

"I'll see what I can do."

"I'm sure James has his number here somewhere."

Pulling on her smock, she studied the groups of stock prescription drug bottles that I had lined together on the pharmacy bench. With Butterman gone, I had taken control of the pharmacy and how it'd be run until he got back.

"What's this?"

"I've been thinking of ways that we can re-organize how we stock the drugs, especially the fast movers. You know, to try and improve the flow when we get busy."

"What's got into you this morning?"

"I've been here a few days and have seen how things work. We can go back to the old way if this doesn't work or James doesn't like it after he returns."

"No, no, no. This is good. We're always trippin' over each other. I've thought we needed to do something, but James, he never liked change."

The store had been open a couple of hours, and business was steady in the pharmacy. Archie talked my ear off that morning. The reorganization of the drug stock took us a little while to get used to, but overall, we both thought it would be a better, more steam-lined system in the long run. We did our best not to fall behind. We had an unusually high number of prescriptions that day for antibiotics, decongestants, and cough syrups. Schools were back in session, and cold and flu season had begun. I showed a young mother who couldn't have been older than sixteen how to dose her toddler with an antibiotic suspension. I helped another mother take the temperatures of her three young kids. It looked as if they hadn't bathed in days. As they waited for prescriptions, I purchased them sample sizes of shampoo, soap, and toothpaste and added them to their order at no charge. The waiting area was slowing filling as Tammy appeared from the stock room after a short break.

"He's out back."

"Who?"

"Johnny Fogg."

"You got a hold of him?"

"Yeah," she nodded, reaching a slip of paper to me. "You were right. I found his number in the rolodex."

"What's his story? Do you know anything about him?"

"He has no story as far as I can tell. He's some guy from the holler who's always hung out around town as long as I can remember."

"Can I trust him?"

"Trust him? Why?"

"He won't lie to me, will he?"

"I'm not the one to ask. I don't know him that well."

"Is he dangerous?"

"Dangerous? Why all these questions?"

"Is he?"

"I don't suppose he is. It's well known that he watched his mother shoot herself when he was just a kid. His dad, who use to beat him 'til he blistered, walked out soon after that. I heard he's scared to death of guns. They say he won't even touch one."

She showed me a puzzled look.

"Why you worried about him?"

"I need to find out what happened to Aaron."

"And you think he knows? Ha!"

"Can you take over here a minute? This won't take long."

I quickly slipped out the back door of the store. The air was damp and cool. The morning's fog still lingered. Nervously pacing and fidgeting, Johnny waited, looking hungover. He had his Pabst beer ball cap pulled down low, nearly covering his eyes.

"What happened to Aaron?"

"I don't know."

"Do you think Butterman killed him?"

"I think he's alive."

"Where is he then?"

"I may got an idea."

"I have a day off on Saturday. Do you think we can find him?"

Johnny nodded.

"Have you talked to Butterman since he left?" I asked as he quickly glanced to the ground.

"No," he said, slightly shaking his head.

He glanced up. I knew he was lying.

"You're telling me the truth, right? You wanted my help," I said as he nodded. "I'll pick you up here at nine o'clock this Saturday morning."

It was about twenty minutes until closing. The drug store was completely empty of customers. It had been a long day, and I couldn't wait to get out of there. As I filled some last-minute call-in prescription refills for the next day, I noticed the front door open. I craned my neck and checked to see who had entered. It was Whitey Blosser. I immediately dropped what I was working on and raced to the front.

"We're closed," I called out before he could get too far into the store.

"I got a few minutes," he responded, checking his watch.

"Out! Get out!"

"I need somethin' filled," he said, holding out a prescription order.

"We're closed. You need to go somewhere else."

"I want this filled."

"I said, 'get the fuck out!'"

"Not 'til I get this filled!"

"Go somewhere else."

"Where?"

I turned to the young clerk at the register in front of the store.

"Robbie, call the sheriff."

"I haven't done nothing," Whitey pleaded as Robbie reached for the phone.

"You're trespassing. Now get out before we call Sheriff Walls."

"So, you're not goin' fill this?"

"We're closed. You need to go. Now!"

"Maybe I'll call Super-Rite headquarters and complain."

"Go ahead. You and your brother are on tape destroying inventory and vandalizing the store."

Whitey stepped forward closer to me. His face was inches from mine. I could spell his sour breath. He grinned, showing me his rotting teeth. I didn't back away or let him move further into the store.

"It's time to go."

He glared at me for a few moments. I glared back, making sure not to look away.

"I'll be back," he warned before leaving.

"Don't bother. You and your business aren't wanted here."

I had settled in for the evening at Butterman's and celebrated my day with a six-pack of beer and a frozen pizza, not really having anywhere else to go. I felt somewhat proud of myself for taking charge at the store and making some changes. But more importantly, standing up to Whitey gave me a confidence and rush of energy I'd never experienced before. Sometime around midnight as I stared blankly at the television, I heard the front door slowly open, having forgotten to lock it. I immediately jumped up and crept towards the door. Uninvited and unannounced, Crystal slipped inside the house. I stared at her without words or a greeting. That time I didn't resist her advances. I welcomed them. We didn't even make it to the bedroom, having settled on the couch- our bodies locked together, our clothes strewn about the living room floor. Her visit didn't last long, less than thirty minutes I believe. I watched her dress in the fluttering light of the television screen. She wouldn't look at me.

"You can stay," I said as I continued to watch, but she never looked back or acknowledged me.

After dressing, she quickly moved to the door as if running late. She stopped at the door, not turning to me or responding, and hesitated a moment before finally leaving. I couldn't tell if she enjoyed our time together. By the end of her visits, she'd change from warm, bubbly, and inviting to cold and uncaring, quickly putting on the best of poker faces to hide any emotion or weakness. She was all business as if completing an assignment. Something was up, and I was determined to find out what it was. But that plan ended up on hold as she disappeared from my life for several days after that night.

Each night over the next week I would lounge in the darkened bedroom under the empty satin sheets, yearning to see her. The anticipation of a possible social call would excite me. So excited, I would be unable to calm myself enough for sleep. So instead of sleep, I would sit alone in bed, wide awake, staring into the darkness, and waiting. I continually would check the clock as night slowly turned into morning. I had quit lying to myself. I enjoyed our naughty, late-night trysts, and at the time, nothing else mattered. But I wanted more. I needed to know her better. I wanted to spend more time together to find out what she liked and what she didn't. I wanted to find out how she spent her time or if she had any hobbies or other friends. Did she travel much? What about her family? But really, what I needed to know the most-what did she think about me? Were there any sincere feelings or was she some hired gun sent late at night to keep me happy or distracted or interested enough to stay in that lonely, isolated place? Or was I making a grave mistake even entertaining the idea that I could have a somewhat normal relationship with her? But she didn't visit any of those nights. And like always, I wondered when or if I'd ever see her again.

I didn't think Johnny would meet me, but he did. We met behind the drug store. Wearing a heavy knapsack on his back, he was a little late, and Rufus, his dog, was with him. I had picked up some coffee and warm homemade doughnuts from the diner. We loaded into my small car and headed for the hollows. Rufus sat in the backseat. We took the scenic route. In no time, we traversed steep, fog-draped mountain ridges through wooded backroads. Reminders of autumn were everywhere. At the higher elevations, the leaves had changed colors. Some had even fallen, kicking up in the air behind us as we drove on. Johnny didn't say much during most of the ride other than to give me directions on how to get to our destination. He mostly snacked on the doughnuts. It didn't seem as if he had been eating much then.

Eventually, we stopped outside an isolated trailer that was somewhat hidden in a thicket of rhododendrons and young pine trees. The darkened trailer looked especially haunted under the morning's overcast sky. Its white aluminum sides were faded and had grayed. The windows were covered with plywood and plastic sheets. Wild ivy covered one end of the trailer. Some vines even reached inside, growing through rips in the metal frame and holes in the roof's lining. Rufus hopped out of the back window before I could park and romped off into the woods as if he had been there many times before. Johnny and I got out of the car and stared at the trailer a moment before approaching the front door. Ever since I arrived in Caldwell, I constantly sensed I was being watched. That time was no different. I glanced back over my shoulder to check the surroundings before we entered.

Once inside the darkened structure, Johnny suddenly became agitated. It seemed he hadn't been back to the place since the 'Tolly' incident. I clicked on a shade less lamp that barely lit the front of the trailer. I immediately noticed brown and rust-colored stains that covered different spots on the floor and wall. As Johnny anxiously paced back and forth through the littered room, I rummaged through a stack of old record albums and dated magazines on a bookshelf.

"Right there," he said, pointing to a table. "I was sittin' there."

"What do you remember?"

"There was yellin' and hollerin'," he answered. "It was Aaron and Tolly, I think. Fightin', maybe."

"Yelling about what?"

"Drugs. It had to be 'bout drugs. I don't know, Michael. I was higher than a kite. I passed out. When I waked up, Tolly is dead, right there! His face was blowed off! And I had to clean it up. I ain't killed no one. Jesus Christ!"

"Who made you clean it up?"

"Goddang! I can't sleep no more. I jus' pass out and pray to the Good Lord the nightmares go away."

"Who made you clean it up?"

We stared a moment, before he glanced away and started to pace again. I sensed he didn't want to tell me, so I didn't press him.

"Do you think Aaron shot Tolly?"

"No, not Aaron. He wouldn't do that."

"Do you think the same person who shot Tolly also shot Aaron?"

"I don't know, Michael."

"What happened to Aaron then?"

"I think he run off."

"Doesn't seem to be anywhere to run to around here."

"I don't know, Michael. I don't know."

Johnny became more agitated. Unable to cope with the horrible reminders of his last visit there, he abruptly left the trailer. Once outside, he started calling and whistling for Rufus who always provided him comfort in times he was distressed. I lingered about inside, searching for something, anything that could help me locate Aaron.

I walked through the other rooms in the trailer. There was a depleted kitchen with a leaky sink and an empty but running refrigerator that no longer stayed cold. The oven was completely gone, appearing as if it had been ripped right out of the wall. The cupboards and drawers were bare. There was a mostly gutted bedroom that looked more like an office with a desk, chair, and notebooks filled with abbreviated addresses, initials, and dates. A soiled mattress without sheets was turned sideways on a beat-up wooden bedframe. I flipped through the notebooks and studied the entries, unable to decipher the codes in the short time I was there. I glanced around, before sliding the notebook with the most recent entries into the back of my pants. I moved into the bathroom and took a piss. The toilet worked, but the hot water to the shower and sink had been turned off. The shower tile was stained and covered in mold. The porcelain sink was cracked, and the mirror to front of the medicine cabinet above it was missing. Evidence of illicit drug use was everywhere. The place was littered with scales, pill bottles, thousands of plastic baggies, used needles and syringes, and an assortment of all types and sizes of lighters and pipes. But I didn't see any drugs. I'm sure they had long been dispensed or consumed.

I turned off the lamp and joined Johnny outside the trailer. A light rain had started to fall as the sky grew darker. The wind had kicked up and whistled through the trees. As Johnny petted and played with Rufus, I snuck to my car and slipped the notebook I had taken under the driver's seat. Johnny called out and motioned for me to follow. He had another place nearby he wanted to show me. I chased after Johnny for ten or fifteen minutes on a well-worn path over multiple hillsides through the woods. Rufus led the way. By the time I caught up with Johnny, he stood over the marked opening to a mine shaft.

"Down there. I dumped Tolly's body there. I wish, by God, I could jump down now, and get it back."

"Who had you dump it here?" I asked, confident I knew the answer.

Johnny grimaced and looked away.

"Who told you to dump Tolly down there? Butterman?"

He wouldn't look at me.

"Is Aaron down there?"

"No, he's alive!" Johnny shot back, turning to me. "I know he is."

"How do you know?"

"I jus' know it. He's important."

"Important to who?" I asked as he again looked away and began to pace. "You wanted my help."

"I know it! He's alive."

"Let's go to the police."

"No police! They'll blame everythin' on me! They think I killed 'em! That's why we needs to find Aaron. He knows the truth. He can save me."

The next stop was a place called Shott's Chicken Palace. I didn't know why we were stopping there. Johnny said something about seeing the Chicken Man for a pick-up. I pulled into a small parking lot that was outside a beat-up double wide trailer. At one end of the structure, an aluminum carport covered several different smokers and deep fryers. All of which were actively being used at the time. There was a simple homemade wooden sign above the door with a painted rooster that read 'Chicken Palace. Smoked Pork'. The rooster's red paint was faded and chipped.

We entered. It was still relatively early in the morning, and it looked as if the place had just opened. Besides us, there was a grizzled and gray gentleman with a lighted cigarette dangling from his lip who sat on a stool behind a bar, staring at a news channel on a wide screen television. I assumed he was the 'Chicken Man'. I scanned the place and checked out its unique décor. The walls were paneled with dark wood and covered with scores of fading team photos of the West Virginia University basketball and football squads as well as assorted calendars from local businesses that spanned decades. The bar had a single tap that poured only Hamm's beer and was just long enough to accommodate seven bar stools that were bolted to the floor. There was small stock of liquor, mostly different whiskeys and flavored vodkas, on a shelf behind the bar. It appeared as if a few of the bottles had been there for years as they were covered with a thick coating of dust. Besides the bar stools, there were three upholstered couches for additional seating and still room enough for a bumper pool table and jukebox. The couches also were bolted to the floor. I guess there was a tradition of burning couches around the state after significant victories by the university's football and basketball teams. And Shott's was not immune from that tradition. Legend had it that the Chicken Man grew tired of replacing the couches from the bar every couple of years.

"Johnny, the usual?" asked the chicken man.

"And with an extra chicken soup," Johnny answered as the old man disappeared to the back.

"This place smells amazing," I said, somewhat distracted by the many decorations on the wall.

"Wait 'til you taste it. Only bar around for thirty miles. It's busy here in the evenin'."

"Do you drink, Johnny?"

"Oh, no. I ain't never touched the stuff. It put a rage on my daddy. I'm afraid it'd do the same to me."

"Where's your dad now?"

"I don't like talkin' 'bout him," he snapped.

The chicken man returned with two large paper bags- one filled with several soup containers and the other with Styrofoam take-out trays. Before Johnny could reach for his wallet, I threw a couple of twenty-dollar bills on the bar.

"That's not enough for this order," the Chicken Man said with a smirk, pushing the twenties back to me.

"I have it," Johnny said, handing him what looked to be two one-hundred-dollar bills folded in half.

"What's in there besides chicken soup?" I joked. "Crack?"

The Chicken Man reached for a bottle of Irish whiskey and two shot glasses.

"How 'bout a shot for the road?"

I nodded as the Chicken Man filled the shot glasses. He raised one up and motioned to the other. I grabbed it, and we knocked back the shots. We both grimaced and shook our heads.

"I'll see you again," the Chicken Man confidently predicted.

Johnny and I drove for ten miles or so deeper into the wooded hollow. We didn't see a soul. With the take-out order on his lap, Johnny had his arms wrapped around the paper bags of food as if trying to protect an unrestrained infant. He didn't say much, and he wouldn't look at me. Rufus slept in the backseat. I followed Johnny's directions but was starting to worry that this trip wasn't a good idea.

"Who's lunch for?" I asked.

"They come like cockroaches in the dark when they heard I've gone to the Chicken Man."

"Who's they?"

"Anyone that needs to eat."

"Aaron?"

"This is where he'd be if I needed to see him."

As we neared our destination, I could hear loud blasts in the distance, perhaps gunshots.

"Hunters?"

"Shootin' range."

I turned the car onto a one lane dirt road and followed it for a few hundred yards. I noticed a small cloud of black smoke ahead, likely from a coal burning stove. We stopped at a gate at the entrance of a non-descript property enclosed by miles of a rusted barb wire fence. Johnny hopped out of the car and unlatched the gate. Driving up to a two-story neglected and decaying house, I recognized a familiar figure, holding a shotgun. I immediately stopped the car and was ready to turn around, hoping he didn't see us. Laughing wildly, Whitey Blosser shot at objects placed on a fence post- an old television, a gallon of paint, a box of light bulbs, and pumpkins, scores of pumpkins.

"Whitey?" I said, shaking my head. "I can't stay! No, no, no!"

"We come this far. We can't turn back. Don't you want to find Aaron?"

Whitey finally spotted us. He stared, not recognizing the car and trying to figure who we were. I looked to Johnny who nodded.

"It's okay. You're with me."

"I don't think that matters."

I hesitated, not at all confident in Johnny's assurance we'd be all right, before pulling the car closer to the house. As Johnny and Rufus got out, I stayed in the car and even slouched in the seat, hoping he didn't recognize me. Holding the shotgun as if ready to shoot, Whitey squinted and studied inside the car. A smile creased his face once he figured who I was.

BOOM!

Without warning, he blasted a hole in the back-quarter panel of my car. Johnny hit the ground, and Rufus dashed off into the woods. Frightened for my life, I immediately jumped out of the driver's seat and hid on the side of the car.

"Christ! You bastard!" Johnny yelled, hopping up and chasing after his dog.

"Jesus, man!" I shouted, kneeling beside the car. "You could've killed that dog! And my car!"

"I owed you one," Whitey sneered, aiming the gun at me as I shuffled, my body bent over, around the car to check the damage in back. "You got a lot of damn balls to show up here!"

Luckily, it didn't appear the shotgun blast did any damage to render the car un-drivable. There was no way I wanted to get stuck there. The back tires were fine, and the gas tank was spared. But one set of taillights was completely gone, and a large hole was blown clear through the spare tire in the trunk. After examining the car, I stood and turned to Whitey.

BOOM!

Again, without warning, he blasted another shot. That time over my head, knocking me to the ground. I immediately ran my hands over my head, chest, and neck, making sure I hadn't been hit. I glanced up to Whitey. He roared in laughter.

"What the fuck, man?"

"Next time, you'll fill my prescriptions," he warned. "If I knew someone wouldn't come lookin' for you, I'd blast a hole clean through your goddamn chest."

As I slowly lifted myself up, Whitey grinned and turned, blasting a hole in a fence post.

BOOM!

Setting the shotgun down, he walked over to my car and pulled out the two bags that we had picked up at the Chicken Palace. He glared at me as he walked by and entered the house. I waited for Johnny who showed up minutes later with Rufus in his arms. He tied Rufus to a fence post and entered the house. I waited outside and peered through a busted screen door, watching them. Besides Whitey, there was one other guy there- an older gentleman with a shaved head named Truman. Tattoos covered his body from his neck to his ankles. Johnny prediction had been wrong- no Aaron.

The place was a disaster. The furniture was badly torn and frayed. Empty green glass wine jugs were everywhere. Soiled plastic and Styrofoam food containers covered the floor and kitchen counters. Whitey swiped everything off a coffee table in the living room and placed the two paper bags down. He and Truman then ripped them opened, pulling out the food containers. They each took a soup and passed the others to Johnny. They then set out the other containers and opened them. Three of them overflowed with pulled barbeque pork and assorted side dishes, like macaroni and cheese, green beans, and cornbread. I stepped closer to the screen door for a better look. The fourth container, the one they were the most interested in, contained small bags of a white powdery substance that they referred to as 'elephant'. Johnny watched them closely. I guess the Chicken Man was famous for something other than slow-cooked meats. With the most courage I've ever had to summon from inside me, I pushed open the screen door with shaking hands and wobbling knees.

"Johnny," I called, not seeing Aaron there, "let's go."

"Let's wait," he said, not taking his eyes off the 'elephant'. "Aaron might show up later. I know it."

Ignoring the food and pulling out syringes from a drawer of the table, Whitey and Truman took a seat on the couch. Johnny quickly joined in, squeezing between them. I wanted to leave, but I didn't want to go without Johnny. I intended to give him twenty minutes, and then I'd be gone, hoping to take him with me.

"Michael," Johnny called out. "Git some food. You won't be disappointed."

As Johnny and his gang started into their drug-taking ritual, I walked over to the containers of food on the table and sampled a couple bites of pulled pork. It was amazingly good. I searched through the bags of food, looking for a spoon in order to taste one of the untouched soups. Not finding one, I went into the kitchen and opened what should have been the silverware drawer. It was filled with nothing but assorted bullets and shotgun shells. I glanced up. The three of them had started injecting themselves with the drug. I opened another drawer in the kitchen. It also was filled with bullets. I opened another- same thing. All the drawers in the kitchen were filled with bullets. I grabbed handful of the bullets and held them up. Johnny looked up and squinted at me. I knew at that point I'd be leaving there alone.

"We don't eat much around here," he said.

Whitey slipped a disc into a CD player. The Johnny Dowd song, "*The Girl Who Made Me Sick*", started to play. I closely watched the three of them for many minutes. It appeared as if they were slowly melting and becoming one with the couch. The expressions on their faces immediately changed. The wrinkles and stress lines on their foreheads and around their eyes gradually faded. Not finding a spoon, I drank from the soup container, still studying Johnny and the others.

"Whoa!" I said out aloud, glancing to the soup. "I didn't know chicken soup could taste that good! Damn!"

"Homemade from scratch," Johnny mumbled, struggling to keep his eyes open as Whitey and Truman drifted off to sleep. "My favorite. Nothin' but deep-fried chicken, made fresh each mornin'. Daddy used to bring it home after work when I's kid."

"You all right, Johnny?" I asked, moving out of the kitchen, and studying him from a seat across the room.

"I'm worried."

"What are you worried about?"

"I killed a man once."

"What?"

"Yeah, I did. I killed a man."

"I don't believe it.

Johnny didn't answer, his eyelids drooping. He fought to stay awake.

"Tolly?"

"No, not Tolly."

"Aaron?"

"I wouldn't kill Aaron," Johnny shook his head- his eyes completely closed. "I liked Aaron."

"Who'd you kill, Johnny?"

"A bad man. He deserved what he got."

"I heard you're afraid of guns."

Johnny immediately opened his eyes wide and stared at me with an angry but distant gaze.

"I had to do it," he said- his eyes closing again. "I had no choice, you know. I had to do it!"

"Tell me, then."

"We was behind the post office in Glady Mills. My daddy was cussin' me like he was always doing."

"How old were you?"

"Eighteen."

"You killed your own father?"

"Daddy was no good, Michael!" Johnny raised his voice. "I had to do it!"

"How did it feel- to take your own father's life?"

"I didn't feel bad like I 'pected to, seein' that he was my daddy, you know. But I wanted to kill again."

"What happened?"

"I shot him in the belly. He laid at my feet, bleedin' real bad. He knew he was gonna die, but he still pleaded for his life."

He paused, opening his eyes but not looking at me. Tears ran down his face.

"I stood over him, bigger than God, you know, and aimed the gun at his forehead. I controlled daddy's whole world. I was the one in control, complete control of somethin'."

He glanced over to me.

"I feel like that when I'm stoned. This junk makes me bigger than God, Michael. Higher than the Eiffel Tower. I like that feelin'. Man, when I'm high..."

He paused and leaned back between Whitey and Truman.

"I pulled the trigger. My daddy had no chance. I wasn't afraid to pull it neither. No sir, by God. I was doin' him a favor, me a favor, the town a favor. I'd do it again. Daddy was no good, Michael! I sent him to HELL where he belonged. I should'a let him suffer..."

Johnny's eyes slowly closed, and he softly began to snore. I scanned the living room of the house but didn't go into any other rooms. I needed to get the hell out of there. Before I left, I finished the chicken soup and checked to make sure that all three of them were breathing. I didn't want to be there any longer, in case more cockroaches showed up.

The drive back to Butterman's house took over an hour. As I passed through downtown Caldwell, my phone suddenly beeped several times. Because I had spent most of the morning deep in the hollows, I had been without cell service. Finally reaching Butterman's place, I pulled into the driveway and checked the phone. There were several calls and messages- all from Meredith. I began to listen to the first message but stopped before it could start. I stared at the phone in my hand for a few moments before turning it off and stuffing it in my pocket. I got out of the car and more closely studied the damage to the rear end before retreating inside the house to disappear for the rest of the day.

It was sometime in the middle of the night. Like a vision, Crystal appeared out of the darkness at the end of the bed, waking me from a deep sleep. I hadn't seen her in over a week. And as always, her visit was unannounced and unplanned. Before joining me in bed, she quietly slipped into the bathroom off the master bedroom. I reached to the nightstand for a glass of water in the dark but accidently knocked her purse to the floor. I leaned from the bed to pick it up and noticed something had fallen out of it. As I reached for the unidentified item, Crystal hit the overhead bedroom lights. I held a 9-mm pistol. I glanced to her, then back to the gun, staring at it.

"What do you need a gun for?"

"What are you doing in my purse?" she asked, approaching.

"What do you need a gun for?"

She ripped the gun from my hands. I studied her. She slowly raised it and pointed it at my chest.

"Bet you never had a gun aimed at you?"

"Well, as a matter of fact, just today…"

"What were you doing in my purse?"

I didn't take my eyes from the gun, not knowing if she was serious or joking around. I never could tell.

"I knocked it off the nightstand by accident. The gun fell out."

"Do you know how easy it would be for me to end your life right now?"

"Put the gun down."

She continued to aim the pistol at me.

"Put the gun down, Crystal."

"Get undressed."

"What?"

She took a step closer and stuck the gun within inches of my face.

"Get undressed."

I didn't move.

"Do it!"

I crawled out of bed and slowly started to take my clothes off but kept my eyes on the gun aimed at me. Once undressed, I slouched in front of her, standing with an awkward, uncomfortable posture. I covered my private parts with both hands. Never had I felt so vulnerable.

"Move your hands."

"Crystal?"

"Move your hands!"

I uncovered my groin area. She studied me a moment.

"Get in bed."

"Huh?"

"Get in bed."

"What are you doing?"

I climbed in bed, taking a seat and leaning back against the headboard. Still pointing the gun, she slowly undressed in front of me, using her other hand. Under the bright overhead light, never had we got such long, close looks at our naked bodies. Most of our encounters before that night were quick hit-and-runs in complete darkness. I couldn't take my eyes off her. She was perfectly shaped in every way. Her bare, tanned skin shined in the light. I had almost forgotten about the gun aimed at me.

"You're not a bad looking guy, Michael."

For several moments, she stood before me.

"Do you like what you see?" she asked.

I didn't say anything. I kept my eye on the gun. Finally, she gently pulled back the hammer of the pistol and clicked it into place, before setting the gun on its side on the nightstand and aiming it towards me. Crawling into the bed, she yanked on my legs and pulled me away from the headboard, before climbing on top of me.

"Don't get too wild," she said as I stared at the end of the barrel of the pistol aimed at us, "you wouldn't want that gun to go off accidently."

She began to rock and grind her body into mine. At first, her movements were slow, easy, and in rhythm with mine. Her brown eyes locked on me. Gradually, she rocked her body faster then harder. The bed began to shake and knock against the bedroom wall. I glanced to the gun. The bed bumped the nightstand, causing the gun to slightly wobble. She dug her fingers into my chest, slamming her body against me. I grabbed for her waist. Out of our control, we climaxed together. She collapsed onto my chest and nearly passed out in my arms. I tried to catch my breath, staring at the gun. After many minutes, I finally eased her sweating body off me. Unexpectedly, she reached for the gun and stuck it in my face.

"What do you say now?"

A million thoughts ran through my head.

"Come on. What'd you need to tell me?"

"I've never, and will never again, meet anyone like you."

"And?" she asked, pushing the gun into my cheek.

"I've never been more turned on."

"Wrong answer," she replied, "but…"

She pulled the gun away and eased the hammer back into the safety position, before getting out of bed. She hid the gun away in her purse as I watched her dress.

"And I was serious about that," I said.

"I know."

After dressing, she quickly left the bedroom and the house. I didn't move from the bed until I heard her Mustang start up and peel away from the driveway. I pulled the covers up to my neck and stared at the ceiling, worried about what I had gotten myself into and not knowing if I could get myself out of it.

It was another Tuesday evening, and I found myself on a country back road that wasn't marked on any map. I was dropping off the last delivery of the evening. As darkness settled, I drove up a long, steep muddy driveway. Parking the car, chickens, dogs, and goats, and even a couple little kids scattered. The yard was cluttered with trash, stacks of worn tires, rusted out automobile parts, and spent appliances. As I approached the rundown wooden shack, I was greeted by an emaciated-looking young woman on a porch.

"I got your prescriptions," I announced.

"What prescriptions?" she skeptically asked, taking the bag and studying the bottles inside.

"Those were called in for you by the clinic. Did you take your kids to clinic today?"

"How much?"

"A dollar-fifty."

"I ain't got that. I have the welfare card."

"Yeah, it's fifty cents a prescription with the card."

"What's it I got?"

"It's medicine for your kids' sore throats and earaches."

She handed the bag back to me and shook her head.

"I ain't payin' for these."

"But your kids need them. They may get a lot sicker if they don't take them."

We stared at each other a moment, before I handed the bag back to her.

"Don't worry about it. Just make sure your kids take all of these."

As I stepped off the porch, a pick-up truck pulled up, and a scraggly young man got out. He carried a case of beer and a carton of cigarettes. He stared at me suspiciously until I got in my car. With glassy eyes, Whitey lifted the plastic that hung over the window and watched me drive away. After I was out of sight, he dipped a sock in a bowl of gasoline and held it to his nose. After several deep inhalations, he dipped the sock back into the gasoline and handed it Johnny Fogg who sat beside him.

Chapter 6
No Promises Have I Made

It had been another zesty, late-night love-making session with Crystal. A trail of her clothes, from a coat, hat, gloves, scarf, shirt, bra, pants, underwear to each shoe, made a path from the front door of the house into the bed. Several empty beers cans were scattered throughout the master bathroom. A smoldering cigarette burned in an ashtray on the nightstand. Crystal lingered longer than usual, her naked body half on mine. She gently rubbed my chest and studied me. I had barely caught my breath as I reached for a beer.

"Do you think I'd make a good mother?"

Taking a sip from the can, I glanced down to her, not knowing how to respond.

"Why?"

"Well, do you?"

"I can't answer that."

"Why?"

"I don't really know you."

"Would you call me a 'good-time girl'?"

I glanced around the sullied bedroom.

"What do you think?" I answered, holding out my arms and pointing around the room.

"I'm being serious."

"I am, too, Crystal. I don't know you outside of this," I said, again, motioning to the bed and our naked bodies tangled together.

"Would you take me to meet your mother and father?"

"Why are you asking me these questions?"

"Would you?"

I hesitated before answering, "no."

"No?"

She seemed surprised.

"I don't have a mother and father."

She glanced up, wanting me to elaborate.

"I was raised by my grandmother."

"What happened to your mother and father?"

"A long story," I answered, not wanting to elaborate.

"Would you take me to meet your grandmother?"

"Yes," I replied without hesitating.

"Why?"

"I think she'd like you."

"You know," she said, motioning to the bed and entangled bodies. "This isn't who I really am."

"Who are you then?"

She studied me for a few minutes before rolling out of my arms. Sitting on the edge of the bed, she started to dress.

"You don't have to do this anymore," I said as she stood and started for the bedroom door. "I'm not the one forcing you to come here."

She stopped at the door but hesitated a moment before turning to me.

"Tell me, who are you?" I asked.

"Do you want me to come back here?"

I didn't answer.

"This is your chance to stop it right now," she said, not taking her eyes from mine. "Do you want me to come back?"

"You know the answer to that."

Studying me for a moment, she finally glanced away. Not once, did she look back to me before she left.

Crystal returned two nights later. She rarely visited on consecutive days. Breathing hard and sweating, I reclined in bed and closely watch as she rushed to dress in the dark. She didn't seem to be in a good mood. More than any other night with her I felt like a prop- an insignificant player in a bad movie. Her visit had lasted only fifteen minutes. She hardly spoke a word or even looked at me. Like most nights, I wondered where she had been before and where she was headed next. She was in a hurry to leave. But I wondered, as I always did after her visits, if there was someone else out there in the night waiting for her.

"Wham bam, thank you, ma'am," I said, "another hit-and-run."

She didn't look at me.

"Why do you always have to leave so soon?"

Grabbing her shoes from the floor, she took a seat on the end of the bed.

"Stay the night. Let's do something tomorrow. I have a day off."

She didn't respond, pulling on her shoes.

"Crystal?"

"I can't," she said, still not looking at me. "I need to go."

"At this hour?"

She shrugged, standing, and checking her appearance in the dresser mirror.

"I don't want you coming here anymore," I said as she rolled her eyes, brushing at her hair. "I'm not into this anymore."

"You were WAY into a few minutes ago."

"I don't need you coming here anymore."

My phone started to ring.

"If that's what you want?" she said, still looking at the mirror and checking her lipstick.

I didn't answer her as my phone continued to ring.

"Who keeps calling you?"

"It's my conscience trying to tell me what a big mistake this has been."

The phone stopped ringing.

"Why are you always in such a hurry to leave?" I asked as she grabbed her purse and slung it over the shoulder. "I'm serious. Don't come her anymore."

"What?" she asked, turning, and studying me.

"I don't want you coming here anymore. It's over."

"I thought we had something special."

"Something special?" I said, throwing the covers off me. "Shit! Coming here in the middle of the night and screwing my brains out. I need a little more than that!"

"I'm out of here!"

"So, this is goodbye?" I asked, hopping out of bed as she turned to leave the room. "Goddammit, Crystal!"

"I haven't promised you anything!"

Before she could leave, I violently swept my arm across the top of the dresser as everything crashed to the floor, startling her. She stopped and stood in the doorway.

"I have nothing here!" I said. "You're all I got. I look forward to these visits. You know that."

She turned to me.

"And I hope you enjoy these visits as well," I said, pausing and wanting her to respond, but she didn't.

"My family and friends bug me every damn day about my decision to come here. Please give me a reason to stay."

"I have to go," she said without emotion, coldly glancing to her watch.

I aggressively yanked open the dresser drawer before she could leave.

"Look," I said, pulling out a large stack of one-hundred-dollar bills. "Look! They're paying me thousands of dollars a week to work here because no one else will! I'm engaged to be married! I was saving this to buy my grandmother a new house! Now, I don't give a shit about the money or anything!"

I threw the money in the air; bills flew all over the room.

"If it wasn't for you, I'd be gone. I don't need any of this," I paused. "You changed everything."

She looked away.

"But some strange shit's going on around here. Please tell me you're not involved."

She turned and slightly shook her head. But I knew she was.

"There's so much more I want to learn about you," I went on. "You act all tough and hard, but your eyes show me a lost little girl."

"I really have to go."

"Will I see you tomorrow?"
We stared at each other a moment, before she left without an answer.

The late October morning was unseasonably warm. Temperatures were forecasted to reach seventy degrees that day which was unheard of for Caldwell County at that time of year. It was my first day off in weeks, and it'd be my last until the end of November. I wanted to go fishing. I was sure there were some great fishing holes, but I just didn't know the area well enough to find them. In Butterman's garage, I dug out a couple of dusty fishing poles and some tackle. I had purchased a container of night crawlers from an old man down the road after work the previous evening. As I strung the poles with new fishing line, a car pulled into the driveway. It was Crystal's Ford Mustang.

"What are you doing?" she asked, getting out of the car.

"I'd like to go fishing."

"Where you going?"

"I have no idea."

"Can I go with you?"

"Do you know of a good stream?"

"I got a place."

The weather couldn't have been more spectacular, and the scenery more brilliant. Behind the wheel, Crystal whipped the Mustang around the winding roadways of Caldwell County, pushing us deep into the rural countryside. She wore black Converse sneakers and a yellow bikini top with the bottoms covered by a pair of tight cut-off jean shorts. With the windows rolled down and the sunroof opened, we both gazed at the scenery. Rows of striking green fir trees lining the roadside zipped by as we raced across Route 44. The leaves of maple, oak and walnut trees scattered in groves on the distant hillsides had started to change color.

After climbing in elevation for twenty miles or so, Crystal slowed the car and pulled onto a narrow gravel road. Bouncing over bumps and holes in the road, we followed it a few more miles. The road eventually wound itself down to a small, forgotten graveyard in the valley where we pulled onto a dusty dirt road that was partially hidden by thick brush and overgrown weeds. We pushed through, kicking up a trail of dust behind us. After a mile or two again climbing in elevation, the road smoothed as the car hopped back onto pavement that split a sleepy, isolated farm in half.

On each side of the road, a few head of cattle and scores of sheep, trapped within miles of rusted wire fencing, grazed on the steep rolling hills. A barking dog appeared and briefly gave chase. We passed a leaning, wooden barn with a tin roof covered with chipped and faded red paint. I studied a dented mailbox with no name that stood alone along the road.

The wide, open fields of the farm slowly disappeared behind us as the road transitioned back to dirt. Slowly creeping along the one lane road, we descended the other side of the ridge in dark shade under a canopy of the tallest pines in the area. I could feel the rough, rocky road on the soles of my feet as the underside of low-riding Mustang bottomed out several times. Below the hill, we reached a rickety wooden bridge that swayed over a rushing river. Crystal cautiously eased the car onto the bridge that shook and creaked as we inched across it. On the other side, the road widened as she pulled to a clearing and parked. As I gathered the fishing gear and a cooler, the muffled but constant roar that sounded like thunder could be heard in the distance.

On foot, I followed Crystal into the woods along a thin dirt trail lined with a thicket of giant ferns and rhododendrons. For a half of mile, we hiked parallel with the river, straight up a steeply angled hill. The heavy cover of leaves above us had cooled and darkened the day. At the crest of the hill, we came upon a small alleyway of water that flowed from the top of the mountain beside us and emptied into the river below. Hopping from rock to rock sticking out of the water, we made it across and continued down a hill into the river valley.

After another half of mile, the path changed directions and led us to a rusted-out iron bridge that crossed the river. As we moved closer to the bridge, the thunderous sound of rushing and pounding water roared louder. I followed Crystal onto the bridge that was at least ten feet above the water. For several minutes, we stared mesmerized by the magnificent untamed and untouched beauty of the vibrant river valley. It felt like heaven.

"What's that noise?"

"You'll find out."

"How do we get there?"

"We have to swim."

"Swim? The water's freezing. It's almost November."

After a couple of beers and baiting the fishing lines, I stood on the iron bridge with Crystal. I leaned in close and wrapped my arms around her, demonstrating how to cast a line into the river. I rested my chin on her bare right shoulder that was warm from the midday sun.

"Your dad never took you fishing?" I asked, slowly pulling her right-hand back that held the fishing pole before awkwardly flipping it forward.

"He never was around when I was young."

The line didn't cast as the bait still hung at the top of the line.

"What'd you do for fun?"

"Boys and cigarettes."

She chuckled as we tried again. I pulled her arm back, and we flicked the pole together. Again, the line didn't cast. Instead, the bait, still hooked to the line, dropped on top of her head as she fell into my arms, giggling. Staring up, she leaned the back of her head on my chest and grinned.

"This isn't that hard," I said, laughing.

After a few more attempts, she finally threw a perfect line into the river. I released my arms from around her. She glanced to me and smiled, slowly reeling the line back in. She repeated this a few more times and had gotten quite good at casting the line. And in no time, a fish suddenly struck the bait, causing the fishing rod to bow.

"Whoa!"

Excited, she frantically tried to reel in the fish, I quickly rushed over and again wrapped my arms around her as we struggled to bring the fish in. After a short battle, we eventually pulled an eight-inch rainbow trout that flipped and flopped at the end of our line out of the water.

"What a beauty!" I said, unhooking the struggling, slimy fish from the end of the line and reaching it out to Crystal.

At first, she was reluctant to touch it but eventually grabbed the fish and held it over her head, grinning from ear to ear. I pulled out my phone and took several pictures.

"What do we do with it?" she asked.

"We throw it back."

"Throw it back?"

"You're not going to eat it, are you?"

"Eat it?" she replied, staring at the fish, struggling in her hands.

"We'd have to clean it."

"Clean it?"

"Yeah, you know, cut it open and take all the guts out, then scrape off the scales with a knife."

She showed me a disgusted, grossed out face and walked the fish to the railing of the bridge.

"This won't hurt him, will it?"

"It won't hurt him," I shook my head.

Before tossing the fish back into the river, she gave it a quick kiss on the lips with a laugh and dropped the fish off the bridge. The trout hit the water with a splash and quickly darted away.

We had fished without luck for hour or so more. Neither of us would catch another fish. After putting the fishing poles down, Crystal and I sat on the railing of the iron bridge, drinking cans of beers and enjoying the scenery of the perfect day. As I reached for another beer, Crystal playfully pushed me off the railing.

"Hey!"

Fully clothed, I awkwardly hit the cool water face first, briefly going under. After resurfacing, I glanced up to the bridge somewhat stunned, whipping my head around to shake the water from my hair. Laughing, Crystal jumped off the bridge into the river. Swimming up to me, I pulled her body close. She couldn't stop laughing.

"Today's the first time I'd ever seen you laugh. It's nice."

She smiled as I leaned in to kiss her, but she pushed away and splashed me in the face with water.

"Follow me," she said, pointing ahead and swimming off.

I swam after Crystal for a few hundred yards in the very cold water until coming to a rock formation that had divided the river into many racing paths of current. She climbed onto the rocks where it appeared the river had abruptly ended. Finally catching up, I joined her on the edge of the rock formation and discovered we were standing over a glorious waterfall. The falling water exploded uninterrupted as it crashed onto the rocks and into the water twenty feet below us. I looked over to Crystal. Beaming, she pointed in the direction below the falls, trying to tell me something. Because of the loud pounding of the water hitting the rocks below, I could barely hear what she was saying.

"We're going over!"

"What?"

"We're going OVER!" she yelled, leaning closer to me.

Shivering, I shrugged and shook my head, acting like I didn't know what she was telling me. She grabbed my arm and led me closer to the edge of the falls. I gazed down to the water pounding the rocks below and continued to shake my head.

"We're jumping!" she hollered into my ear.

"I don't think so," I said, shaking my head.

"Yes, we are," she nodded, taking my hand. "We're going over, together."

"What?"

"Right there," she pointed, "in the clearing, away from the rocks."

As I studied the spot of swirling water in which she was pointing, she squeezed my hand tighter and, without warning, pulled me off the rocks and away from the falls. I let out a scream as we plunged downward, feet first. It felt as if the air in my lungs had left me and my stomach was in my throat. Within a second or two, our bodies roughly smacked the water with a wild splash, causing me to release her hand from mine. Once underwater, everything turned dark, and the roar of the falling water became muffled. I opened my eyes to thousands of tiny bubbles scrambling around me. I didn't remain underwater long as I popped up twenty or thirty feet away from where I had entered. I searched for Crystal. She was pulling herself up onto a large grouping of rocks on one side of the river. Feeling numb from the cold water, I quickly swam to her.

"Dammit, it's cold!" I called to her, breathing heavy, as she helped pull me onto the rock. "My damn landing gears have gone up into my belly, if you know what I mean?"

"That was great!"

"Don't do that to me again."

"You know you loved it."

"Hardly," I said, pulling off my soaked shirt and shoes.

"Caldwell would be so boring without me."

Under a brilliant cloudless blue sky, we stretched out together on the sunbaked rock to dry in the warm autumn sun. The tanned skin of her long, slender body glistened. Small droplets of water dripped from her brown hair and the yellow bikini she wore. She had unbuttoned the cut-offs and pulled them off her waist a bit. At her feet, she had kicked off her black Converse sneakers to dry. My wet shirt and shoes were spread out beside me. I reached over and softly rubbed the outside of her thigh. She took my hand. Hypnotized by the sound of falling water from the nearby waterfall, we couldn't help but slip in and out of sleep, napping with what was left of the afternoon.

Dry and warm as the day turned to dusk, I opened my eyes from sleep and turned to Crystal. She stared back. Beads of sweat hung from her upper lip. Small freckles I hadn't noticed before dotted her nose and cheeks. Never had she looked so young and innocent.

"How old are you?" I asked.

"Twenty-two."

"Twenty-two, really?"

"Twenty-two."

"Going on thirty-five."

She briefly grinned and stared a moment, before turning serious.

"What happened to your parents?"

"Huh?"

Your parents- what happened?"

"My father walked out after I was born. My mother died soon after that."

She studied me a moment, before asking, "so, you never knew them?"

"I never knew them."

"Tough break, huh?"

"I think of them every day."

She continued to study me. Her eyes never strayed from mine.

"And, you have a fiancée?"

I didn't initially respond, glancing away from her probing eyes.

"What's her name?"

"Why?" I asked, looking back.

"What's her name?"

I hesitated, before answering.

"Meredith."

"Is she smart?"

"Very smart," I replied, her eyes still locked on mine.

"Is she pretty?"

"Yeah. I think so."

"Prettier than me?" she asked, moving her face closer to mine.

"What do you think?"

"Tell me," she whispered, gently rubbing her salty lips against mine and tightly squeezing my hand.

"You know the answer," I said, softly kissing her.

"Tell me."

She pulled back. We studied each other.

"I want you to say it."

"No one's prettier than you."

I leaned in closer for another kiss. She stared at me a moment before turning away and letting go of my hand.

"Are you going to tell your fiancée about me?"

I hesitated a moment, before answering, "of course."

She stared deep into my eyes. I tried not to look away, but she knew I was lying.

"We need to leave," she said, sliding from me. "It'll be dark soon."

The long shadows of late afternoon had moved in. A cool breeze had started to blow. The temperature was falling fast as we dressed. It felt good to put dry clothes back on. We had a long walk back to the car and even longer drive home. But neither of us said much. Not wanting the day to end, I talked her into making one last stop for a bite to eat.

By the time we got to Shott's Chicken Palace, it was nearly dark. Crystal parked the Mustang and pulled on a loose-fitting flannel shirt to cover her bikini top. Out of the car, the evening air had grown cooler with the falling sun. The smell of fried chicken and smoked pork filled the valley, stopping us in our tracks. White smoke billowed from a series of smokers and deep fryers on the covered patio at one end of the joint. We lingered outside and enjoyed the savory scent of the slow-cooking meats.

"How'd you find this place?" she asked, opening the front door.

"I can't believe you've never been here."

I didn't expect the place to be so crowded. Every bar stool was taken, and each of the couches were occupied. The lone beer tap flowed freely. "*There Stands a Glass*" by Webb Pierce blared from a jukebox filled with nothing but classic country standards. The ever-present haze from too many smoked cigarettes greeted us as we stepped inside. It was immediately apparent that Crystal was the lone female there. As the door closed behind us, every head in the place turned. Conversations paused. The song on the jukebox ended. You could hear a pin drop. All eyes were directed at her. She was everything the regulars anchored to the bar stools were not- young, vibrant, confident- a bright light in their gray impotent world. Me, on the other hand, I was forever invisible. With her by my side, I basically blended in with the bar's dreary décor, lost in the thick plume of secondhand smoke. I was as drab and boring as the bar's dated wood-paneled walls.

We worked our way to the bar and ordered draughts of Hamm's beer. The Chicken Man remembered me and gave us two shots, compliments of the bar.

"I knew I'd see you again," he said as Crystal and I knocked back the shots of Irish whiskey. "How'd you like the soup?"

"Wonderful!"

"You two eatin'?"

"Yeah, what do you recommend?"

"The Palace Special."

"I'll take two."

Noticing the bumper pool table was open, I broke some one-dollar bills into a fistful of quarters and quickly claimed the table. As we waited for our sandwiches, we played several games of bumper pool. I'm pretty sure I won every game, but I don't think Crystal tried very hard. Each time it was her turn, I constantly spied many different men gawking at her, especially when she leaned over a shot facing away from the bar. Crystal noticed their stares as well, but she didn't seem to mind. And neither of us felt threatened while we were there. She was used to the attention and appeared to thrive in it.

Our order was finally ready, so we finished our beers and headed outside. Because we were both quite hungry, we decided to eat the sandwiches there and looked for a spot to sit. The darkening sky and poor lighting in the parking lot made it difficult to see much. After scanning the lot, Crystal motioned for me to get in the car with her as she moved the Mustang several hundred yards away, parking it in what looked to be an abandoned football field. We got out of the car. The grass on the field was overgrown and wet from the early evening dew. Crystal held a blanket. From there, we could clearly hear the music from the jukebox and the chatter from the bar. We also heard the crack of bumper pool balls striking each other and the Chicken Man shouting out food orders.

"Can you help me up?" she asked, pointing to the hood of her car.

"You want up there? Won't we dent the hood?"

"It'll be all right. Help me up."

With my hands on her side, I lifted and eased her onto the hood of the Mustang. She spread out the blanket on the windshield and carefully slid herself on it.

"Come on."

"I don't want to hurt your car."

"It'll be okay."

I tossed her the bag of sandwiches and leaned on the side of the car, hoisting myself onto the hood, being careful not to dent it. I gently slid my body next to her on the blanket that the covered the windshield. She immediately tore into the bag and pulled out the sandwiches. They steamed when we took them out of the foil. I lifted the bun off mine to check it out. The Palace Special was a 6-inch thick piece of deep-fried chicken breast covered in red hot sauce, blue cheese dressing, and pickles on a toasted Kaiser roll. I glanced over to Crystal. She had already bitten into her sandwich. It was funny as I watched her eat. I wasn't used to seeing her engage in normal everyday activities we all do, such as eating. She looked to me as I took the first bite of the sandwich and held her sandwich up in appreciation.

"Pretty good, huh?" she said.

"The best," I enthusiastically nodded before taking another bite.

And it really was the best. I couldn't ever recall any other sandwich as good. I had never tasted fried chicken as moist and flavorful. The outside breading was perfectly spiced and crispy with just the right amount of zing. I looked back to Crystal. She had almost finished the entire sandwich as I could barely eat half of mine, wrapping the rest for later. Some sauce from the chicken still lingered on her lips and cheek. I reached over and wiped them with my sleeve.

"We should've gotten some beers," she said, sliding herself closer to me.

We gazed up into the dark October night. The sky was clear and smeared with stars. It was a new moon, and without the accompanying moonlight, the stars were especially bright and more plentiful than I've ever seen them before. We leaned back onto the blanket, resting our heads on the windshield, and stared above. The stars glittered and shimmered, almost as if alive and breathing. I pinched myself and was again convinced this was heaven. Neither of us said word for a few moments. I couldn't help but wonder what Crystal was thinking. Still a mystery, she was as curious to me as all the secrets hidden among the stars over us.

"This is truly a beautiful place," I said, breaking the silence and still staring at the sky. "And, it's the first time I've noticed the stars here. After growing up in all the noise and chaos of the big city, I've never seen or appreciated anything like it- this simple natural beauty."

"Sadly, much of this area, and even some of the people, have become scarred with warts and bruises," she said, referring to washed out logging and oil roads, the hollowed out and topped off hillsides from decades of coal mining, and a worsening drug problem. "You just have to find the time and look up every now and then."

I could tell she was a little cold, so I pulled her closer to me and wrapped the edge of the blanket around her.

"But you could live anywhere," I said. "Why do you stay here?"

"Where would I go?"

"There's a great big world out there. You'd be a star."

"A star? Of what?"

"Anything you wanted."

"Why do you say that?"

"You seem like a girl who gets what she wants."

"Maybe I like it here."

"Weren't you ever encouraged to move on like a lot of other young folks around here do? You know, see what it's like somewhere else."

"My father needs me here."

"I still don't know what he does or what you do for him?"

"Does it matter?"

"What about your mother? Do you have any brothers or sisters? What about hobbies?"

"We really should have gotten beers to go," she said, having no interest in answering my questions.

"Like tonight, after all the time we've been together, this was the first time I've seen you eat. Most couples when they get together…"

"So, we're a couple now?"

"Okay, friends and family then, when they get together, they usually go someplace to eat..."

"I like what we do better."

"That's not what I'm saying. There's more to a relationship than that. I'm trying to find out a little more about you. Like, what do you do in your free time?"

"Oh, brother," she rolled her eyes. "If there's one thing I don't like about you- you ask too many questions. Just enjoy the moment. Hasn't today been fun? Look at those stars. You'll never forget this day as long as you live. And all you're worried about is whether I have a brother or sister. Who the hell cares? You may never be in a setting like this again. Please enjoy it. All the other bullshit, does it even really matter?"

She spoke the truth. I had no answer as we gazed at the stars. She rolled her body closer into mine and pulled more of the blanket over her.

"Neither of us know how any of this will end," she went on, "please don't ruin it now."

We stayed another hour or so but didn't say much. It was getting late. We needed to go. Both of us were cold. I helped her climb down off the hood of the car. We could hear the muffled conversations and muted laughter coming from the bar. The jukebox still played. Both of us immediately recognized the next song- the slow tear-jerker, "*He Stopped Her Loving Today*", by George Jones. I headed for the passenger side of the car.

"Wait," she ordered, "don't get in the car."

I stopped

"Come here," she said, reaching her arms out. "One dance before we go."

I joined her. She grinned, and I took her in my arms. In a tight embrace, we slowly swayed our bodies together to the backbeat of the country classic. She rested her head on my shoulder. Neither of us said a word while we danced. Like every time I was with her, I didn't want the night to end. I glanced to her face. Her eyes were closed. She smiled. It was sincere. She finally opened her eyes and glanced up, studying me. I leaned my face forward. We kissed. She quickly pulled away. I searched for her eyes- a reaction, anything. She shot a look to the ground. That kiss felt different. Although brief, she delivered it with more meaning. It took her a moment to look back. The feeling behind it appeared to have frightened her.

"You know why he stopped loving her?" she asked as the song ended. "He killed himself. He couldn't have her, and it was the only way her could deal with his love for her. Love can be an awfully cruel beast."

For several minutes, Crystal and I sat in her Mustang in Butterman's driveway. It was nearly midnight. The engine was running. The car was dusty after having spent most of the day on dirt and gravel backroads. I didn't want to get out of the car, and I certainly didn't want her to drive away. I stared at her. She wouldn't look over. Never had I felt closer to her, but as always, she had a way of pulling me in before shoving me away.

"You all right?" I asked.

She glanced to me and nodded but showed no expression or any emotion.

"You won't something to drink? A water? Coffee? It's been a long day."

She shook her head.

"Do you want to come in, hang out a little while?"

"I can't."

"Why?"

"I don't know, Michael," she snapped. "I just can't."

"Who are you Crystal?" I asked as she glanced away. "I let you in. Why won't you let me in?"

I stared at her. She wouldn't look at me. Finally, I got out of the car.

"I had a great time," I said, leaning into the passenger side window.

She nodded still not looking at me.

"How about you?"

"Sure," she replied without any enthusiasm, briefly glancing to me.

I wanted to say much more, but I didn't. There was no reason. I leaned back from the car. She glanced to me one last time, before hitting the gas and leaving in a haste without saying a word.

Chapter 7
All This I've Done for You

I arrived at the pharmacy early that morning. The drug store wasn't open yet, but a line had already formed outside the front door. One of the pharmacy phones had started to ring. I tried to ignore it, telling myself that I wouldn't answer until the store opened. But it didn't stop ringing. I had a fairly good idea the call was from Meredith. I had been negligent about returning her calls or following up on her messages. I avoided speaking with her for the obvious reasons that I was actively unfaithful to her and was too much of a coward to address it. I kept lying to myself that I'd find some time to visit and confess to her face-to-face, but I hadn't yet made a serious effort to follow through. Also, I was positive that my so-called relationship with Crystal wasn't sustainable in its current arrangement and would surely end at any time. It may have already ended as far as I knew. I hadn't seen her in weeks. I started to believe the best-case scenario for me was to give up any hope that Crystal and I could thrive in a more normal, compatible relationship and confess it all to Meredith, praying she forgave me. I certainly understood if she never wanted to speak or see me again. I also wouldn't blame her if she wanted to hit me in the head with a shovel. I deserved that at least, and probably much more.

I took a deep breath and reached for the ringing phone as the front door to the drug store was unlocked. A stream of patients steadily flowed towards me to the pharmacy in back.

"Super-Rite Pharmacy," I spoke into the phone's receiver.

"Please answer me when I call you."

"What do you need? We just opened."

"This is your last chance," Meredith said over the other end of the line.

"Last chance?" I asked, believing she referred to the end of our relationship.

"They're giving your medical school spot away today."

"I can't take it. You know that. Not this year."

"This is your chance to get out of there."

"Maybe I don't want to get out of here."

"We could be together again."

Tammy entered the pharmacy and stared at me as I faced away from the patients at the counter with the phone stuck to my ear. Archie suddenly appeared and started yapping to anyone who would listen.

"They'll let you start for the winter term. But you must call them today. The dean of the med school is only doing this as a favor to my father. You don't know what my dad had to do to get that spot for you."

I didn't respond. Neither of us said anything for a few moments.

"Sorry, Meredith. The store just opened. I have to take care of some patients."

Mr. Morris had hobbled to the pharmacy and leaned on the counter, trying to catch his breath. A cantankerous and an irascible elderly woman, Cecile

Dawson, appeared behind him and began loudly tapping her empty prescription bottle on the pharmacy counter. Holding the phone to my ear, I glanced to them both and held up my finger, indicating that I'd be with them shortly.

"Why don't you answer my calls or messages?"

"I'll call you tonight."

Mrs. Dawson began to bang her bottle harder against the counter, ignoring my sign for to be patient.

"You say that every time," Meredith reminded me, "but you never call back."

Tammy re-appeared. I put my hand over the receiver of the phone.

"Deal with her!" I angrily snapped out loud, pointing at Mrs. Dawson.

Tammy showed me a sour face as if to say back to me, 'what's wrong with you?'

"I really have to go," I spoke into the phone.

"The only time we talk is when you're working," Meredith said. "But you're always too busy."

"Meredith?"

She abruptly hung up the phone.

"Shit!" I exclaimed, slamming the phone down.

Tammy quickly turned and slid by me, holding Mrs. Dawson's prescription bottle.

"She's all yours. I'll take care of her prescription. You take care of her list."

I stared at Tammy who glared back and shrugged.

"And Archie and Mr. Morris need their blood pressures taken."

Archie started to babble at me. Distracted, I didn't pay attention to what he was saying.

"I hear the state started naming the puddles in the potholes on 15," he ranted. "They're jus' as deep as lakes."

Drool spilled from the side of Mr. Morris' right cheek onto the counter by the cash register. Mrs. Dawson shook a piece of paper at me. She always had a list- a long list of items that she needed from the store. And she insisted every time that someone, specifically the pharmacist, had to go around the store with her to pick out these items. This was never an easy task, and as hard as any of us at the store tried, we could never please her.

I grabbed an alcohol wipe and cleaned the drool spot on the counter, before giving Mr. Morris a napkin for the drool hanging from his mouth. I looked to Mrs. Dawson.

"Let me check Mr. Atwater and Mr. Morris' blood pressures real quick and then I'll help you with the list."

"I was here first," she said. "They can wait."

"I believe they were in line before you. It will only take a minute or two."

"I'm in a hurry!" she insisted. "Help me with my list."

I came out from behind the cash register and helped Mr. Morris wipe his mouth, before leading him to a seat in the waiting area.

"Archie, can you come back in a little while?" I asked. "We'll have more time to talk then."

"Who should I call about the potholes?"

"Did you try the sheriff's office?"

"My list!" Mrs. Dawson loudly spoke.

"I'll be with you shortly, Mr. Morris," I said. "Archie?"

"I see ya' in an hour," Archie said.

I turned and approached Mrs. Dawson, grabbing the list from her hand.

"Let's go shopping," I said sarcastically.

The first item on her list was soap. I escorted her to the soap section.

"Okay, soap. Which kind do you want?"

"Dove."

I grabbed the three-pack of Dove soap bars from the shelf and tossed it into her basket. She quickly pulled the three-pack out of the basket.

"I only want one bar," she said, putting the three-pack back on the shelf.

"But it only comes in a three-pack," I said, taking the soap from the shelf and tossing it back into the basket.

"I only want one," she said, lifting it out of the basket.

"If you want Dove, you have to buy three."

"I only want one."

"It's much cheaper this way."

"I only want one," she said, still holding the soap.

"If you want Dove, you have to buy three bars of soap!" I said, raising my voice.

Several shopped glanced at us. I looked to the pharmacy. Tammy stared at me, shaking her head.

"But I only want one. I always get it this way."

"Not from here."

"I always get it here."

"Okay," I said, yanking the soap from her hand and knowing she wasn't right.

I ripped one of the bars of soap from the three-pack and slammed it into her basket.

"There. Are you happy?"

She picked the bar of soap out of the basket and studied the price tag on it.

"I'll jus' charge for the one!"

She slightly nodded and placed the single bar of soap back into the basket. I looked to Mr. Morris in the waiting area. He had fallen asleep. I glanced back to Mrs. Dawson list.

"What else?"

An old-time salve remedy called Bag Balm was next on the list. Super-Rite hadn't carried that product for many years.

"I'm sorry, Mrs. Dawson. We don't have Bag Balm."

"The hardware store does."

"But we don't. I can order it for you, and you can get it next time you're here or you'll need to get it at the hardware store."

"I need it today."

"Then you'll have to get it at the hardware store."

"I'm not goin' to the hardware store today."

Much of the next twenty minutes with Mrs. Dawson went that way. As the prescriptions piled up in the pharmacy, I tried to rush Mrs. Dawson along. Finally, the shopping list was cleared, and I got her on her way. I quickly returned to the pharmacy waiting area to take Mr. Morris' blood pressure. He was not only sleeping, but snoring, and loudly, with his mouth wide open. The front of his jacket was stained and covered with thick drool that dangled from the side of his mouth. I looked to Tammy.

"Should I wake him?"

"Nah, come help me catch up with these prescriptions first."

So, I let him sleep. He didn't wake until later that day. Periodically, we'd check on him to make sure he was breathing.

The day flew by. Tammy had just left. The store didn't close for two more hours. Like I had oftentimes before, I wondered if I'd ever see Crystal again. And that drove me crazy. Desperate, I did a search of her name on the pharmacy computer. I discovered that she had a patient profile in the Super-Rite system that hadn't been updated in quite some time. There was only one entry for her from years earlier, showing that she received an allergy medicine that was prescribed for hay fever. Despite the old entry, I saved the home address that was listed on her profile into the GPS app on my phone. I would make a visit after work. For my sanity, I needed to see her.

Closing time couldn't come fast enough. After having made the decision to go and search for Crystal, I was both anxious and excited, like waiting for a first date to start. The last hour of my shift dragged. Sharon from the nursing home stopped. We chatted briefly. She didn't stay long. She could sense I was distracted. To fight my nervous energy and kill time, I studied the drug ledger that I had taken from the trailer on the trip with Johnny. I had snuck it into the pharmacy with me that morning. The pages in the notebook were filled on both sides of every page with hundreds of entries. And that was only one of many more ledgers. The entries began with two letters and a

159

space, followed by a single letter with a number, another number, then what looked be a price, and finally a date of transaction, such as BE X2.0 #30 50.00 091518. I suspected the first two letters to be the initials of the buyer, the single letter and number to be the drug and its strength, and the next number to be the quantity purchased. The interesting thing that jumped out if I deciphered the code correctly was that different buyers were charged different prices for the same amount of the same drug. I guess these dealers apparently knew their market. They knew who to gouge and who not to. The person with the initial's BW was gouged the most, and by a great margin. It just happened that the sheriff's wife was named Beverly Walls.

At exactly eight o'clock, I hurried out of the store and dashed to my car. I set the GPS and followed the directions for several miles south of Caldwell. I came to a stately two-story brick building that appeared to one-time house some type of government agency, such as a health department. The building had an official, clinical-look to it. It since had been converted into what appeared to be two rather large apartments with one on each floor.

I pulled into the empty driveway. Both apartments were dark and quiet. It didn't seem as if anyone was home at either place. I got out of the car and checked the mailbox next to the door of the bottom floor apartment. Crystal's name was taped to the front of the box. I assumed she still lived there. I knocked a few times on the front door, but no one answered. Too hyped to go home, I stood there a minute and scanned the area around the building, hoping she would suddenly somehow and magically appear in the driveway. But she didn't, so I decided to go to the Frank's Supper Club instead of home.

Frank's was mostly empty. Three guys sat at the bar. One of which was Jack Chub. The stage lights had been turned off. The jukebox played low. Nobody said a word. A cloud of cigarette smoke hung in the air. As I approached the bar, Jack squinted his eyes, seeming to recognize me. I ordered a draft and slid onto a barstool. Jack soon joined me.

"I's good at faces," he said, closely studying me, "but very bad at names."

"Michael."

"Michael, yes," he said as his face lit up. "You's the druggist."

"Right."

He suddenly hopped off his barstool and duck-walked around the bar, holding his lower back and grimacing as if in severe pain.

"My back's been a' hurtin' ever since I's a kid, shit," he said, returning to his stool at bar, "that's when I performed the prettiest of swan dives right smack into the mud of the shallow end of a pond back home in Georgia. Lordy, lordy, my back ain't never been the same. You gots anything for that?"

"Yeah, there's stuff for that- muscle relaxers…"

"Muscle relaxers! That's it! That's what I need! If anyone ever needed to relax. Do I have to go to a doctor?"

"I'm afraid so."

"Can you help a poor fellow and good friend out?"

"Sorry, wish I could."

"But I don't do doctors."

"I'm sure Dr. Valenzuela can hook you up without much…"

"Fuck that guy!" he interrupted. "That quack gives me a cough syrup once that wrecked my vocal cords. I couldn't sing for weeks. Thought my career was over!"

I shrugged and took a big swig of beer. Jack motioned to the bartender, holding up two fingers. Two shots of whiskey were quickly placed in front of us. Jack grabbed one and slid the other to me. He nodded as we slugged back the shots.

"So, how you doin'?" Jack asked.

"Not bad," I said, cringing from the whiskey.

"What brings you out tonight?"

"Mostly bored."

"Yeah, you right. I knows that."

"By chance, have you seen Crystal Foley in here recently?"

"Um, not for weeks," he shook his head, before turning to bartender. "Sam, have you seen Crystal Foley?"

Sam shook his head. Jack looked to the other two guys at the bar. They also shook their heads and shrugged.

"No performances tonight?" I asked.

"I already did one. My heart wasn't in it. And," he motioned to the empty tables in front of the stage, "nothin' sadder than performin' for an audience of no one."

"How's business?"

"Always starts to slow this time of year. But it'll pick back up for the holidays."

I took another big swig of beer and scanned the bar. The bar was quiet, and I felt awkward and little out of place. I spotted a jukebox in the corner that was softly playing when I came in.

"You don't mind if I play some tunes, do you?"

"Not at all," he beamed. "As a matter of fact, I'll picks some with ya'."

I finished my beer and got another one. Jack grabbed a fresh whiskey and cashed a twenty into some fives and ones, before joining me at the jukebox. He flipped through and stared at the selections, picking a few songs as we went along. I expected Jack to select old fifties' hits and rhythm and blues tunes like the ones he's known for singing. Instead, he selected heavy from the more roots, rock, and blues era of the Rolling Stones, like *Sticky Fingers* and *Beggars Banquet*. He had me stall on the Stones' classic record, *Tattoo You*, as another Stones' song *"Tumbling Dice"* from *Exile on Main Street* started to play.

"Sam!" he shouted out. "A little volume, please!"

With eyes closed, his face turned towards the ceiling, and the veins in his neck and forehead bulging, Jack wailed along to the chorus of the song in his sweetest, most soulful voice. I glanced to the bar. Sam and the other two fellows were all smiles, listening closely to the tune as Jack sang along.

"Got to roll me! Got to roll me! Keep on rollin'!"

He lowered his head, opened his eyes, and turned to me.

"Listen to that! Can you hear it?" he excitedly asked. "I'd give a million damn dollars to back-up on that recording! Shit!"

Jack stopped singing for a moment. We both listened to the next verse. He glowed in the light of the jukebox, obviously lost in a pleasant memory of another place and another time. A smile creased his face. Tears formed in his eyes, not tears of sadness, but joyful tears- likely reminders of youth and former loves. A time when he still had hope and dreams. He was in heaven. As the chorus came around again, he pointed to the bar, threw his arms into the air, and started to sing. The volume of the jukebox was turned up. Sam and the regulars joined along as we all sang together.

"Keep on rollin'!" Keep on rollin'! Roll-roll-roll me, call me the tumblin' dice!"

The song ended. We cheered ourselves. Jack staggered around, wiped his sweaty forehead, and fanned himself, before dropping to his knees. He acted as if he'd been overwhelmed by the power of the Holy Spirit.

"Goddamn! Goddamn! Goddamn!"

I helped him up. He grinned and again leaned over the jukebox, ready to play more songs. I clicked the button that moved the selection tile to the next page.

"Wait! Wait! Wait! Go back!"

I hit the reverse button. He again fixated on the Rolling Stones' *Tattoo You* album.

"Did you make any records yourself?" I asked.

"Nah, man. Wish I did, though. I'd have somethin' to show for myself," he said, still staring into the light of the jukebox and studying selections. "I's always on the road. You made more money on the road."

He turned and leaned away from the jukebox.

"I made twenty-thirty dollars a night. Back then, that was a lot of damn money, 'specially when you playin' every night 'cept Sundays."

He paused and shook his head, before looking back to the jukebox.

"Shit! I ain't got nothin' now. I blew it all. Women. Booze. On shit I put in my body that I ain't never been proud of. On shoes..."

"Shoes?"

"Nobody had badder shoes than me, buddy." His face lit up as he turned to me. "No sir! Not the rich white woman in the fancy hotels! Not even Carl 'fuckin'' Perkins!"

He returned his attention to the jukebox.

"It cost money to make a record, you see. You has to pay for studio time. You has to pay a producer, your manager. Then you has to pay to get the damn things pressed. Shit! I always liked the road better," he paused. "Way more fun and no damn rules, at least not with the dudes I's with."

Jack still studied the *Tattoo You* record in the jukebox.

"What's so special about that album?"

"I wants to play all these, startin' with the "*Worried About You*" track."

"*Worried About You*?"

"On the record, side B begins with *Worried About You.*"

"Side B?"

"Yessir. Side B of *Tattoo You* is twenty-one minutes and twenty seconds of pure lovemakin' mmm-mmm-mmm! The greatest 'make-out' side to any record ever made. I'll argue that with anyone 'til the day I die. And twenty minutes is about all I got, and all I need."

I selected the five songs he wanted to hear in order.

"When this record come out, I was seein' this pretty little thing. And we was all kinds of in love. We did the nasty to side B jus' about nightly 'til we worn the goddamn thing out."

"Thing? Your thing?"

"No! But it sure felt like it some nights," he said with a roaring belly laugh. "The record!"

The song, "*Worried About You*", started. It was slow ballad-type number. Jack stopped talking, looked up in the direction of the ceiling, and closed his eyes.

"Worried 'bout you," he mumbled quietly along with the song with his eyes still closed, before turning to me. "The sexiest thing you could ever tell a woman is, 'I'm worried about you.' Ain't nothin' better than knowin' someone out there in this crazy fucked-up world is concerned, thinkin' 'bout you, you know. This song would start. I softly, gently, start strokin' her hair, her arm, her hand, her ear. I'd whisper 'I'm worried about you, baby.' Mmm…"

His voice drifted off as we closely listened to the words.

"It was so excitin' and sad with that young gal then, knowin' each time we was together might be the last."

"The last?"

166

"She was white and ten years younger. Her daddy wanted to hang me from a big ol' oak tree in their damn front yard."

As *"Worried About You"* ended, he glanced back to the jukebox.

"We made love like there would be no tomorrow. God, I miss that girl."

The next song, *"Tops"*, started to play. Jack returned his attention back to the music playing.

"Tops! My god! This is when shit gets real. I'll take you to the top, baby. I'll make you a star. Come on! The lights are turned down low. The clothes start comin' off. I'll take you a million miles from all this!"

He sang along with the song, then looked to me. "At this point, everyone's turned up, if you know what I mean, and dialed in. Nothin' out there in the world but you and your girl. Mmm-mmm-mmm."

The next song, *"Heaven"*, began to play.

"Damn! We's in heaven. Feels so good. Feels so right. We's gone to fuckin' heaven. Kissin' and runnin', kissin' and runnin', kissin' and runnin' away.

"'Til we's standin' right in front of fuckin' God, man. Christ!"

He chugged the rest of his whiskey and held the empty tumbler in the air. I grabbed it and went to the bar to get him another one. As Sam filled his glass, we stared a moment at Jack singing aloud to the song, shaking our heads and grinning.

The next song, *"No Use in Crying"*, came on the jukebox as I handed Jack his drink.

"Volume up, Sam," he called out, talking into the jukebox glass. "You're grindin', man. You're on top of the world, but deep in your soul you know it ain't goin' work. There ain't no train comin', baby. I ain't never comin' back."

With his eyes closed, he quietly sang with the rest of the song to himself.

"You listen to this record a lot, don't you?"

"Nah, man. It's makes me too sad. That little sweetie was the only one who ever made me cry. And it was cryin' about everything good, always. It was never bad with her."

"What happened?"

"She moved to Ohio with her folks to look for work. There ain't no jobs here, man. Never was. Even less now. But shit! Think about it. She left me for Ohio! Fuck!"

"You didn't stay in touch?"

"I tried, man. But I was too stubborn. Mad at the world. Played the victim. I never saw her again. What a mistake. No one's ever moved me like she did."

He sucked hard on his whiskey as the last song we chose started, *"Waitin' on a Friend."* It was a cheery, less intense number. A smile quickly returned to Jack's face.

"Now, you's all finished with the sexy-sexy, lovey-dovey, in each other's arms, sharin' cigarettes, gigglin', happy, singin' together. Everything's all well in your world. The pressure gone, and the steam released. Ain't no place you'd rather be. Damn! Been a long fuckin' time since I been there."

He draped one of his arms over my shoulder and raised the other one to the bar. We all sang along with the tune. We again cheered ourselves when the song ended. Jack immediately whipped around to the jukebox to make more song selections.

"I got to piss," I informed him, tapping him on the back before disappearing in the cramped and dingy bathroom.

As I urinated into the rust-stained porcelain trough, the door to the Men's room busted open. I turned. It was Jack. I nodded, before looking back to the urinal. Not waiting for me to finish, he practically snuggled up against me and joined me at the trough. As he unzipped his pants, I awkwardly looked to the ceiling as I finished nature's call. Nearly done, I glanced to Jack and caught him staring below my waist.

"Nice helmet," he remarked as I reached to zip my pants.

"Huh?"

"Nice helmet," he again commented, still staring below my waist, before looking up to me.

"Uh, thanks, I guess," I mumbled.

I left the restroom without even washing my hands. It was time to go home. I hustled to the bar to pay my tab. The jukebox blared with the tune Jack has just selected- another Stones song, "*Memory Motel*." As the bartender returned with my change, Jack joined me. I threw a twenty-dollar bill on the bar.

"Get him another whiskey," I said to Sam. "Keep the rest for yourself."

"Oh, man, Michael! You can't be leavin' are you? Was it somethin' I said?"

"I got to be up early for work in the morning."

"We still got songs left on the jukebox."

"I need to go. I got a little bit of a drive ahead of me."

"Don't be a stranger now, okay? I'm here every evenin'."

"I won't."

"I had me a good time with you tonight."

"Yeah, I did too. I'll see you soon."

I started to leave but stopped and turned.

"Hey, if you run into Crystal, can you give me a call at the drug store?"

"Absolutely."

"You haven't seen her?" I asked again.

"I promise you I haven't."

I sat outside in the dark on a deck off the living room of Butterman's house, sipping at a can of beer. The air was heavy and damp. A dense fog obscured the sky, hiding the stars and moon. A gusty breeze howled, stripping what leaves were left off the trees. I pulled the hood from my sweatshirt over my head. Winter was close. Even though it was late, I wasn't ready for sleep. I stared to the empty road, searching for a sign of life- anything. The silence was unsettling. The insects, the birds, everything had moved on. I was alone, waiting- disconnected from the rest of the world. Ever since I met Crystal, I spent most of my free time waiting for her. That night was no different. I awoke a few hours later in the chair on the deck, damp from the morning dew with several empty cans of beer at my feet, still waiting.

The area was in the grips of cold and flu season, and the pharmacy was as busy as I had ever seen it. Tammy and I were busting our asses trying to keep up. With an overflow of patients in the waiting area, she looked over to me as she filled prescription orders and shook her head. I grinned and shrugged, almost chuckling at the absurd number of prescriptions we were filling for antibiotics, decongestants, and cough syrups, particularly cough syrups with codeine. And nearly all the prescriptions were coming from Dr. Valenzuela's office. Some of the people waiting were actually sick, but I knew many were not. They faked sickness to get a six-ounce bottle of the codeine cough syrup that could give quite a buzz alone or mixed with Sprite or even added to vodka. It also was good for fending off opiate withdrawal when area supplies were depleted or dealers were unavailable due to arrest or overdose, which happened a good bit of the time then. Also, most of the sickness at that time of year was due to the common cold or influenza virus, and antibiotics don't do a thing about killing viruses.

"Tammy?" I asked, scanning the waiting area.

"Yeah," she answered not looking up from the orders in front of her.

"Have you seen Crystal Foley recently?"

"Who?"

"Crystal Foley."

"Why?"

"Have you seen her?"

"Why?" she asked again, looking up to me. I didn't answer.

"She's bad news, I hear."

"Have you seen her in here?"

"No, not for many weeks."

We returned to filling the orders and ringing customers up. After many minutes, I asked, "Why's she bad news?"

Tammy stared at me a moment, seeming disappointed that I even asked about Crystal.

"She has a reputation," she said, then briefly paused before whispering. "She gets around."

"What's her story?"

"Why? You interested?"

"Do you know what her father does?"

"I didn't know that she had a father."

"I've met her. She told me she helps her father with his business, but she wouldn't tell me what business."

"I don't know. I wouldn't trust her. I've heard rumors."

"She seems interested about me staying in Caldwell and other long-term plans of mine."

"Maybe it's because there's not many young professional men around here. Maybe she's interested in you."

"No, I don't think it's that."

"Whatever it is I'd stay away from her. Besides, you got yourself a nice gal back home."

Evelyn suddenly appeared at the pharmacy counter. Along with coffee for both Tammy and I, she handed me a small package wrapped in decorative Christmas paper.

"What's this?"

"Open it."

I ripped at the paper and opened the package as Tammy watched me, grinning. Evelyn giggled like an excited child at a birthday party. It contained a knitted gold and brown winter hat and a pair of matching mittens.

"What the…?"

"I made them for you. It took me weeks."

"What?"

"It's startin' to get cold."

"You didn't have to do this."

"I wanted to."

"You're too kind to me," I said, then looked to Tammy, "and us."

"I have a set as well," Tammy smiled.

"This is the first time anyone's ever made something like this for me."

"I hope you like them."

"I love them!"

On her knees, Crystal, in a sparkling and very revealing cocktail dress, vomited into a stained toilet of a filthy bathroom. Nauseous, she turned away from the toilet into a sitting position and tried to catch her breath in between dry heaves. Her eyes and nose were red from crying. She kicked off the spiked heels she wore and pushed at the purse beside her. Its contents spilled out- lipstick, a pack of cigarettes, breath mints, several one-hundred-dollar bills, and a gun. She reached for the gun and studied it a moment, checking to see if was loaded. She used the sink to pull herself up and stared at her reflection in a clouded vanity mirror, holding the gun at her side. Slowly, she raised it and held it against her face for many minutes, still staring at her reflection and weeping. Finally, she slammed her fist holding the gun into the mirror. The shattered glass shredded her hand. She brushed at her hair that had fallen over her eyes, leaving stains of blood on her cheeks and forehead. Blood poured from the deep gash across the back of her hand and knuckles. She lowered her damaged hand as the sink quickly filled with blood.

It was December. Thanksgiving had come and gone. I had worked every day for weeks. Time flew by. My small world on the ridge off Route 15 suddenly looked and felt very different, having changed almost overnight. The frozen ground was covered with layers of dead leaves. The branches on the trees were bare and exposed. The nights were longer and darker. The mornings were frosty, dreary, and gray. There still was no sign of Crystal. I would drive by what I thought was her apartment every two or three nights after work. Each time, the place was blacked out and lifeless. I began to believe she no longer lived there. I also believed she was gone.

Her absence drove me crazy. And every night I waited for her, I found myself doing things I'd never thought or cared about before. My behavior had changed. One night at Butterman's place I came across a half-pack of unsmoked cigarettes. I smoked three of them. It took me awhile, but I eventually choked them all down. And they were disgusting. It took me days to get the awful taste out of my mouth. As I smoked the cigarettes that night, I stared outside the open front door into nothing, waiting for something, anything. Of course, nothing happened, and Crystal didn't show up. On another night, I brewed a pot of coffee at midnight, and nearly drank all of it in little more than an hour. I fidgeted and paced the empty house for most of the night, alone and bored with nothing to do, waiting for something to happen. Again, nothing did. And another night, I stared until dawn at obscure television channels I found on the satellite. I watched west coast professional basketball games late into morning before switching over to a soft porn channel. I couldn't decide which was worse- the NBA or me watching cheaply produced pornography alone in a stranger's house. I guess some people got aroused by the porno channel. It just made me feel lonely and awful, watching couples seeming to have more fun than I was. For the first time since I had moved to the Caldwell area, I felt isolated and disconnected from everyone I cared about and all the things I enjoyed. I knew I wouldn't make it much longer if I continued to live that way.

Wearing sunglass and in a Speedo, an oiled-up James Butterman sat beside a pool, enjoying an exotic fruity adult beverage. His fat body glistened and baked in the hot Florida sunlight. Two fit and handsome young men sat with him, also reveling in the bright sun and adult beverages. A sandy white beach was only steps away. The gulf was unusually rough that morning. A tropical storm was several miles off the coast. Dark, ominous storm clouds had formed in the distance and slowly approached. As Butterman stared at the choppy blue ocean, his phone rang. He lowered the sunglasses and checked the number before rolling his eyes.

"Excuse me, boys," he said, standing and clicking on the phone.

"This better be important," he mumbled into the receiver, walking away from the table. "This day has started off too perfect for any bullshit from up there."

"A state detective's snoopin' around," said Sheriff Walls on the other end of the line. "He's talked with Phyllis and the Morgan kid's mother. He's wantin' to speak with Johnny next."

"Johnny Fogg?"

"Yeah, but he hasn't been able to locate him yet. He also wants to search your house. Don't worry about that. I'll have my staff do the search."

"Okay. Okay. I'll get ahead of it. I know what to do. Keep me posted if anything else comes up."

Butterman powered off his phone and returned to his young friends by the pool. With the sunglasses positioned on top of his tanned bald head, he looked lost, staring blankly into the pool water.

"Something wrong, James?" one of the young men asked.

"Not at all, boys," he said, shaking his head and smiling. "Nothing that a couple phone calls can't solve."

Butterman lowered the sunglasses over his eyes and scanned the pool area.

"Now, where's our server? We need more of these tasty drinks. Am I right?"

Not paying much attention after a long and tiring day at work, I entered Butterman's house through the front door. Once inside the house, I suddenly heard a shuffling sound from the kitchen as if I had surprised someone. The door in the kitchen that led to the backyard opened and closed with a slam. I scrambled through the house to the kitchen and stepped outside. I heard the engine of a four-wheel, all-terrain vehicle rev a couple of times before speeding through the yard. Because it was dark, all I could see were the vehicle's red taillights as they disappeared into the woods that extended away from Butterman's property.

I rushed back into the house. The door to Aaron's room had been kicked opened. The wooden door frame was busted and splintered into pieces. The door swayed, hanging only from a broken hinge. I quickly entered the room. The drawers to the nightstand had been pulled out. The gun and bottles of morphine all were gone. I ran back into the kitchen and an opened a small cupboard door above the refrigerator where I had hidden the notebook I took from the trailer. It too was gone.

"Crystal!" I shouted, pounding the refrigerator with my fist.

The lights to the sparse, desolate apartment were off. Gloria Morgan watched television from bed. A cigarette burned in the ashtray beside her. She held a pint glass filled with vodka. It had been days since she changed out of the heavy wool nightgown she always wore. It had been longer since she left the apartment. There was a knock at the door. At first, she ignored it. There was another knock. After an initial hesitation, she sighed, pushed herself up, and mope-walked to the door, checking the peephole. Her face immediately lit up. She excitedly pulled the door open. Aaron stood before her. He looked incredibly stoned and disorientated.

"Aaron? My God! My prayers have been answered!" Gloria cried out, hugging him with all the strength left in her soul. "My baby boy has returned!"

She started to cry. Aaron wrapped his arms around his mother and held her tightly. She leaned her face away to check him out more closely. Unkempt and struggling to keep his eyes open, he appeared as if he hadn't slept or bathed in days. They stared for a moment until the barrel of a handgun suddenly appeared over his shoulder, aimed at her face.

"Sorry, ma."

Before she could respond, a shot rang out. Aaron held tightly to his mother's lifeless body, preventing it from dropping to the floor. Gunpowder had burned the side of his neck and cheek. But he didn't feel a thing with all the dope flowing through his body. Blood poured like an open spigot from the gaping hole in the back of his mother's head. He wrapped a towel around her face and head and carried her into the apartment as the trigger man disappeared down the hall. Aaron eased his dead mother onto the bed and rolled her body in its sheets and blankets, before cleaning the mess off the door and hallway floor.

Due to a looming snowstorm, the county was sending the school kids home early. Most of the downtown Caldwell businesses were already closed for the afternoon. The Super-Rite corporate offices were shutting the drug store down three-hours early. I had let Tammy leave before that, so she would be home for her kids when they got off from school. I scrambled around the pharmacy and frantically filled the rest of the many new and refill prescription orders that had been called in earlier. At a few minutes before five o'clock, I walked to the front of the store and locked the door to the main entrance.

Wearing the knit hat Evelyn had made for me, I stared outside. The heavy gray clouds were low, and the sky was black. A light snow fell and had started to accumulate on the sidewalks and cars parked outside. I stayed late for another thirty minutes with Robbie, the young store clerk, who waited for his ride. We had heard that the roads in the more rural areas of the county had already become icy and treacherous. He was the last one left in the store. I wasn't going to leave until I knew he had a way home.

"Isn't this a little early for snow?" I asked him.

"We always seem to get a big storm or two like this in early December."

"How much are they predicting?"

"I think someone said eight to ten inches."

"The whole county's been shut down."

"They don't mess around. With the hilly roads, it's easy to get stuck."

"They don't treat them?"

"They try, but the county jus' don't have enough trucks, and they lost most of their drivers to the oil and gas companies. They pay 'em a lot more than the state can."

"Do you think we'll be open tomorrow?"

"Probably. They may delay when we open. That's what they did last year."

Finally, a snow-covered pick-up truck pulled to a stop outside the store. I unlocked the front door.

"You be careful, Robbie," I said as he bounded out. "I'll see you tomorrow."

The drive to Butterman's house normally took thirty minutes. The trip that night took over an hour. The roads were slushy in most places and initially not too bad. But as darkness fell and the temperature dropped, the pace of the falling snow quickly picked up, and the roads had gotten worse. By the time I was about three or four miles from Butterman's place, the roads had become icing and were covered by over an inch of snow. I shifted into low gear, took my time, and white-knuckled it the rest of the way. I didn't know which was worse, fishtailing and struggling to peak a hill or skating down the other side. Either way, I was all over the road, trying like hell to keep the little car in its lane. Luckily, no one else was out.

As I neared Butterman's house from the south, I noticed a set of fresh tire tracks in the snow that had approached his place from the north and turned into the driveway. I pulled in behind the tracks and followed them to the garage door. But there was no vehicle. The tracks appeared to back up and turn around, before exiting the driveway via the north. I initially assumed that someone had gotten lost and used the driveway as a turning point. That was until I looked up and scanned the property. A porch light over the deck off the living room had been turned on. I had never used that light before.

Wearing the knit hat and matching mittens, I shut off the car, stepped through the freshly accumulating snow, and entered through the garage. Thinking the culprit that stole the gun and drugs from Aaron's room had returned, I grabbed a four-iron from Butterman's old golf bag and tiptoed up the stairs to the kitchen. They mustn't have expected me at that time because of the store's early closing. But they would've heard my car drive up. I slipped into the darkened kitchen and immediately smelled something- smoke. It was cigarette smoke. I peeked into the living room and walked towards the smell. All the lights in the house were off. I could see the sliding door to the deck was slightly propped open.

I crept over to the sliding glass and peeked to the deck, raising the four-iron. As the falling snow swirled around her, Crystal inhaled deeply on a cigarette, blowing the smoke into the cold air with her arms tucked in tight against her body. She looked different. Her hair was shorter and lighter in color. Her right hand was heavily bandaged. I dropped the club and rushed outside.

"Shouldn't you be at the drug store?"

Not answering, I aggressively grabbed the front of her shirt, causing her to drop the cigarette.

"What are you doing, asshole? Get your hands off me!"

I dragged her inside as she struggled, throwing wild punches in the air and kicking at me. I pulled her into the living room and pushed her onto the couch. She tried to stand. I shoved her back onto the couch.

"What the fuck happened to you? Bad day at work?"

"Someone broke in here recently. They knew about the drugs and gun in Aaron's room. Did you take them? Did you?"

"Where'd you get that stupid hat?" she asked, staring at me with a funny look.

"What?"

181

"That stupid hat and those mittens."

I pulled the hat off my head and glanced at the mittens on my hands.

"You look ridiculous."

"I like them."

"They're hideous."

"Whatever. Did you take the gun and other things from Aaron's room?"

"No!"

"Do you know who did?"

"No!"

"Bullshit! What's going on here in Caldwell?"

"I'm in trouble."

"Cut out the bullshit!"

"I really am this time!"

"Come on!"

"That's why I'm here. I need a place to hide."

"Bullshit!"

"I tried to stay away from you, but…"

"But, what?"

"Can I stay here tonight?"

"You need to tell me what the fuck is going on around here!"

"I'll tell you everything I know."

"How'd you get in the house? Steal the key again?"

"The side door to the garage was unlocked."

"I've never unlocked that door."

"Well, it's unlocked now."

"Who dropped you off?"

"There you go with all the questions. I thought you'd be excited to see me."

"I saw tracks in the snow. It looked like from a truck. Who dropped you off?"

"A friend."

"What friend?"

"You don't know him."

"Who'd you tell him you were coming to see?"

"I told him I was coming to see you."

"Does he know anything about me? Or us?"

"No."

Shaking my head and looking away, I didn't believe her.

"The Mustang's parked in front of my apartment. I want people to think I'm home."

"What people?"

"I've been helping a friend the past month. And he got in over his head a little bit and skipped out of town for a while. I just need to lay low a few days."

"What friend?"

"You don't know him."

"Butterman?"

"Ha," she laughed. "If anything, the problem around here has gotten a lot worse since he's been gone."

"What problem?"

"There's been a shooting and a bad batch of killer drugs floating around. And not to mention, Aaron and a couple others are missing."

"How are you involved?"

"My friend, kind of used my car, in runs to Detroit and Baltimore."

"For drugs?" I asked as she shrugged. "He 'kind of' used it?"

I started to pace around the room.

"Things will settle down," she tried to assure me.

"What'd you get out of the deal?"

"Gas money."

"Bullshit! I don't believe a thing you're telling me."

"Is your dad the friend you're talking about?"

"Ha!" she laughed again. "No."

"Are you in danger?"

"They don't care about me. But they're probably watching my house. They're using me to get to him. They want my friend."

"Must be some friend."

"What do you mean by that?"

"Sounds like a close friend."

"Oh, brother. You're jealous?"

"Am I involved in any of this?"

"Yes."

"Yes! How the fuck am I involved?"

"Quit looking for Aaron."

"Why?"

"Just quit. That's all I'll say now."

"Who took the gun and morphine?"

"I told you. I don't know!"

"Why should I believe any of this?"

"Don't. I'm just warning you."

"Butterman's behind this. I know it."

At that moment, the lights in the house flickered a couple of times as if Butterman was listening. Eventually, the power went completely out and so did the furnace. We heard it shut down with a bang, a knock, and then a loud thud. We glanced around the darkened house, hoping the lights would come back on. They didn't.

"The power may be out a while," I reasoned. "The storm's only going to get worse, and I need to keep the house as warm as possible."

"What are we going to do?"

"You're not staying here."

"Where am I going go now, at this time, in this weather?"

"Goddammit, Crystal!" I said, looking away and pacing around the room. Knowing I had no other option, I glanced back to her. "Please tell me I can trust you."

"You can, Michael. I'll only stay tonight."

We studied each other a moment. I still didn't believe her.

"There's a stack of wood behind the house," I said, pointing to a fireplace that looked barely used. "We'll need to start a fire."

"I'll look for some blankets," she said.

"How's the charge on your phone?"

"Less than half."

"Me, too. I better shut mine off. I'll need to call the store in the morning to see if we're open."

The temperature quickly dropped in the big drafty house. With little time to waste, I had brought several loads of wood into the living room and set them next to the fireplace. Crystal had found some blankets and a couple of sleeping bags as well as an assortment of sweat clothes and heavy flannel shirts. Candles lit the room as I started a fire. Crystal prepared some snacks and brewed hot tea. We put on the additional clothing and arranged the blankets a few feet in front of the fireplace. The wood was damp from being stored outside and took some time to catch fire. We sipped at the tea and stared at the fire that struggled to thrive.

"I'm calling Butterman," I said, breaking the silence, not giving up on our previous conversation. There was so much more that I needed to ask her.

"That'd be a mistake."

"Why?"

"I don't want to talk about it anymore tonight."

"What happened to your hair?"

"I needed a change."

"A change in appearance?"

"Maybe."

"And your hand?" I said, pointing to the bandage.

"I cut myself shaving my legs."

"Right."

"Believe what you want."

"Where've you been?" I continued, ignoring her request and still wanting to press her with questions. "It's been weeks."

She didn't immediately answer, taking the cup of tea from my hand and setting it aside. We rearranged the blankets and slid our chilled bodies under them. She held me tightly. I looked away. She turned my head towards hers. We stared at each other, our faces inches apart. She stroked my forehead and cheeks. I tried to resist. She gently kissed me.

"The day on the river. The chicken place. In the field under the stars," she said, before briefly pausing. "I wasn't supposed to do any of that."

"What do you mean- 'not do any of that'?"

"It wasn't part of the script."

"Script?"

"I was given one rule," she said, gazing deeply into my eyes, "don't fall in love."

I didn't know how to react. Her responses caught me off guard- 'script?', 'don't fall in love?' The comments stunned me. I looked away and stared into the growing fire that popped, cracked, and sparked. I glanced back to her. She beamed in the orange glow that lit the room. He eyes were as bright as stars.

"I'm cold, Michael," she whispered.

Not knowing what to do next, I pulled her body almost completely under me, trying to keep her warm and safe as best I could- all the time hating myself for it. We were dressed in hoodies over flannel shirts and sweatpants and buried under a pile of blankets and sleeping bags. I could hear the gusty wind, knocking at the windows. I could feel her heart, beating against me. Through the sliding glass door, I watched large flakes of snow pouring from a black stormy sky. I wanted to believe she belonged in my arms, under me. To make it all work with her, I needed the outside world to go away and the power to the house to stay off forever. Never in my life, under those blankets, alone with her in a lost wilderness, had I been so comfortable in a moment, in a place, and in a time. I was king for a night. I was giant. But I couldn't trust her, and man, I really, really wanted to. I knew she was lying.

"I ran away when I was fourteen," she said, breaking the silence. "I've been running ever since."

"Huh?"

"I ran away from home. My dad left my mother when I was nine or ten. I never knew why. I still don't."

She rolled her body around in my arms and faced me. We stared.

"My mother's new boyfriend soon moved in with us after my dad was gone. They got married. He was then my stepfather, and he...," she suddenly stopped and turned away from me, trying to compose herself, unable to continue.

"It's all right," I whispered, gently patting her on the back. "You don't have to say anything else."

"No. No. You wanted to know."

She was silent for a minute or two.

"He had a thing for little girls," she finally confessed with a sigh.

"Crystal."

"It wasn't every day or even every week, but it was regular."

I pulled her tight against me and massaged her arms and back- still she looked away.

"I don't know if he did anything to my sister, but I'm sure he did."

"You have a sister?"

"She never said anything."

"You never said anything?"

She faced me and shook her head. I wiped away a tear that hung from her cheek. I could tell she wasn't lying about her past.

"Not until now. You're the only one who knows."

"Have you seen your mother or sister?"

"Not for years. I hardly speak to them. I don't want to."

"Not even your sister?"

"Nope, and I don't know why. Maybe because she stayed and let him get away with it. I don't know."

"And you?"

"I wasn't putting up with that shit. He wasn't going to ruin me anymore that he already had."

"So, what'd you do?"

"I ran away. Stayed at a friend's house for a few days," she said, before pausing and taking a deep breath.

"It's okay..."

"Feel my back," she interrupted.

She took my hand and directed it to the small of her back under the several layers of shirts she wore. I softly ran my hand over her warm, bare back, feeling three raised ridges of scarred tissue I hadn't noticed before.

"I made my friend whip me with an extension cord. She beat me so hard my back was blistered and bleeding. It scared her. She bawled and bawled as she beat me. She cried harder than I did."

"God, Crystal."

"I turned myself into the police station and told them my stepfather had beat me, and I wanted to go live with my real father."

"So, what happened?"

"My mother and stepfather show up. It was a complete drama shit show with the crying and the denials and all the lies and promises."

"And your mother let you go away?"

"She had no choice. I ended up here."

"And now?"

"Once I turned sixteen, I got my license and my father got me an apartment. I've pretty much been on my own ever since. But...," she paused, looking away from me.

"But, what?" I asked, practically smothering her in an embrace.

"I just want to go home."

She pushed more of her body into mine. I rested the side of my face on the back of her head. I nibbled and softly kissed at her ear. The fire we built roared and kept us warm. We didn't say another word the rest of the night. Our relationship suddenly seemed different. In no time, we were both asleep.

I awoke out of a deep sleep. Crystal stood over me. It took a moment to gather my thoughts and process where I was and what had happened. It was still dark outside. I was warm and comfortable under the blankets. I hadn't slept that well since I'd arrived in Caldwell.

"I gotta go," she informed me.

"Gotta go?"

"My ride's here."

"Ride?"

The power to the house was still out.

"What time is it?" I asked.

"Not yet five."

"How much snow did we get?" I asked, sliding out from the blankets that covered me.

"Over a foot."

"Wow."

I wiped at my sleepy eyes. She appeared worried.

"You going be all right?"

"I'll be fine."

"You sure?"

"Yes."

"You can stay another…"

Before I could finish, she leaned in and kissed me. And it wasn't just a 'so-long-I'll-see-you-later-peck-on-the-cheek'. That kiss was more- even more than the one at the Chicken Palace. It took my breath away. She pulled back. I studied her.

"Don't worry," she tried to reassure me. "We'll be all right."

"All right?"

"All this I've done for you."

"All what?"

"You'll understand later."

"Understand what?"

"I need to go."

She left in a hurry. I rushed to the front door and watched from a window, having no idea what she was trying to tell me. An idling tow truck waited in the driveway. She stomped down the stairs at the front of the house through the deep snow that had accumulated overnight and hopped in the passenger side of the truck. Because of the darkness, I couldn't get a good look at the driver's face. Within seconds, they were gone.

I turned away from the window. The dark house was empty and quite cold. According to the thermostat in the living room, it was a frosty forty-one degrees inside. I moved to the fireplace and jabbed at the lone smoldering log with a cast iron poker. The charred log sparked and soon rekindled a small flame. After adding a couple more logs, I powered on my phone and checked the messages. I had several voicemails from Meredith and one from Super-Rite headquarters. I saved the ones from Meredith for later and only listened to the Super-Rite message. I found out that the drug store would be closed that day and would open with a two-hour delay on the day after. I powered down the phone to preserve what little battery life was left. I knew it might be a day or two before the power to the house would be back on, and I had to make sure that I had some connection to the outside world.

I returned to the fireplace to warm myself. The fire quickly swelled. I crawled back under the blankets and sleeping bags. I easily fell back to sleep, remaining under the covers for most of the day, only leaving their comfort and warmth a few times to add more wood to the fire. I didn't feel alone. The scent of Crystal lingered with me under the blankets.

Chapter 8
Too Far Down

The power to the house came back on sometime before daybreak. The rumbling sound of the furnace restarting woke me. I peeked my head out from under the layers of blankets and sleeping bags that covered me and stared at the fireplace. One last charred log smoldered. A single lamp lit the room. I was too warm and comfortable to move. Even though I still had to clean the snow off my car, the front steps of the house, and possibly a path in the driveway to get the car out, I wasn't in a hurry to go anywhere. The opening of the drug store would be delayed for two hours that morning, so I had plenty of time. I thought.

As I lazed in the warmth under the blankets waiting for the temperature in the house to rise, my eyes were drawn to the photograph of Butterman's daughters on the mantel. After a several minutes, I finally slid out from the blankets towards the fireplace. I grabbed the metal poker and stabbed at the smoldering log, restarting a small fire. I added another piece of wood and stood in closer to the building flames, before reaching for the photograph and studying it closely. Without setting it down, I suddenly was compelled to search through all the drawers, cupboards, and storage spaces in the entire house. I wasn't sure what I was looking for, but I was quite certain I would know when I found it.

I started in the living room then the kitchen. I moved into the master bedroom and rummaged through every dresser and nightstand drawer. I found a small antique desk that I hadn't noticed before in a spare bedroom. I pulled open a bottom drawer and discovered what I had suspected and didn't want to believe. In the top of the drawer, I found a checkbook belonging to Butterman from a Florida bank. Underneath the checkbook, there were stacks of stuffed envelopes. I opened one. The envelopes contained returned, cashed checks each written to Elizabeth Foley for $2500. There were checks for every month, and the dates of the envelopes spanned nearly a decade. Alimony was handwritten on the subject line for every single check.

A pit that seemed the size of the nearby New River Gorge immediately formed in my gut. I glared back at the photo I still held, taking special notice of the younger of Butterman's two daughters. I collapsed back into the chair of the desk, continuing to stare at the photograph. Shaking my head, I slammed the photo to the ground, shattering the glass of the picture frame. I had been played. Before I could think about what to do next, there suddenly was a knock at the front door.

"Crystal...," I grunted under my breath.

The knocking continued as I stomped to the front door, jerking it open.

"What?" I yelled, expecting it to be Crystal.

To my surprise, it wasn't her at all. It was Meredith, instead.

"Surprise!" she beamed.

Without even thinking, I scanned the snowy and frozen landscape around Butterman's property behind her.

"I thought you'd be more excited to see me," she said, trying to frown but unable to hide her smiling excitement.

"I am. I am. It's been a couple crazy days here," I said, not looking her in the eyes and still checking the road and driveway for Crystal. "The power went out the night before and just came back on a few hours ago..."

"Can I come in?" she asked, interrupting me.

"Sure. Sure. Sure," I said, grabbing her travel bag and leading her inside. "This is a surprise."

"I canceled my classes. Drove through the night, and here I am. I needed to see you."

I took an additional quick scan of the property outside before closing the front door.

"I drove through a snowstorm to be with you. You seem more concerned about something else," she said, motioning towards the door. "Aren't you even a little bit excited to see me?"

"I am. I am. It's just I don't have any free time. I need to be at work soon and still have to the clean snow off my car. I won't be back until later this evening. And I have to work again tomorrow."

"I don't care. I wanted to see you, Michael. Even if it's only for a few hours."

An awkward silence followed as she stared at me. I had trouble making eye contact.

"You seem distracted."

"No. no. no," I said, trying to reassure her that everything was all right.

"Tell me, what's going on here?"

"This really is a surprise. It is. And a good one. But I need to get ready for work," I said, as I turned away, took a seat, and started to put on a heavy winter coat and boots. "They can't open the drug store without…"

"I love you, Michael," she interrupted as I looked up to her. "I came all this way to tell you that."

"I'm sorry, Meredith. My life here's gotten a little complicated."

I stood. We hugged.

"Please leave this place," she whispered in my ear. "Come back home with me. We can start over."

"I wish it was that easy."

I pulled away from her. We studied each other before I grabbed a snow shovel and stepped out the front door. Sadly, I was suddenly in a hurry in get out there. She followed with a broom.

"What are you doing?"

"I'm going to help."

"You don't need to do that."

"I want to."

"Go back inside and rest. You have to be tired, driving all night."

Ignoring me, she started to sweep off the porch and iron steps at the front of the house as I cleaned the snow off my car. I started it to warm it up for the drive into town. I shoveled a path in the snow behind the car to make it easier to pull out of the driveway. The two of us worked outside for over thirty minutes. I occasionally would glance to the main road in search of Crystal. After Meredith and I were done clearing the snow, we went inside and had enough time to share a cup of coffee and catch up with some idle chit chat as I got ready for work.

"I brought some groceries," she said. "I'll make lasagna and homemade sauce while you're at work."

"My favorite. You're too kind."

Before I could leave, we hugged at the front door. I pecked her on the lips. Though, she wanted more. And I was gone.

Parked on the street in front of the florist in downtown Caldwell, Crystal took several deep breaths. As she waited for the florist to open, she suddenly felt nauseous. Peering down the street, she noticed the drug store hadn't opened yet either. She needed to get something to calm her stomach, but by then her skin instantly had turned cold and clammy. She again took several quick, deep breaths. Everything in her stomach, which wasn't much, suddenly felt in her throat. Unable to hold back the contents of her gut, she threw open the car door and violently vomited in the pile of snow that had been plowed against the sidewalk. Slowly sliding out of the car, she kneeled on her hands and bended knees in the slush of the sidewalk, yakking up nothing but a thick, red-orange substance, likely a combination of bile and stomach acid. She tried to catch her breath. The muscles in her belly had contracted and cramped as she began to dry heave uncontrollably. Finally, after many minutes, the dry heaves stopped. She crawled into the back seat of her car. The knees of her slacks were soaked and stained. She rested until the flower shop opened, which turned out to be an hour later than usual because of the storm.

Along with the sudden stress of Meredith's surprise visit, I was worried about the potentially treacherous drive into town that morning after the snowstorm. For the most part, the main road was slushy where it had been treated and snow-packed in the other areas. The drive wasn't as bad as I expected it to be. I was terribly distracted and stressed about my collapsing world. Meredith's surprise visit was one thing. And I couldn't wrap my mind around the fact that Crystal was Butterman's daughter. I knew at that point she was scheming me. But I wasn't sure about her father. He had to be, and I needed to find out why. Once I got to the drug store, I immediately called Johnny. We planned to meet in the coming days. I would be off from work through the weekend after two more shifts at the pharmacy. Later that morning and still confused and distracted, I reached for the phone. I had dialed Super-Rite headquarters to tell them I was quitting. Maybe it was time to go back to Pittsburgh with Meredith. I was put on hold and after waiting several minutes before someone of authority answered, I eventually hung up.

Soon after I had left for work, Meredith brought a couple bags of groceries into Butterman's house from her car. She had planned to make a special dinner that evening while I was at work. Once she put the groceries away, she walked through the house giving herself a tour. With her travel bag slung over her shoulder, she stopped at the threshold of the master bedroom and peered in, making note of the gaudy design and messed bed. It's sheets and bedspread balled up and twisted together, and the mattress nearly half off the exposed box springs. She turned away without entering. Instead, she took her bag into one of the spare bedrooms and set it down on the bed. Noticing the broken picture frame in the middle of floor, she found a broom and dustpan in the kitchen and swept up the glass, dumping it into a small garbage can next to the desk. She reached for the wrinkled photo on the floor and briefly examined it, before crumbling it up and tossing it away in the trash with the pieces of glass and broken wooden frame. She returned to the living room and begun to straighten up the blankets and sleeping bags on the floor in front of the fireplace. As she folded one of the blankets, she caught a whiff of the fruity fragrance common in women's shampoo as it brushed near her face. She immediately dropped the blanket as if it had suddenly caught fire. With a disappointed almost defeated look, she balled up the blankets in the sleeping bags and dragged them to the master bedroom. She pushed them in the room, before closing the door.

As homemade tomato sauce simmered on the stove, Meredith chopped vegetables and prepared dishes for dinner in Butterman's kitchen. Music played as she quietly sang along with the tunes. Suddenly, there was a knock. Meredith wiped her hands with a towel and stared at the front door with a puzzled look. She turned down the music. There was another knock. She threw the towel on the counter and walked to the door, cautiously pulling it open. It was Crystal. She held a large bouquet of red, yellow, and white roses.

"Oh, my," Meredith said with a smile, reacting to the flowers, "let me help you with that."

She took the flowers from Crystal.

"These are beautiful!"

"They're from Michael Young," Crystal said as Meredith examined the flowers more closely. "He picked them out himself."

Not taking her eyes from the flowers, she stepped back into the house, before glancing back to Crystal.

"Do I owe you anything?"

Crystal shook her head as they closely examined each other for the first time. The surprised and delighted look on Meredith's face gradually changed. She had to know I was unfaithful. She also had to know that Crystal, who stood before her with a smug grin, had to be the one. Neither of them knew how to react. Crystal stared back. Her fists were slightly clenched; she was ready for a fight. Meredith's first thought was to slam the door shut, but for some reason, she couldn't. With her face suddenly flushed, she glared at Crystal, wanting to smack the smirk off her face.

"It is odd, though," Meredith said as Crystal shrugged, continuing to grin, "as long as I've known Michael, he's never given me flowers before. That's not his thing."

"He must've been awfully bad," Crystal said still smirking, before turning and starting to walk away.

"Oh, wait a minute," Meredith called out. "Come in. Come in."

Crystal stopped and followed Meredith who walked inside to retrieve her purse. As Meredith dug through the purse, Crystal quickly scanned the living room and kitchen.

"Wow, smells great in here."

"Yeah, making a special dinner."

"For Michael?"

"His favorite, lasagna," Meredith said, pulling a twenty-dollar bill from her wallet. "I'm surprised that anyone would be out in this weather. You know- making deliveries. The roads must be awfully slick."

"It didn't matter. He wanted me to get these to you as soon as possible."

Meredith handed Crystal the money.

"How much snow did we get out here?" Meredith asked, trying to ease the tension with small talk.

"I don't know, fourteen-fifteen inches."

They stared at each other. Neither looked away. Crystal again clenched her fists.

"How well do you know Michael?"

"Pretty well. I see him nearly every day."

"Every day?" she asked, still not looking away.

"Caldwell's a small town. There's no secrets here."

"Secrets?"

"Everyone loves Michael at the drug store. You're a lucky woman. I would do anything to trade places with you."

The tension between the two grew. Meredith's face reddened even more; her hands slightly shook. Her immediate thought was to get in her car and drive home, but she wanted to confront me first. Crystal's grin widened, knowing she had pinched a nerve.

"You're too kind," Crystal taunted, holding up the twenty-dollar bill as Meredith looked ready to push her out the front door. "And we're all thrilled to hear that Michael has made a commitment to settle in Caldwell."

Crystal backed outside. They continued to stare at each other before Meredith finally slammed the door. Before Crystal left, Meredith rushed to one of the front windows and watched. Crystal stood by her Mustang with the door open and briefly stared at the house, before getting in and driving away. With her hands still shaking, Meredith walked to the flower arrangement and yanked out the card that came with it. She read it aloud:

"May these roses brighten your day! Love, Michael."

She crumbled the card into a ball and violently threw it into the trash.

"Gag me," she mumbled, knowing the flowers hadn't come from me.

She glared at the trash a moment or two, then reached in and pulled out the wrinkled card, sticking it back into the flowers. She then moved the rose arrangement to a coffee table near the fireplace.

Sometime after sundown, Crystal pulled her Mustang into the downtown public parking lot a few blocks from the drug store. After parking, she pulled a large hunting knife from under the driver's seat and got out of the car. Sticking the knife in the back of her denim jeans under a heavy down jacket, she walked with a confident gait in the direction of Super-Rite. Passing by the entrance of the store, she continued around the building to the back where the employees parked. Without hesitation, she walked to my car and scanned the lot, before pulling out the knife. Leaning down, she stabbed the front tire on the driver's side of my car- not once but multiple times. Calmly, she pulled herself up, scanned the parking lot again, and hid the knife, before leaving the scene.

I had about fifteen minutes before closing. The store was extremely slow that day. All of Caldwell County was buried in snow. Archie, Evelyn, or Sharon didn't visit that day. Mr. Morris however did make it in. I helped him put drops in his eyes for his glaucoma and took his blood pressure. I also bought him lunch that was delivered from the diner. He then slept most of the afternoon in the mostly empty pharmacy waiting area. I had filled less than twenty prescriptions. I wished that I had the authority to close the store. There was no reason to be open. I could've spent the day with Meredith, trying to repair the damage I'd done to our relationship. I was anxious about the night ahead. I was excited to see her and spend time with her for sure. But at the same time, I had to tell her about Crystal and that scared the hell out of me. Also, I had to worry about Crystal. I never knew when she would make a visit, and it didn't need to be that night. I couldn't predict either of their reactions if they were to meet by chance. But something told me, Crystal already knew that Meredith was in the area.

As I wrapped up the paperwork for the day, Robbie came out from the back-storage room and walked up to the pharmacy counter.

"Hey," he called out. "You know you got a flat?"

"What?"

"One of your tires is flat. I was gettin' ready to go home and jus' saw it."

I followed Robbie out of the store to the lot in back. I leaned down and grabbed at the several pieces of shredded rubber that hung from the flattened tire.

"That don't look like no accident," he said.

I nodded, knowing exactly who did it. My assumption was right. Crystal knew Meredith was around, and I should've predicted this would be her reaction. I pulled out my phone to let Meredith know that I'd be late.

"Do you want me to check the surveillance video?"

"There's no need," I shook my head as I dialed the phone.

"What happened to the back of your car?" he asked, noting the damage in the back from Whitey's shotgun blast.

"Freak accident."

"Deer hunter?"

"Maybe," I mumbled, opening the trunk.

"No spare?"

"There's a spare, but it's filled with holes."

"Well, let's at least get the flat off the front."

Meredith was disappointed after I informed her about the tire. She had spent most of the day preparing a special meal for us, and it was nearly ready. It seemed she didn't believe me about the tire at first, so I took a picture just in case I needed conformation. As Robbie watched, I pulled out the jack and lug nut wrench. Robbie helped me position the jack and lift the front side of the car enough to get to the flat tire. The lug nut wrench that came with the car was single-shafted and practically useless. Both of us tried to remove the lung nuts, but because of the single shaft of the wrench neither of us could get enough torque to remove any of them. Most likely because they had been overtightened automatically by a bolt gun as opposed to by hand. We stood there for a few moments helpless, staring at the shredded tire suspended off the ground.

"My friend, down the road a ways, has a regular X-shaped kind of lug wrench and probably a spare you can have that'll fit," Robbie said. "I can get 'em."

"You don't have a wrench?"

"No, I lost it in a snowbank someplace last winter. I keep forgettin' to get a new one."

"How far down the road?"

"Maybe a mile."

"Is he home?"

"He's always home. He doesn't got nowhere to go."

I glanced back to the flat tire.

"Okay."

Robbie quickly hopped into his truck and drove off. He came back to the parking lot in twenty minutes. It took us another half-hour to replace the flat tire with the spare, a temporary 'doughnut' that was smaller than the regular tire and made of what seemed to be a hard-plastic material. Both of us took turns standing and jumping on the wrench after it was attached to each lug nut to finally loosen them. We both were filthy at that point. Robbie had saved me. I shook his hand, and offered to pay for his help, seeing that he stayed an extra hour after work.

"Thank you. Thank you, Robbie. Let me give you something. Come on."

"It's all good. I'd hope someone would help me the same I did for you if I needed it."

"You stayed an extra hour. What's Super-Rite pay you an hour? At least, let me give you that."

"No, you don't have to do that."

"I know I don't, but I want to. How much do you make an hour?" I asked, pulling my wallet from my back pocket."

"No, no, that's all right. Really it is?"

"How much do you make an hour?" I pressed him.

"Eight dollars and fifty cents," he reluctantly answered, almost embarrassed about the amount.

I stared at him a moment, not realizing what little money he and probably most of the others at the drug store made besides myself and Butterman.

"Shit, man," I shook my head, pulling a one-hundred-dollar bill from my pocket, "go out and have some fun this weekend."

His eyes lit up as he studied the bill that I held out to him. But because of his kindness that was all too common among the generous folks in Caldwell, he adamantly refused to take the money. After he left, I phoned Meredith to tell her I was on my way. She didn't sound too pleased about the delay, but she understood.

By the time I got to Butterman's, it was nearly ten o'clock. I slowly and reluctantly entered the house. The place smelled amazing from the wonderful meal Meredith had prepared. Upon entering, I glanced around, searching for her in the darkened house. She sat alone at the end of the long dining room table covered with assorted dishes of food and a half-empty bottle of wine in front of her. The several candles that illuminated the room had mostly burned away.

Melted wax from the candles spilled over the edges of the holders that supported them and onto the table. Crystal looked exhausted and defeated. It was all my fault.

My serving of lasagna had already been plated. Her eyes followed me from the time I walked through the door from when I washed my grease-stained hands in the kitchen sink until I sat down at the table. She didn't utter a single word the whole time. She didn't need to. She was already finished with her meal when I finally I cut into the lasagna on my plate. It was delicious but cold. I ate a few bites. She continued to closely watch me. I shoved another bite of food into my mouth and smiled. Her expression never changed. Finally, she broke the ice.

"How's the lasagna?"

"Fabulous!"

"What happened to your tire?"

"I don't know," I said, shrugging, "but it was shredded pretty good. The roads around here…"

My voice drifted off as she looked away and finished her glass of wine. She poured herself another without offering any to me.

"I haven't eaten like this in a long time. The lasagna, the garlic bread, everything's wonderful."

"It's all cold."

"No, no," I shook my head. "It's fine. Really, it is."

She glared at me with a shake of her head. I continued to eat, mostly in silence. She stared at me, not saying a word until I finished.

"Why so quiet?" I stupidly asked.

"I feel I've lost you."

She immediately stood, not allowing me to respond, and started to gather dishes from the table before disappearing into the kitchen. I followed her.

"I need to know about your commitment to Caldwell and the drug store," she said, not looking at me.

"Commitment?"

"Didn't you make a commitment to stay here?"

"I have made no commitment to anyone!" I snapped. "I'm here until next fall, and that's it."

"No commitment to anyone? You sure about that?"

"That's right. No commitment!"

"What about me?"

"I wasn't talking about you, us," I snapped back, shaking my head as she started to rinse the dirty dishes in the sink.

"You've changed."

"No, I haven't!"

"Please come home," she said, turning to me. "You can get another pharmacy job there."

"I have to stay here at least until Butterman gets back from Florida."

"You don't want to leave!"

"That's not true. Please be patient. At least until spring…"

"It'll be too late," she interrupted as she started to load the dishwasher.

"Meredith?"

She wouldn't look at me or say another word until later that night, abruptly ending the conversation. Because of the delay with the flat tire, it was nearly eleven o'clock. She was obviously very tired, having driven most of the night and didn't seem in the mood to talk anymore. She wanted to go to bed soon after dinner. She fiercely refused to sleep in the master bedroom where I suggested. I was pretty sure I knew why. She wouldn't even step in there, and it had nothing to do with garish décor.

I took a seat on the bed in the spare room as she prepared to turn in. I had forgotten about the broken picture frame I left in the middle of the room that morning and suddenly wondered where it was. Meredith opened her bag. She didn't bother to change into the sexy negligée that was at the top of the other items in her bag. Instead, she set it aside and slipped into a sweatshirt and baggy pair of pajama bottoms. I also noticed an unopened bottle of champagne she didn't bother to take out of the bag. She pulled down the covers of the bed, and I joined her. It felt as if a concrete wall a mile thick separated us. I was ready to tell her everything.

"Is there a florist in town?" she asked before I could speak.

"Um, yeah."

"Have you been there?"

"No, not yet. Why?"

"Oh, I was just wondering if they had any Christmas arrangements out yet. I thought this place could use a wreath or tree or something for the holidays."

I glanced over to her. Her eyes told me everything I needed to know. I was a terrible liar and a horrible cheat. And she knew it. I slid closer. I wished I could have erased the last few months. I wanted to say something. And she waited. I was lost her in glare. I wanted her to reach over and hold me. She didn't allow me to touch her.

"I'm sorry," I finally whispered.

Her expression didn't change. We stared at each other a moment longer until she turned away and shut off the lamp beside the bed.

We both struggled to sleep. At some point in the middle of the night, she left me for the solitude of the couch. I didn't follow. She didn't want me to. It must have been after four when I finally dozed off before being roused from sleep just before daybreak by an aggressive pounding at the front door. With a concerned look, I glanced around, alone in bed and afraid to leave it, pulling the covers over my head. I obviously assumed it was Crystal.

"Michael!" Meredith called in a concerned tone. "Michael?"

I heard the front door open.

"Michael! You better get out here."

With some hesitation, I joined Meredith at the front door. Unexpectedly, I was greeted by Sheriff Walls and a handful of deputies.

"Sir, we have a warrant to search the premises."

I looked to Meredith who had already dressed and packed her bags.

"Goodbye, Michael," she said, reaching for her purse and travel bag.

"Meredith! Hold on. Hold on," I pleaded as she stepped out the front door.

"Can we come in, sir?" Sheriff Walls asked, moving aside on the porch to let Meredith leave the house.

"Yeah, yeah," I nodded, chasing after Meredith in the snow in bare feet. "Meredith, wait!"

I rushed after her, nearly slipping down on the icy, snow-covered stairs at the front of the house. But she didn't turn or wait for me. I stopped at the bottom of the stairs as she got into her car and started it up. Without a single look in my direction, she backed out of the driveway and was gone. I kicked at the snow in my bare feet and tromped back up the stairs to the house. The sheriff waited for me at the front door as his officers searched the house.

"Will this take long?" I asked.

"Shouldn't be more than a couple of hours."

I had to call the pharmacy to inform them that I'd be late. We legally couldn't open the drug store without a licensed pharmacist on the premises. I first phoned Tammy.

"I'm going be late. The sheriff's here. They have a warrant to search Butterman's house."

"To search his house? What in God's name for?"

"Likely something to do with Aaron."

"And Butterman's involved?"

"I have no idea. They think the search will take at least two hours. I can't leave to open the store until they're done."

"I'll put a note on the front door about the delay until you get here. But you better call headquarters and see if they're all right with it."

"Okay, okay. I'll talked to you soon."

As I dialed the phone, I saw a flower arrangement that I hadn't noticed the night before near the fireplace mantel. I walked over and checked it out more closely. I pulled the crumpled card that went with the flowers and read it with a sigh. Setting the card on the mantel, I noticed a ring beside the flowers. It was Meredith's engagement ring.

I finally made it to the drug store, two and half hours late. I had no desire to work. It felt as if I'd been struck by a speeding truck that stopped after hitting me before backing over my broken body a few more times. I spent most of the day in a chair in the corner of the pharmacy hidden from the patients. Tammy assumed I was sick. I was, but it had nothing to do with any bacteria or virus. I had her take care of all the prescription orders. She would bring the filled prescriptions to me to check and approve them. Luckily, it was a slow day as most people in the county were still trying to dig out from the recent snowstorm. The pharmacy did receive the three quarterly checks that Butterman was so concerned about- one each from the nursing home, Dr. Valenzuela's clinic, and the rehab hospital. I filed them away that afternoon. I didn't have the energy to walk a couple of blocks to the bank to deposit them. Thankfully, I had the next several days off. I planned to spend them in Pittsburgh and try to straighten out the mess I had created. Tammy was especially interested in the search of Butterman's house. That was the only thing she wanted to talk about.

"What'd the sheriff say?" she asked.

"He didn't say anything to me."

"What do you suppose they were lookin' for?"

"I don't know, but they pretty much emptied the room where Aaron stayed."

"Do you think James is in trouble?"

"No."

"No? Why not?"

"I have a feeling that Mr. Butterman can do whatever he wants around here. No one will say a word."

Tammy stared at me, looking somewhat disappointed, not sure what I meant. I wasn't necessarily saying anything bad about Mr. Butterman. I was just stating what I thought to be true. And I firmly believed that the sheriff went to the house to protect Butterman, taking anything that could incriminate him regarding Aaron's disappearance. He didn't even ask me about the broken door and frame to Aaron's room.

Because I had to save my relationship with Meredith, I didn't bother to go back to Butterman's house after work that night. I drove straight to Pittsburgh like a madman- on a temporary 'doughnut tire' for over five straight hours without stopping. I pushed the little car as fast as it could go, even with the front end badly out of alignment due to the abnormally small tire. The speed of the car topped out at eighty-five miles per hour at which point the steering wheel would shake so badly I could barely hold onto it. I wanted to get to Meredith's apartment well before she could leave for work the next morning.

During the drive, I had plenty of time to dwell on all the trouble I caused in the short time since I had moved to Caldwell. I likely had lost my fiancée. I was aware enough to know that my trip to Pittsburgh that night was a last-ditch, end-of-game 'Hail Mary' pass, a longshot horse winning the Triple Crown. And I also knew that longshots mostly came through only in books and movies and rarely in 'real-life'. All this trouble because I couldn't resist the lure of the local 'good-time' girl, 'Queen of the County', the 'Belle of the Hills'. I lusted after her Siren's song and wrecked myself when I tried to get too close, knowing the entire time it was a mistake. I was a willing subject of her scheme as she slowly and expertly bludgeoned and hacked away at my integrity with the precision of a butcher, leaving me nothing but a hollow shell with little soul left. I couldn't sink any lower. I had hit rock-bottom. I was too far down. Part of me wished I had stayed in Pittsburgh in the first place. The other part wasn't too sure how to feel yet.

It was sometime after three o'clock in the morning when I reached the driveway of Meredith's apartment building. After parking, I dashed from the car and pounded on her front door.

"Meredith!" I called. "Meredith!"

Eventually, the door slowly opened. She blocked the entrance, so I couldn't enter.

"I drove five straight hours on a busted tire to see you."

She didn't immediately respond and slightly shook her head.

"I got here as fast as I could after work."

"You wasted your time."

"You don't mean that."

"You're too late."

"Meredith?"

"You should have done this weeks ago, and maybe....," her voice drifted off.

"Let's talk about it."

"What's there to say at this point? I could almost understand if it were a one-time thing, but you kept it going."

"Meredith..."

"And behind my back."

"When did you know?"

"I always knew."

Her steely, cold glare bore a hole through me. I had trouble making eye contact. I pulled her engagement ring from my pocket and reached it out to her.

"Here, this is yours. Please take it. Put it back on."

"I don't want it," she shook her head. "I want you to keep it as a forever reminder as to what a horrible, selfish mistake you've made."

I bowed my head. I could no longer face her.

"And for what? A little freedom? A piece of ass?"

She paused until I finally looked her in the eyes.

"And I also want that ring to be a reminder to never ever put someone else you supposedly love through the bullshit I've had to endure these past many weeks. All the while, giving you the benefit of the doubt and hoping you'd come to me to talk. I wasted enough tears on you, Michael. No, there's nothing to talk about. You're too late, way too late."

I closed my eyes as she calmly and gently closed the door on our relationship, leaving me to stand alone, holding the engagement ring.

I suddenly had nowhere to go. With the next few days off, I had hoped to spend the free time with Meredith to repair our fractured relationship. I even thought about speeding right back to Caldwell. Instead, I found myself in the driveway of my grandmother's house, licking my wounds and tightly grasping Meredith's engagement ring in my pocket. Even though it was quite early, my grandmother appeared to be awake. I knocked and entered through a side door into the kitchen. She sat at the table, drinking coffee, and reading the Post-Gazette.

"What a surprise!"

She stood as we hugged. It had been over a month since I had talked to her, and even longer since I had seen her.

"You drove all night jus' to see me?" she asked.

I slightly nodded, not wanting her to know the real reason I was there. I was getting use to hiding the truth at that point. She continued to hug me and rub at my back. I couldn't help but think what a fool I was not come back and visit her more. And I was an even bigger fool to have betrayed Meredith.

"I miss you, grandma."

And that wasn't a lie. I deeply missed the comfort, shelter, and most importantly, the love she always provided.

"How 'bout some breakfast? You must be hungry."

"I don't feel like eating."

She proceeded to make me a large breakfast anyway, just like she did on weekends when I was young. Our Saturday morning breakfasts use to always include eggs, fried potatoes, bacon, assorted fruit, and coffee- lots of coffee. Sometime during middle school, she allowed me to drink coffee, but only on Saturdays. As she prepared the breakfast that morning, we caught up on each other's news. She hadn't missed Sunday mass since I had left and was spending two or three nights a week at the senior center in town. She tried not to drive as much. She felt great and was sleeping and eating normally. In turn, I told her everything there was to tell about the pharmacy and Caldwell. I did my best to try and convince her that I was doing fine. She especially liked some of my stories about the regulars at the drug store- Evelyn, Mrs. Dawson, Mr. Morris, and Archie. She loved my matching knitted hat and mittens. I didn't say a word about Crystal. Or Meredith. But by the way she studied me, I could tell she was concerned.

"Have you been eating?" she asked. "You look thinner."

"I try, but…"

"You need to eat, and healthy food, too," she interrupted. "I know you're busy, but please find time to eat."

I nodded and looked away.

"And sleep? You look tired. You have to get your sleep."

And she was right. She had no idea how exhausted I was.

"Are you goin' see Meredith?" she finally asked, but I didn't respond. "You know she's stopped here several times to check on me since you've been gone."

"I didn't," I said, shaking my head.

"She's changed some light bulbs for me. Picked up groceries. Took me to the dentist. She even helped me replace the filter on the furnace."

"She's the best."

"Yes, she is. You're so lucky."

In the driveway, Crystal sat in the idling Mustang and stared at Butterman's blacked-out house. My car was gone, and I normally would have been home at that time in the morning, getting ready before work. After a few minutes, she peeled away and sped towards downtown Caldwell. She arrived at the drug store about twenty minutes later and parked on the sidewalk in front. The store had just opened, and she hurried to the pharmacy in back. Tammy was quick to greet her.

"Is Michael here?" Crystal asked with some urgency, glancing behind the counter and noticing a much older gentlemen who was the fill-in pharmacist for the day.

"He went home," Tammy answered.

"Home?"

"To Pittsburgh."

"Is he coming back?"

"We hope so. He's scheduled to work next week. He needed to take care of some issues he said."

Crystal sighed, seeming somewhat relieved but still appearing concerned.

"Is there anything we can do for you this morning?"

Crystal shook her head.

"Are you all right?"

"I'll stopped back when Michael's here."

After poking at a fried egg and picking at some bacon, I found comfort on the couch, spending the next couple of hours falling in and out of sleep to the morning news, random talk shows, and the Price is Right game show. I intended to stay a couple days after rightfully getting shredded by Meredith. But like a junkie craving his next fix, Caldwell, and especially Crystal, were calling me back. Sometime later that morning, I gathered myself, kissed my grandmother goodbye, and raced back to Caldwell. I was determined to find out what fate Crystal and her father had in store for me.

Although the temporary tire nearly melted off the rim, I made it back to Caldwell in record time. I drove directly downtown to the bank. I needed to deposit the three large checks the pharmacy had received the day before. I parked the car and hurriedly entered. One of the tellers I knew, Kelly Stalnaker, was available. I handed her the three checks.

"I want to deposit these. They're made out to Super-Rite Drug and are stamped on the back."

"I jus' need you sign them as well," she said, sliding the checks back to me through the teller's window.

"Sign them? My name?"

She nodded as I started to sign one but stopped.

"Are you sure? This isn't my money."

"Mr. Butterman makes these deposits quarterly."

"And my name's on the account?"

"Yes," she answered, after taking the checks to look up the account number on the computer. "Michael Young, right?"

"Can I ask who else is on the account?"

"Uh, let me see. There's Mr. Butterman, yourself, Aaron Morgan, and uh, Crystal Foley."

I stared at Kelly for a moment.

"You know what, can I have those checks back?" I asked as she slid them to me and nodded. "I don't want to get myself or Mr. Butterman in trouble. Since this is my first time making this deposit, let me call him to make sure I'm doing this correctly."

"Sure," she said, nodding.

Tightly grasping the checks, I hustled a few blocks up the street to the drug store and made a beeline directly to the pharmacy in back, not stopping to say a word to anyone. I nodded to the fill-in pharmacist. Looking puzzled, Tammy's face lit up upon seeing me.

"Hey! I thought you went home for a few days?" Tammy asked as I pulled a large three-ring binder off a shelf. "What are you doin' here on your day off?"

I flipped through the files in the folder, ignoring her. I studied the paperwork over the past several years, then stared at the checks in my hand for $16,000, $19,200, and $15,700.

"These just don't add up," I mumbled to myself.

I slammed the binder shut and returned it the shelf, before filing away the three checks. As I started to exit the pharmacy, Tammy tried to get my attention.

"Hey, what's goin' on?"

I didn't answer, leaving the pharmacy area.

"Crystal was in here, lookin' for you," she called out, causing me to immediately stop in my tracks.

"What'd she say?"

"She seemed worry."

"Are you in trouble?"

"I'm not sure, yet."

Before she could press me with more questions, I rushed out of the pharmacy and sped off. By the time

I reached Butterman's house, the car was no longer drivable because of the damaged spare tire. Knowing this would likely be a problem, I had called Johnny Fogg before I left downtown and arranged for him to pick me up at Butterman's place as soon as possible. He was waiting for me in his truck with his dog by his side as I skidded my car to a stop in the driveway. I hopped out of the car and quickly got in the truck.

"They're playing me, Johnny."

Johnny glanced to me, then looked away without responding.

"They're playing me, and I fell for it, all of it."

I had him drive me to the clinic at Dr. Valenzuela's office. Johnny parked his truck in the lot. We watched folks that appeared to be from all ages and economic backgrounds mill around in front of the clinic, smoking cigarettes or vaping and talking on their phones. I studied the license plates of the vehicles parked around us. There were numerous cars with out of state plates, mostly from Ohio, and even a couple from Pennsylvania and Maryland. Business it seemed was good for Dr. V and James Butterman.

"Butterman's selling stock drugs purchased by Super-Rite to the clinic, nursing home, and rehab hospital at elevated prices and keeping the difference," I said.

Johnny looked to me from the corner of his eyes, then quickly glanced away.

"He has you and the Avon Lady selling pills on the side. All the money he's made is in a special account."

Johnny wouldn't look at me.

"Can you do something for me?" I asked as he glanced to me with an unsure expression. "Can you walk into the clinic and see if you can get something for pain?"

Johnny smiled as I pulled out my wallet.

"I jus' needs thirty," he spoke up.

I handed him the money. He slipped out of the truck as if he had a sore back, slowly limping the entire way to the entrance of the clinic.

With a puzzled look, Crystal pulled into Butterman's driveway and parked her Mustang behind my car. She got out and studied the warped and scorched spare tire before looking up to the dark house. Pulling a key from her pocket, she entered through a side door off the garage, quietly stepped the set of stairs that led to the kitchen and entered. She scanned the living and dining rooms, before walking through the rest of the house. She entered the master bedroom, then the spare bedroom with the desk. She glanced down and noticed something in the trashcan. She bent down and reached for the broken picture frame. Looking back into the trashcan, she pulled out the wrinkled photograph of herself and her sister. She studied the picture a few minutes and softly ran her finger over her sister's smiling face. Keeping the photo with her, she suddenly got up and hastily left the house. She rushed back into downtown Caldwell and checked the drug store again. The replacement pharmacist was the only one present in the pharmacy. Tammy had gone home for the day. Crystal then raced across the street to the motel and stomped up the stairs to my rented room. She pulled a key card from her coat pocket and slid it in the slot, slowly pushing the door open. The room was empty. She returned to her car with a sigh, trying to figure out where to look next.

Slumping in the passenger seat of Johnny's truck with his dog, Rufus, I waited for a short twenty minutes in Dr. Valenzuela's parking lot. Holding a small paper sack, Johnny practically ran back to the truck. Hopping into the driver's seat, he handed me the bag. It contained an unlabeled pill bottle with ten generic Vicodin tablets.

"No prescription?"

"You can visit Dr. V once a month on your insurance or welfare card," Johnny said, shaking his head. "He adds a thirty buck service charge for ten pain pills if you needs it."

"You know that's illegal?"

"Dr. V don't care. The inspectors, the judges. He knows they've all paid off by the drug companies. And if you got cash, you can visit as much as you want."

"To pay the office visit and the drug service charge?"

"Yep, and he don't keep no records. At least, not honest ones."

"How much is the office visit with cash?"

"Hundred bucks."

"Plus, the thirty-dollar drug service charge."

"Yep."

"So, I guess Butterman isn't the only one making a fortune here."

Johnny fired up the truck and glanced over to me.

"Where you need to go next?"

"I'm sure not, yet," I answered, watching scores of supposed patients going in and out of the clinic.

"How 'bouts a beer? There's some dudes at Frank's who would love to knowed that I'd seen the doctor."

In Johnny's beat-up, old truck, we rattled, bounced, and rolled our way over the busted backroads for the next fifteen minutes or so. Neither of us said much. Johnny's was nearly salivating over the fact that he had a bagful of opiates in his possession. I was trying to figure out what I was going to do next. At that point, I hadn't a clue. With the next several days off, I had plenty of time to think about it. I also considered moving out of Butterman's place and going back to the motel room. As we pulled into Frank's parking lot, I stared at Johnny a few moments until he looked over at me.

"I've been meaning to ask you. Did you really shoot your father?"

"I ain't shoot no one," he quickly and definitively answered, before easing the truck into a parking space. "I's scared of guns, and I wish I weren't, though."

"You said you did."

"When?"

"At Whitey's."

"Whitey's?"

"When I was there. You guys were getting stoned."

"Oh, that was nuthin' but big talk for Whitey."

"Hell, he was passed out."

"He was? Shit. I jus' want Whitey to like me. Ain't no one important ever liked me."

224

"I don't think Whitey's that important," I said as Johnny looked to me. "But I like you, Johnny."

Bringing his backpack and Rufus with him, I followed Johnny to the entrance of Frank's. We pushed open the heavy front door. The regulars that circled the bar shielded their eyes from the outside light of the late afternoon sun, trying to see who was entering. Standing over the jukebox, Jack turned and raised him arms in excitement as we took seats at the bar. Staying close, Rufus eased himself down underneath Johnny's barstool.

"Michael! Michael! My friend! Johnny! Come in! Come in!" Jack said, walking towards us. "Sam, get Michael a beer and a shot of whiskey on me!"

Jack quickly joined us, sliding onto a barstool and leaning in close to Johnny who showed him a wink and a nod.

"The ship's done come in," Johnny whispered.

"What's you got?"

"Special V. Ten of 'em."

"How much?" Jack asked as Johnny's phone started to ring.

"How many you want?" Johnny asked, retrieving his phone from the heavy backpack he always carried.

"All ten."

"Fifty," Johnny responded, checking his phone as it stopped ringing.

"Johnny. Johnny. Johnny. It's me, Jack."

"Forty."

"Sam," Jack called out. "Get me a couple tweenies from the register."

Johnny and Jack secretly exchanged the money and the pill bottle under the bar. Before politely excusing himself, Jack opened the bottle and handed Johnny two of the tablets. Slipping the tablets into his shirt pocket, Johnny's phone began to ring again. He checked the number and studied it with a curious stare.

"You all right?" I asked.

"I gotta get. You need a ride?"

"Nah, I think I'll hang out here. I have nothing else going on."

"How you gettin' back to town?"

"I'll figure it out. I'm off for a few days. I'm not too worried."

Johnny nodded and headed for the door in a rush as Rufus followed.

"Johnny?" I called out before he could leave. "Be careful."

He nodded and was gone. From inside the bar, I could hear his old truck start with a rumble and pull away with a loud roar. I was never much of a drinker, but I felt like getting drunk that night and listening to some jukebox music with Jack. I picked up the shot of whiskey and tossed it back. As I set down the shot glass, the front door to the bar opened, and Crystal stepped out of the light that suddenly flooded the place. She immediately joined me at the bar but didn't sit.

"Drink?" I asked her.

"Let's go."

"Nah," I shook my head, pointing at my nearly full beer. "I'm staying here."

"Let's go, Michael."

"I don't think so," I said, reaching for my beer.

"I'm not telling you again," she said, firmly tugging at my shirt collar and pushing the mug of beer away from me. "LET'S! GO!"

I turned to her.

"Come on. Let's go for a ride."

Reluctantly, I stood and followed her out of the bar.

At a dangerously high rate of speed, Crystal's pushed her Mustang to the limit, squealing around the winding turns of the rural backroad. Neither of us said much for the first few minutes of the drive. She tried to scare me, but I wasn't afraid anymore. And she knew she was losing her control over me. She kept glancing at me, but I wouldn't look back. Finally, she broke the silence.

"I thought you went home. What are you doing back here?"

"This is all I got."

"All you got? You want me to feel sorry for you?"

"Your flower trick worked. You ran her off."

"You ran her off. Don't blame me."

"So, I guess I'll be staying here awhile," I said, finally looking over to her. "That was the plan, right?"

"I don't care what you do."

"Let me out of the car."

"What?"

"Let me out of the fucking car! I'm going back to the bar."

She looked over to me and stared.

"Stop and let me out of the car!"

She continued to stare.

"Stop the fucking car!"

She suddenly slammed on the brakes, causing my body to violently jolt forward.

"I'm done, Crystal!"

"What?"

I threw opened the passenger side door.

"I'm done. The game's over. I'm out!"

As I started to pull myself out of the seat, she stomped her foot on the gas, causing me to awkwardly tumble to the hard-frozen ground as the passenger door swung shut, and the car raced away. I got up and brushed myself off, watching Crystal's Mustang disappear in the distance. From the fall on the asphalt, I had ripped the sleeve of my shirt and one of the knees of my pants. Rubbing at the scrape on my knee, I looked back in the direction from which we came and studied the challenge of the sharp curves and steeps hills in the road without much room to walk on either side due to the plowed snowbanks. There still was another hour or so of daylight left. I figured I had about a thirty-minute walk back to the bar and could get there before dark. But I didn't get too far. My phone started to ring. It was Johnny.

"Johnny, you all right?"

"I'm down by the river. I think it's trouble."

"What?"

"I don't feel right about this."

"Where?"

"Right off the same road from Frank's, not too far. My truck's parked by the road. There's clearin' down to the river."

"I'm on my way!"

Unsure of how far I had to go, I started to jog, sticking out my thumb when an occasional car or truck came upon me from behind. But no one stopped. Suddenly, I heard tires squealing around turns in the distance ahead of me. Crystal's Mustang appeared and sped in my direction, before screeching to a stop and nearly striking me.

"Get in, asshole," she ordered through the opened passenger window.

"Johnny's in trouble," I said, climbing in the car.

"Huh?"

"Johnny's in trouble!"

With a puzzled look, Crystal stared at me.

"Drive!"

Crystal continued to stare at me.

"Drive, dammit!"

A heavy coating of undisturbed snow covered the ground from the recent snowstorm. Johnny and his dog walked over a set of abandoned railroad tracks that one time fed and connected a series of bustling coal towns. The tracks ran alongside the raging Big Tug River- its rushing, white-capped waters spilled over the riverbank. A brisk and frosty wind blew from the north through rows of tall fir trees that lined the other side of the Big Tug. Johnny slowed his pace as his dog slowed behind him.

"What's a matter, boy?"

Spooked, the dog suddenly stopped. Puzzled, Johnny whipped around as the dog scampered away.

"Mr. Butterman?"

Butterman appeared on the tracks as if expecting to meet Johnny. He raised a shotgun and aimed it at Johnny's chest.

"I can explain!"

"That won't be necessary, Johnny."

Crystal pulled her car to a stop along the road next to Johnny's truck. I hurried out of the car and quickly glanced around. As Crystal followed, I pointed to a fresh set of footprints in the snow leading to a trail through a dense wooded area. She hesitated as I started for the trail. I stopped and turned to her. She approached me and put her hand on my shoulder, shaking her head. She knew something bad was about to go down. A gunshot instantly echoed through valley.

Next to the river, Johnny had ducked and fell to his knees on the railroad tracks after the gun blast. He had covered his ears with both hands as he scanned the area with dart-like looks in every direction. He glanced over his shoulder. He was surprised to discover that Butterman had been shot. Johnny again scanned the area, searching for the shooter as Butterman, bleeding from the head, staggered to the river's edge and clumsily stumbled into the frigid rapids. A rustling sound in an area of heavy brush caught Johnny's attention. He dashed towards the thicket as if chasing after someone.

Crystal and I hurried towards the sound of the gunshot. Johnny's dog galloped by us in the opposite direction. I slid down a slippery, snow-covered hillside, before fighting through a nearly impenetrable overgrowth of gnarly brush.

"Johnny! Johnny!"

"Michael?" Crystal called out, chasing behind me. "Wait! Michael! Stop!"

I climbed two small hills buried in snow until coming to sloping meadow that ended at the railroad tracks. Out of breath, I reached the tracks and glanced around.

"Johnny!"

I noticed a trail a blood in the pristine white snow that led to the river. I rushed to the river's edge and spotted something floating in the distance- a man's body. Crystal ran up behind me.

"Michael, don't."

"Johnny!"

The body bobbed and dipped on the surface of the rushing river.

"No! Johnny!"

The body quickly disappeared downstream, riding atop the surface of the rushing whitewater.

Chapter 9
Dead Set on Destruction

In a forgotten hollow a long way from anywhere that mattered, the dark foreboding sky hung low over the surrounding hills. Phyllis Moody repeatedly slammed the gas pedal of her pink-customized Jeep Wagoneer complete with pristine white leather interior and Avon decals on the back window. The Jeep also had a personalized state license plate that read 'AVON LADY'. The back wheels of the Jeep spun unhindered in a deep, muddy rut in the road. She rolled down the frosty, driver-side window for a look behind. The wind howled, and the snow flew. With her head out of the window and watching, she hit the gas again. Wet, slushy mud kicked up behind the Jeep. It wouldn't move. She was stuck on a lost hollow road that hadn't be used for days, or maybe worse, weeks.

She checked the gas gauge and turned up the heat inside the Jeep. Her phone was useless as that part of the county was without cell service. Holding her crossed arms tight against her chest, she pondered her next move, worried about her safety. Suddenly, the headlights from a moving car danced in the distance, bouncing off a nearby hillside and heading her way. She breathed a sigh of relief as the car approached. A beat-up, early model Plymouth pulled behind her with two people inside. Phyllis studied the car. The driver got out. It was Whitey. She rolled down the window and poked her head out.

"Thank God, you showed up."

Whitey studied the stuck Jeep and glanced inside it. The backseat was filled with numerous Avon paper sacks of different sizes, all stapled shut.

"I never thought I'd get hung up in this thing."

Whitey moved to the driver's side of the Jeep and slowly lifted a handgun from his ragged flannel coat. He stuck the gun in Phyllis' face.

"Gimme the keys."

Phyllis showed him a puzzled look.

"The KEYS!"

She nervously fumbled with the keys, trying to get them out of the ignition until he reached inside the Jeep and yanked them from her. Throwing the Jeep door open, he aggressively grabbed the back of the fur collar of her winter coat and roughly pulled her out. She awkwardly fell face first to the ground in the snow and mud.

"Please!" she begged, pushing herself up into a sitting position. "Don't hurt me!"

With the heel of his boot, Whitey shoved her back down, again face first into the mud. He ripped the expensive coat off her back and rolled it up under his arm.

"Shut the fuck up!"

"God! Please! Oh, God!"

Whitey opened the back door of the Jeep and started collecting the shopping bags. Sobbing and starting to hyperventilate, Phyllis gathered herself, staggered up, and tried to escape as Whitey loaded his car with her winter coat and the bags filled with controlled prescription drugs.

"Christ," he mumbled, turning to Phyllis who tromped through the mud, stumbling away from her Jeep.

Whitey raised the handgun, aimed, and shot at Phyllis. She immediately dropped, falling head first to the ground. She'd been shot in the neck. As Whitey emptied the Jeep, she wailed in the distance.

"Oh, God! Please! Please help me!"

Whitey reached the gun to the passenger in the Plymouth who had been slumped down low as if trying to hide. It was Johnny Fogg.

"I didn't 'tend to shoot her," Whitey confessed, "I was goin' to leave her here to freeze."

Whitey reached the gun closer to Johnny who shook his head.

"Here. Take it."

Johnny continued to shake his head.

"You work for me now, Johnny."

Johnny reluctantly took the gun and stared at it.

"Be a man," Whitey pressed as Johnny glanced up to him. "Finish her off."

Slowly, Johnny walked towards Phyllis. She was on her back like a turtle that had flipped onto its shell. Her legs and arms flailed helplessly. The rate of the falling snow had picked up. Reaching her, she sobbed for her life. Johnny stood tall over her, but he couldn't look her in the eyes.

"Please! You must help me! Johnny, please!"

She gurgled with each breath as blood poured from the wound in her neck and flowed from the side of her mouth. Johnny raised the gun and aimed it. Her body squirmed in the freezing mud. She wept uncontrollably, staring at the gun. Johnny still couldn't look her in the eyes. The gun shook in his hand. He closed his eyes and tried to the pull the trigger. His hand tremored more violently. He reached for it with his other hand to hold it steady.

"Please! Oh, God! No!"

Again, he tried to pull the trigger but couldn't. Finally, lowering the gun. Phyllis sighed, wiping at the tears and blood that stained her face.

"Johnny, you got to get me out of here! I'm dyin'! I need a doctor!"

Suddenly, out of the pouring snow, Whitey appeared and ripped the gun from Johnny's hand, pulling the trigger. BANG! He blasted Phyllis in the face with a single gunshot.

"Shit, boy! You ain't good for nuthin', nuthin' at all."

In horror, Johnny dropped to his knees, staring at Phyllis's dead body. A steaming pool of warm blood quickly puddled around her head.

"Your 'pa was right. You ain't nuthin' but a coward."

Johnny looked up as Whitey flipped him the keys to the Jeep.

"Those are your only way out of here."

Johnny caught the keys and briefly stared at them, before glancing to Phyllis' dead body.

"And don't forget the Avon Lady."

Whitey quickly retreated to his car and sped away, taking all the stolen Avon bags of controlled drugs with him. Johnny studied the body a moment then looked to the Jeep that was about fifty feet away.

Pulling a ski cap from his coat pocket, he kneeled over Phyllis and looked away, before covering her head and unrecognizable face with the cap. He then took a frayed piece of rope from his pocket and tied it tight over the ski cap. Hesitating a moment, he finally grabbed her feet, one in each hand, and started to slowly drag the heavy body through the thick mud and accumulating snow towards the Jeep. As he dragged the body, a sweater and shirt balled up around Phyllis' neck and chest, exposing the gray skin of her bare fat belly. A trail of blood followed. At the Jeep, he reached underneath the armpits of the mud-caked body and hoisted it up, leaning it into the backseat. Taking her feet, he pushed and shoved at the lifeless lump of dead weight into the back of the Jeep enough to where he could slam the door shut.

He hurried into the driver seat and started the Jeep. Before pulling away, he glanced to the dead body in the back. A mix of blood, mud, and melting snow soiled the immaculate leather upholstery. He put the Jeep in drive and hit the gas. The back wheels violently spun, but the Jeep didn't move. He put it in reverse, the same. He tried quickly shifting back and forth between reverse and drive. Still, the Jeep didn't budge. He finally got out and studied the back tires, buried in deep mud. Scanning the desolate landscape, he gathered an armful of heavy sticks and fallen tree branches and placed them under each back tire. After several minutes of rocking the Jeep back and forth from drive to reverse, he was able to free it from the mud.

As he pulled onto the main road, he checked the fuel gauge. The muddy Jeep was full of gas. He figured he could travel pretty far on a full tank. He considered turning west and just driving as far as he could.

"What's the worst that could happened?" he mumbled to himself. "I get arrested."

And that may have been his best option at the time. His other prospects weren't good. He needed to get sober, and he certainly didn't want to end up at the bottom of the mine shaft with the others. And he knew he didn't have the constitution to help Whitey with the all the dirty work planned for him.

The pink Jeep hadn't been on the Route 15 more than a mile or two when a speeding car quickly pulled up close behind. He squinted in the rear-view mirror trying to determine what type of car was tailing him in the dark. Without warning, a blue light flashed, and a siren sounded. Johnny's first instinct was to stomp the gas pedal and try to outrun the cop car behind him. Instead, he found a clearing and eased the car off the side of the road. Glancing to Phyllis' dead body in the back, he figured he was going to jail, likely for a very long time, if not forever.

Aiming a flashlight at the driver's side window, a county deputy approached slowly. Johnny powered the window down and looked out, nearly blinded by the bright beam of light.

"What the hell? Johnny 'mother fuckin'' Fogg? Who went and named you Avon Lady for the county? You've the last person I expected to see behind the wheel. Where in the hell you take this thing?"

Johnny didn't say a word as the cop studied the mud-caked exterior of the pink Jeep.

"I wouldn't be out committin' crimes in this. You ain't no wallflower drivin' a pink car."

Wanting the whole charade that was his crumbling life to end, Johnny discretely signaled to the cop with his eyes to check the backseat. The cop showed him a puzzled look. Johnny motioned with his head towards the backseat. The cop flashed the light to the back end of the car. A bloody handprint and several splotches of blood stained the handle of the back door on the driver's side. The cop aimed the light inside the back seat. Seeing the desecrated body, he nearly fell over, dropping the flashlight on the ground. The cop shook his head, fumbled with the flashlight, and checked the backseat again, taking a deep breath. He stared for many minutes at the hooded, bloated body in the back. He then glanced several times to the empty roadway in each direction, before sticking the flashlight within inches of Johnny's face.

"I don't know what you got goin' on or who you're workin' for 'cause I know you're not capable of doin' somethin' like this on your own. But you better get the hell out of here. And if someone asks me, I ain't seen a thing."

Johnny stared at him a moment.

"Now, get the fuck out of here!" The cop shouted, ramming the flashlight into Johnny's face.

Johnny peeled away in the pink Jeep. The cop again glanced multiple times in each direction of the roadway, before hopping back into his squad car and speeding away in the opposite direction Johnny had taken.

In the kitchen of Butterman's house, I paced as Crystal sat at the table. We both were wearied and looked ragged. I was desperate. I had no idea what I'd do next and was scared for my life. She wouldn't look at me until I pounded my fist on the table. She finally glanced up.

"We're not safe here!"

"We're fine."

"Bullshit!"

"Just relax!"

"Relax? Johnny's dead! They may be coming after me next. Who did it?"

"I don't know."

"Yes, you do! Now tell me. Who killed Johnny?"

She looked away.

"How much is your dad paying you to yank my chain?"

"It's not what you think."

"You and your dad have made hundreds of thousands of dollars illegally selling drugs here."

"Not me."

"I saw the accounts. Your name's all over them."

"I never sold any drugs."

"Come on! Don't fucking lie to me anymore!"

"I just helped him with the other things."

"An accomplice, then."

"Whatever."

"I was brought in to work the drug store while your dad tended to his other activities, but he needed something to keep me distracted and occupied."

She looked back to me.

"And that's where you came in."

"You have quite the imagination."

"Well, the game's over. Aaron knew too much. He's missing. Johnny was starting to talk and now..."

I again slammed my fist on the table.

"Who's next, Crystal?"

"I don't know what you're talking about."

"I'm going to the police."

"Don't!"

"I need to save myself."

"Wait!"

She stood and approached me. I turned away.

"I'm not waiting anymore!"

"Not yet! Please!"

"Why?"

"I need your help, first."

"Help you? Why would I ever want to help you?"

A heavy snow poured from the black winter sky. Emotionless, Johnny stood, staring into the hole of the abandoned mine shaft. Snow quickly accumulated in the empty, blood-stained wheelbarrow beside him. Festive bluegrass music blared in the distance where the trailer convulsed from wild dancing in celebration. Phyllis Moody's muddy Jeep was parked outside. Johnny aimed his face to the sky and caught the falling snowflakes on his tongue. He was in no mood to celebrate with the others.

Crystal and I had hunkered down for the night at Butterman's house. I didn't feel safe, so I turned off all the lights and spent part of the night watching out the front window for anything that looked unusual or suspect. Crystal spent the night on the couch. I continually pressed her about what she knew of her father and his connection to the disappearance of Aaron and Johnny's supposed murder. She didn't say much, maintaining her ignorance regarding the details as well as denying any involvement. After several hours and unable to fight exhaustion any longer, I finally joined her on the couch sometime in the middle of the night. She had already fallen asleep. I snuggled in close to her and pulled a blanket over us. Sometime around daybreak, I slid my body away and stood over her, staring. I had come to a decision after agonizing about it for most of the night. I was left with no choice. Crystal opened her eyes as I pulled on my coat.

"Where you going?"

"I need to go to the drug store."

"I thought you were off today."

"I have to take care of something before the store opens."

"You're coming back, right?"

I slightly nodded as we stared at each other. She had to know I was lying. But she trusted I wouldn't turn her in to the police.

A thick fog darkened the frosty valley, blocking out the rising sun. All was quiet at the trailer. Morning had yet to arrive. The place was a disaster. Whiskey bottles, take-out food containers, and empty beer cans were strewn about on the tables and floors. Whitey slept in a chair with his head thrown back and a shotgun across his lap. On the couch, Dorsey, barely clothed, was entangled with two young local women from a nearby hollow who liked to party. Johnny was passed out on the floor. His dog, Rufus, was snuggled

241

up beside him, trying to keep warm. The front screen door squealed as it slowly opened, waking Whitey. He tightened his grip on the shotgun and raised it off his lap. Rufus quietly growled. Natural light quickly flooded the dark trailer. Squinting, Whitey aimed the gun at the visitor. Aaron Morgan stepped out of the light. Whitey grinned and lowered the gun.

"Good mornin', buddy. I didn't think you'd show. Are you ready?"

The roadway was quiet, but visibility was poor due to the early morning fog. Driving at a high rate of speed on the still damaged spare tire, I fiddled with the radio dial, searching through static and poor reception for a news station. Finally, I dialed in a local, all-night public broadcasting station and turned up the volume.

"...The lead story- a man's body was found late yesterday evening on the banks of the Big Tug River. Authorities have not yet identified the body. Foul play is suspected..."

Upon hearing the news, I drove faster. I was headed to the closest state police barracks. After arrival, I rushed into the chaos of the small but bustling office. I approached the front desk near the entrance. The officer at the desk hardly acknowledged me.

"Someone will help you in a minute," he said, not looking up.

Pacing and fidgeting, I nodded and took a seat. The officer jotted notes on a yellow notebook pad with one hand and held a phone receiver in the other.

Another officer in a different part of the office stood at his desk and turned.

"We got an ID on the body," he announced as the room got quiet. "It's a James Butterman. The pharmacist in Caldwell. He'd been shot in the head."

"What the…," I mumbled to myself, sliding from the chair and quietly slinking out of the office.

I fishtailed the speeding car in the snowy driveway of Butterman's house and skidded to a stop, nearly sliding into the garage door. I dashed up the icy stairs to the front door without taking time to shut off the engine or close the driver's side door. I burst into the living room, waking Crystal who slept on the couch.

"Crystal! Come on!"

She rolled over and looked up to me.

"Get up! Come on!"

Ignoring me, she rolled back over.

"We need to get out of here!"

I aggressively grabbed the back of her shirt, trying to pull her off the couch. She whipped around and batted my hands away.

"Take your fucking hands off me!"

"Come on we need to go!"

"I told you not to touch me like that!"

She stood and shoved me in the chest.

"We got to go! You don't understand!"

She tried to push me again, but I grabbed and held tightly onto her arms.

"Let's go!"

She struggled in my arms as I tried to hold her still.

"The body in the river..."

I paused as she fought to free her arms.

"It was your dad," I said as she glared at me with a blank stare. "We're not safe here. The state police are on their way."

She shoved me again, but this time harder, knocking me backwards.

"You're lying."

"We've got to go. Now!"

She tried to push me again, but instead, collapsed in my arms. I held her tightly.

"It can't be."

"We need to go."

Because of the bad tire, we took Crystal's Mustang as I sped over the rural highway. She sat beside me, lost in a daze. I headed to downtown Caldwell to the motel room. We needed a place to hide. With flashing lights and blaring sirens, multiple state police and county sheriff cars zipped by us, driving in the opposite direction. I glanced to Crystal.

"It was supposed to be Johnny," she mumbled, staring straight ahead.

"What?"

"It was supposed to be Johnny."

"So, you knew about this?"

"I need to call my mother."

"We're in trouble."

"How did this happen?"

"You tell me. You were part of all this."

"I need to call my mother."

"Where in the hell is Johnny?"

"There has to be a mistake," she said, shaking her head, still not looking at me.

"Why was your father back from Florida?"

Crystal glanced to me, not answering my questions. "You better start talking."

"Why'd you come back for me?" she asked as I glanced to the road but didn't respond. "You could've gotten out of this whole mess."

Aaron and Johnny were stoned and sat close together on a couch in the cluttered living room of the decaying trailer. The light from a muted, black and white television lit the room. Whitey loaded multiple shotguns. He was dead set on destruction. The haunting Johnny Dowd song, *"The Devil Don't Bother Me"*, played on an AM radio station. Bags of drugs, stacks of money, and a cache of guns and bullets were scattered around Whitey. Plastic garbage bags had been taped over the windows to block out the sun and, more importantly, hide them from the world.

"Aaron?" Whitey called out.

Struggling to keep his eyes open, Aaron glanced over.

"You ready to come back from the dead?"

Aaron didn't respond as his eyes slowly closed shut. Whitey looked to Johnny who glanced away.

"I need you, Johnny," Whitey said. "You'd be dead man, you know that?"

Whitey picked up a shotgun and reached it to Johnny. Fidgeting, Johnny nervously took the gun.

"We'll never pull this off without you. I need you, Johnny."

Johnny grimaced, staring at the shotgun, refusing to look at Whitey.

Crystal and I entered the motel room. I checked behind us to see if anybody had followed. The hallway was empty. I hadn't been in the room in weeks. It was spotless. The motel's lone maid had kept the room in order despite my absence. I pulled the heavy plastic curtains closed, darkening the room. Crystal sat on the bed as I turned on a lamp.

"I have to go out," she said, digging through a knapsack.

"You can't."

"I need cigarettes."

"What was your dad doing back from Florida?" I asked, pacing the floor.

"I'm going out," she said, standing.

I pushed her back on the bed. She gave me a dirty look.

"You can't keep me here."

She returned to digging through the knapsack, finally finding a single cigarette.

"What was he doing back here?"

"I don't know."

"Come on."

"I don't know!"

"He was trying to cover his tracks. But something went wrong, didn't it? What was it, Crystal?"

Not looking at me, she lit the cigarette and took a drag.

"Who killed your father?"

"I said, I don't know! I need to call my mother."

"You're not calling anyone until you tell me what in the hell's going on around here!"

"I told you. I don't know."

"I'm going to the police."

"No!"

"You better start talking then."

"My father was a control freak. He came here and took over the lives of everyone around him," she paused, taking a hit from the cigarette. "He used three things to take control."

"Drugs?"

"My father knew Aaron and Johnny and all the others would do anything for a fix."

"Sex?"

"He would fuck anyone or anything that helped him get what he wanted."

"Money?"

"He set up the bogus drug store account to hide the drug money. He put our names on the account to incriminate us all when we used it. So, you see, you can't go to the police."

"I never used the account."

"But you did. You signed and deposited the checks from the clinics."

"I never deposited them. When I saw your name on the account..."

"You didn't deposit the checks?" she interrupted, stubbing out the cigarette as I shook my head.

"Nope."

"I need more cigarettes."

She stood. I stepped in front of her and blocked her way.

"You can't keep me here."

We stared at each other a moment.

"If you didn't deposit the checks, just call the police. Turn me in."

"I tried, believe me."

"Why don't you do it?"

She glared at me for a few moments until I eventually moved out of her way. She slung the knapsack over her shoulder and left the room with a slam of the door. I thought I'd never see her again.

Phyllis Moody's pink Jeep was covered in mud. Large spots of dried blood stained the white leather interior of the backseat. Cigarette butts and empty cans of energy drink littered the floor. Whitey sat in the driver's seat; Johnny sat beside him; Aaron was in the back. All three looked haggard. None of them had bathed or changed clothes in weeks. The Jeep was parked across the street from the Caldwell Savings and Loan. Whitey continually checked the rear-view mirror.

"How much can you withdraw?" he asked Aaron, spying the entrance of the bank.

"I... I don't know."

"What do you mean you don't know?"

"I don't know!"

"Your name's on the fuckin' account!"

"I only made deposits."

Whitey glanced to Johnny who looked away.

"What are you spooked about?" Whitey barked, seeming anxious. "I should've fuckin' left you at home."

Whitey turned to Aaron.

"Here," he said, holding out a handgun- the same one used to kill Butterman, Phyllis, and Gloria. Aaron shook his head.

"Take it."

"What'll I need it for?"

"Take it!"

"No!"

"Take the goddamn gun!"

Aaron reluctantly took the gun, stuffing it in his coat pocket, and slowly got out of the Jeep. Whitey and Johnny intently studied the busy downtown street. Adjusting the knapsack on her shoulder, Crystal suddenly exited the bank and glanced to the Jeep. Holding a pink Avon telephone, Whitey watched until she disappeared around the corner. He dialed a number and put the phone to his ear.

"I would like to report a bank robbery in progress. The man is armed and appears to be whacked out on drugs."

Johnny showed Whitey a concerned look. Whitey shrugged.

As I paced around the motel room, Crystal entered, smacking an unopened pack of cigarettes against the palm of her hand. She threw her knapsack over the back of a chair and sat on the bed, opening the pack and pulling out a cigarette.

"I didn't think you'd come back."

"Michael, come sit with me," she said, lighting the cigarette and taking a long drag off it. "I need to tell you something."

I approached and stood over her.

"I've been afraid to tell you this."

"What?"

"I should've told you this sooner."

I continued to stand over her.

"Sit, please," she ordered, puffing the cigarette.

I finally took a seat beside her on the bed. She hesitated a moment before speaking.

"I'm pregnant."

"Huh?"

"I'm pregnant."

"Pregnant?"

"I've been sick for weeks."

"Are you sure?"

"I took the test three times."

"Positive?"

"All three times."

"I bet there's a dozen guys who could claim it."

"No, it's you."

"Bullshit."

"It's you."

"How are you so sure?"

"I haven't been with anyone else since I met you."

"Is this part of the script?"

She shook her head and showed me a serious look.

"No way. You're sure?"

"The is real, Michael. I'm completely, absolutely one-hundred percent pregnant."

"Shit, Crystal."

I fell back onto the bed and stared at the ceiling. Crystal snuggled up beside me. I wouldn't look at her.

"You okay?"

"I never imagined I'd find out that I'd be a father like this."

"With me?"

I glanced to her.

"You going to have it?"

"I don't expect anything from you," she said as a series of sirens suddenly blared outside.

"They're not coming here, are they?"

I hopped up from the bed and pulled aside the curtains. Several state police cars raced by the motel.

"They're headed to the bank."

Crystal joined me at the window.

"What do you think's happening there?"

As I glanced to Crystal, the door to the room unexpectedly banged open. She screamed as Whitey and Johnny barged in, carrying shotguns. I stepped in front of Crystal as they approached. Whitey raised his arms and violently cracked me in the forehead with the butt of a shotgun, knocking me unconscious. It would be the last thing I remembered that afternoon.

Leaving Phyllis Moody's Jeep behind, Whitey sped by all the flashing blue and red lights at the bank in Crystal's Mustang. Every available state police and sheriff's car in the county must have been there. Crystal sat beside Whitey in the passenger seat, and Johnny was in back. I was unconscious, bound, and gagged next to Johnny. He kept looking at me. The bruised knot on my forehead was bleeding.

"Why'd the fuck you kill my father?"

"More for us, baby."

"That wasn't the plan!"

"What's the big deal? You never liked the asshole."

Whitey glanced to Johnny.

"He was going to kill Johnny, and I like Johnny. Ain't that right?"

Johnny nervously nodded as Crystal checked Michael.

"What do you see in homeboy anyway?"

"You didn't need to hit him so hard."

"If it was up to me, I would've shot him."

Crystal glanced away and stared out the window.

"Everything's done," Whitey boasted. "Butterman's out. You made the withdrawals and closed his accounts. Aaron's out. They got the gun. The cops ain't got nothin' on us."

Crystal looked back and studied Michael.

"We have only one thing left."

She glanced away.

Groggy with blurred vision, I struggled to open my eyes and keep them open. I had no idea where I was or what had happened. I felt as if I had been drugged. I was still gagged and had been tied to a chair in a corner. I had trouble breathing with a dirty rag taped inside my mouth. Because I faced the wall, I couldn't tell what exactly was taking place behind me. I did recognize the voices of Whitey and Crystal as they talked in an adjoining room of a trailer.

"As long as lover boy's alive, he's trouble," Whitey said as he and Crystal divided out large stacks of $100 bills.

As I began to regain more of my senses, I was able to turn enough of my body around to witness what they were doing. Crystal occasionally would glance over to me as they counted the money. Johnny held a shotgun and watched.

"Don't do anything until I'm gone," she said to Whitey.

"He's a dead man by mornin'."

I stared at Johnny, trying to get his attention. He wouldn't look at me. I glanced to Crystal who filled a knapsack with what must have been over a half of million dollars. She finally looked to me. I glared back. She showed no expression or offered any apology with her eyes. She turned away and left me nothing. Johnny quickly followed her as I tried my hardest to scream and shake myself free from the chair. I was able to bounce and shake the chair a few feet where I was close enough to bump myself against the wall to make a knocking noise. Hearing the noise from the other room, Whitey rolled his eyes around as if inconvenienced, before rushing in and nailing me in the middle of the face with a hard punch that busted the bridge of my nose open. Blood flowed over my face and shirt. He slammed the door to the room as he left. Gagged and nearly suffocating, I struggled to breathe through the broken nose.

Whitey was huddled next to Johnny on the couch in the front room and excitedly pulled the coffee table closer to them. Whitey opened a fresh bag of insulin needles and syringes and fumbled with a lighter, before tossing a small square of heroin wrapped in aluminum foil on the table. Crystal watched them, pulling on coat.

"You doing that now?"

"Come on, Crystal. Join us. You used to love to party."

Ignoring him, she threw the knapsack of cash over her shoulder.

"You'll be broke by the fourth of July," she said, stepping through the littered trailer.

"Hell, I could be dead tomorrow," he said as Crystal reached for the front door causing him to ask, "where you goin'?"

"A long way from here."

"You'll be back," he predicted as Crystal hesitated at door. "You always came back."

At an excessive rate of speed, Crystal sped the Mustang across the dark, deserted rural highway and headed south. She kept checking for the knapsack of cash in the passenger seat beside her. It was still there. She also continually checked the rear-view mirror. No one followed. She had planned to go to Florida for a new start. Suddenly, she wasn't so sure. As she drove away from Caldwell, she expected to feel much different. She thought she'd finally be free. Instead, she felt the opposite, shackled to the past and burdened by an overpowering emotion she'd never experienced before or ever wanted. Whitey was right, and she knew it. She couldn't leave Caldwell- not yet anyway. As much as she despised the idea, she had to turn back.

As the car raced on, Crystal screamed aloud, pounding the steering wheel with her fists. She slammed the brakes as the Mustang shimmied over the yellow line into the other lane, before shrieking to a stop. Tightly grabbing the wheel, she violently shook it several times before taking a deep breath. After a few moments, she slammed the gas pedal, made a sweeping wide, left-hand turn on a narrow stretch of backroad, and headed north. She had never been in love before, and as she retreated to Caldwell, she especially hated how it had seized control of her life.

Crystal gently pushed open the front door to the trailer and peeked inside. Whitey and Johnny were both passed out on the couch. Johnny's dog softly growled as Crystal entered. She put a finger to her lips, signaling to the dog to keep quiet. She crept to the backroom and cautiously entered, closely the door behind her. Still tied up and covered in blood from the busted nose, I squirmed in the chair and tried to scream, knowing someone had entered the room behind me.

"Ssssh," Crystal whispered, blowing her warm breath in my ear.

She ripped the tape from my mouth as I spit out the rag and took several deep gasps for air. She then took both my numbed hands that felt like pin cushions and gently caressed them back to life. I squeezed her hands back, finally letting go as she produced a long hunting knife.

"Why'd you come back?" I whispered as she frantically sawed at the rope bound around my wrists with the knife.

"You got to get outta here."

"I'm going with you."

"You can't."

Click! Whitey cocked a shotgun and placed the end of the barrel against the back of Crystal's head before she could untie my arms and legs.

"No one's goin' nowhere!"

The Johnny Dowd song, *"No Woman's Flesh but Hers"*, blared at an ear blistering level from a console stereo. On an uncovered, stained mattress, Whitey had tied Crystal, spread eagle, to four bedposts. He roughly yanked and pulled, tightening the ropes around her ankles and wrists. I was still bound to the chair. Both Crystal and I were gagged.

"I want you to watch this," Whitey grinned, dragging the chair I was tied to up against the bed.

Clutching the hunting knife that Crystal used to try and free me, Whitey quickly hopped onto the mattress and crawled on top of her. He continually grinded and humped his pelvis into her body- starting at her legs, then moving over her stomach and breasts, and finally against her face. Turning her head away, she violently thrashed her body and ripped and kicked at the ropes around her arms and legs, trying to free herself. Whitey smacked her face to get her to calm down, before grabbing her throat.

"Settle down, bitch!" he grunted, straddling his crotch around her legs- his legs bent backwards.

He slapped her again across the face. She stopped moving and glared at him. With the knife, he pricked her cheek, drawing blood. I tried to scream, hopping up and down, still tied to the chair. Whitey look over and laughed at me. The blood rolled into Crystal's mouth. As she turned trying to wipe her face against the mattress, Whitey proceeded to slowly slice her clothes open, hacking off each button of her blouse with the blade. In the adjoining room, Johnny awoke upon hearing the struggle coming from the bedroom.

With his pants unbuckled, Whitey ran his hand along the front of Crystal's jeans, while grinding on her legs. Her struggle become more violent as he slipped his fingers inside her jeans and underwear. I again hopped up and down in the chair as he nibbled her ear. Laughing, he pulled his hand from her jeans and stuck his fingers in my face and shoved them in my nose. Crystal kicked and flailed her body under his. I tried my hardest to turn my head away.

"I bet you miss the smell of this?" he sneered.

Unexpectedly, the door to the room burst open. Turning, Whitey hopped off Crystal, dropping the knife. Sweating and shaking, Johnny rushed into the room, holding a shotgun. Whitey grinned and shook his head, his trousers unbuckled. Johnny stepped forward and raised the gun at Whitey.

"Put the gun down, Johnny."

Johnny didn't move,

"I saved your life. Remember?"

Johnny still didn't move.

"Gimme the gun."

Johnny shook his head and closed his eyes. I looked to Crystal who stared back at me. Whitey shuffled a few steps closer to Johnny who glanced to me. I shook my head. Johnny glanced to Crystal.

"Remember, Johnny?" Whitey said, pointing to Crystal who shook her head. "It was her dad. Her DAD who lied to you! Remember? Her dad wanted to frame you for murder."

Johnny shook his head and looked to Crystal. Whitey eased a step forward. Johnny glanced back to him and lifted the gun higher.

"Put the gun down."

Johnny slowly started to lower the gun, before glancing first to me, then to Crystal. We both shook our heads.

"We're friends, Johnny," Whitey continued, again stepping forward. "You know and I know, you're a nice fellow. You don't want to hurt no one."

Johnny glared at him, shaking his head.

"Besides, it takes guts to kill someone, Johnny," Whitey said, stepping even closer to Johnny. "I don't believe you got the guts. Your daddy was right. You don't got the guts to do nuthin'."

Johnny shook his head several times and gritted his teeth.

"You're a coward."

Johnny pulled the trigger. Pop... Nothing happened. He tried the trigger again but squeezed it tighter that time. Pop... The gun was unloaded. Closing our eyes, Crystal and I audibly moaned and dropped our heads. Whitey smiled and laughed out loud.

"Goddang! I thought of everything!"

Whitey yanked the shotgun from Johnny who looked both stunned and helpless.

"Fuckin' punk! I saved your ass!"

Whitey pulled two shells from his pocket and loaded the shotgun, glaring at Johnny.

"You're next!"

Whitey angrily shoved the gun against my forehead.

"I should've done this already."

Crystal pleaded with him, trying to scream and talk through the tape. Whitey violently ripped the duct tape from across her mouth. The pain nearly took her breath away.

"Wait!" Crystal pleaded. "He's done nothing to you!"

"It don't matter," Whitey shook his head, pressing the barrel of the gun harder against my forehead.

I closed my eyes and lowered my head. 'Get it over with' was my initial thought. As hard as I tried not to, I couldn't help thinking about Meredith moving back to Pittsburgh. I should be there, planning our wedding and watching football in a warm living room instead of waiting for my execution.

"Take me instead," Crystal pleaded.

"Oh, I will, not 'til we have fun some first."

Whitey looked back to me. I glanced up and did my best to stare him down. He grinned.

"This is so fuckin' easy for me. You don't even know."

Visions of my grandmother flashed in the many thoughts rushing through my head. I didn't want her to know I'd been murdered. I knew I was destined for the mine shaft to be lost forever. Hopefully, someone will get her the few thousand dollars of cash I had saved for her from Butterman's house. I then glanced to Crystal, who cried, shaking her head. He ripped off the tape that covered my mouth.

"Any last words, lover boy?"

"No!" she screamed as I lowered my head and closed my eyes again.

In a flash and without warning, Johnny lunged forward, scooped up the hunting knife off the floor, and plunged it deep into Whitey's back. Whitey jerked up with a groan, firing the shotgun into the ceiling. Shards of the fiberglass and cardboard from the ceiling rained down on me as Whitey collapsed to his knees, the knife still stuck in his back. Johnny violently ripped the knife out as Whitey fell forward with a shriek, followed by a loud thud at my bound feet. Johnny reached for the shotgun and kicked Whitey over onto his back. Blood streamed from the side of his mouth. Tears rolled from his eyes. Johnny aimed the gun at Whitey who grinned.

"If I was you," he mumbled, struggling to breathe- his face turning gray. "I'd make me suffer."

"I'm only doin' you a favor."

Without hesitating, Johnny pulled the trigger as a loud blast followed. BANG!

He immediately dropped the smoking gun, staring at Whitey. I sighed, wanting to get the hell out of there as fast as I could. Blood poured from a large hole in the middle of Whitey's chest and flooded the floor.

"Johnny!" Crystal called out.

Johnny moved to the bed and cut Crystal free. She immediately took control of the situation. First, she retrieved the shotgun from the floor. She went around the room, gathering up unspent shotgun shells that had fallen out of Whitey's shirt pocket. Reloading the shotgun, she looked at a despondent Johnny who again studied Whitey's dead body with a trance-like gaze.

"Johnny," she said, grabbing the end of one of Whitey's leg and bracing the shotgun between her side and one of her arms. "Help me move him."

Johnny didn't budge from his spot as if hypnotized by Whitey's corpse. I watched, still tied to the chair, waiting to be set free.

"Get the other leg," she ordered. "Johnny!"

Eventually, Johnny snapped out of the trance and approached Whitey's lifeless body. He hesitated initially before grabbing the other the leg. The two of them squatted, pulling the body into the front room of the trailer and leaving it just inside the screen door. Crystal then grabbed a set of truck keys on a table by the door and tossed them to Johnny.

"Now, get out of here," she said as Johnny caught the keys and stared at them in his hands. "Get out of here, Johnny!"

He glanced up to her, then looked over to me.

"Go, Johnny! I'm serious! Get the fuck out here!"

Johnny didn't move still staring at me, searching for a sign about what to do next. I shrugged as Crystal set down the shotgun and violently grabbed the back of Johnny's flannel shirt.

"I said, 'get the fuck out of here'!" she yelled, dragging him towards the door.

She kicked open the screen door and released his shirt from her grasp, pushing him outside.

"It isn't safe, Johnny," she said. "You need to get out of here and never come back."

I continued to watch still tied to the chair and wondered what Crystal knew that Johnny and I didn't. After Johnny drove off in the truck, Crystal returned to the bedroom. I thought to free me. Instead, she turned the chair that I was tied to around and pushed it to the wall next to the bed. I no longer faced the door to the bedroom.

"What are you doing?"

"You'll thank me later," she answered, hurriedly pulling the ropes tighter around my wrists and ankles, nearly cutting off the circulation to my arms and legs.

"Crystal!" I violently shook the chair with my entire body, unable to see what was happening behind me. "Untie me!"

"Calm down!" she loudly screamed in my ear causing me to cringe.

She reached for the additional pieces of rope from the bedposts and began to tie one side of the chair to the head bedpost and frame, securing it in such a way that I couldn't move it.

"Crystal? Hey! What are you doing? Untie me!"

She didn't say a word, turning off the lights to the room as each of my legs started to go numb. For several minutes, which seemed like hours, I sat silent in the darkness. Nothing in the trailer moved or made a noise.

"Crystal?" I whispered into the dark. "Crystal?"

Finally, the screen door slowly screeched open then slammed shut. I couldn't tell if someone had entered or exited the trailer, but it sounded more like someone had just left. I hoped that it wasn't Crystal, leaving me alone to suffer, or even possibly die. Johnny was the only other person who knew that I was there, and Crystal scared him away. But why did she come back for me in the first place when Whitey was still alive?

The screen door opened and closed again. It sounded as if someone had entered the trailer that time. I sat as still as I could. Along with my legs, my arms had started to go numb as well. The light to the bedroom suddenly flashed on. I didn't move. I wanted to call out, but I couldn't. I sensed someone's eyes all over me. I prayed it was Crystal, but I was expecting the worse. Nearly ready to break and scream out, I heard Crystal's voice.

"I'm sorry."

A loud shotgun blast rang out, shaking the trailer and knocking the chair I was in askew. Behind me, a body hit the floor with a thud. Silence followed. Within seconds, blood flowed across the floor and underneath the chair, soaking into my shoes and the bottoms of my pant legs. My limp body hung from the chair angled to the floor- the ropes tearing at the skin of my wrists and ankles. My first thought as I tried to process what had just happened was that Crystal had shot and killed herself.

"Crystal!" I screamed. "Crystal! Crystal!"

There was no answer or any other sound. I didn't recall hearing anyone leave the trailer after the blast. Frightened for my life and ignoring the pain, I tried to free myself from the chair, ripping and tugging with my entire body, using what little strength I had, to try and loosen the ropes that bound me. It was to no avail. Desperate and losing hope, I started to hyperventilate. Then, I gagged and dry-heaved as fresh blood continued to pool under my feet. My heart palpitated; my legs and arms went dead. I finally vomited a mostly clear liquid, having not eaten for hours. The pain in my wrists and ankles had become unbearable after I rubbed them raw, attempting to escape. Eventually, I blacked out, still bound to the chair and struggling to breathe.

I didn't regain consciousness until sometime in the morning. Although overcast, the light from the new day woke me. I was still in the chair, but it had been returned to its upright position and untied from the bed, facing the doorway to the room. It didn't appear as if anyone was in the trailer. The dead bodies had been removed, and the pools of blood had been mostly cleaned up. My lips were badly chapped. I struggled to open my mouth that was parched from not having anything to drink for over a day. I noticed that the ropes around my wrists and ankles had been loosened. I was able to easily slip my stiff and sore arms and legs free from the chair. It took me a few moments to get my legs to work enough so that I could stand. Shaking my arms to try to bring them back to life, I staggered like a drunk to the bathroom sink and immediately stuck my head under the running faucet, desperately drinking at the warm, metal-heavy water. Never had a drink tasted so good.

After re-hydrating, I walked into the front room. Everything was gone- the money, the drugs, the guns, everything. I took a seat on the couch and stayed there motionless for almost an hour, trying to regroup and comprehend what had happened to me the previous forty-eight hours. I worried I was still in danger. I hoped and prayed that Crystal was alive. I wondered if anyone would come back for me. But someone did at some point in the night to clean up the mess and unbind me from the chair. They then must've wanted me to get out of there.

Gradually gaining my strength back, I slowly moved to a window in front of the trailer and gazed out. Johnny Fogg's red pick-up was parked outside. I glanced around the inside of the trailer before stepping out. Without hesitating, I sprinted to the truck and pulled at the driver's side door. Luckily, it was unlocked. Taking a deep breath, I checked the ignition. The keys were there. I hopped into the driver's seat with a slam of the door, started the truck, and punched the accelerator with my foot. I couldn't get out of there fast enough. I followed a beat-up and muddy dirt road for several miles, hoping that I was traveling towards a main route or highway and not deeper into the hollow. I also hoped that I wouldn't encounter any other vehicles that perhaps were headed back to the trailer. In no time, I found myself on an unfamiliar part of Route 15.

After a thirty-minute drive, I entered Caldwell and parked the truck in a non-descript public parking lot on the edge of downtown. I remained in the truck for a few minutes, surveying the area and checking to see if anyone was around. I reached for a hooded jacket on the seat that must've belonged to Johnny and slipped it on. Finally, when it appeared the street was mostly empty, I slowly got out of the truck, leaving the keys in the ignition. I flipped the hood over my head, trying my best to hide my face. At a quick pace, I walked directly to the motel, avoiding eye contact with the few people on the streets I encountered. Once in the motel, I stopped at the entrance of the diner. The smell of coffee and fresh-baked pastries froze me in my tracks. I quickly made a beeline to the counter and put in an order.

"What happened to your face?" the lady at the register asked, not seeming to recognize me. "Car accident or something? Those roads have been nasty."

"Yeah," I mumbled, not looking her in the eyes and pulling more of the jacket's hood over my head.

"Looks like you hit your face pretty good," she said, handing me a large coffee and a box of warm cinnamon rolls and homemade doughnuts.

Luckily, I didn't have to work in the pharmacy for the next few days as I disappeared into the motel room, locking the door. The rope burns on my wrists and ankles were blistered and swollen. Some even bled. Not having any kind of medicated cream or ointment and not wanting to be seen in the drug store, I grabbed several wash clothes from the bathroom and soaked them in very hot water before wrapping them around the wounds to soothe the sores. I found a small bandage and applied it the oozing cut on the bridge of my busted nose. I then eased myself into a desk chair and quickly devoured the entire box of pastries, gulping at the coffee in between bites. Unable to hold off sleep any longer, I crawled into bed nearly paralyzed from what I had just experienced. On my back with little energy to turn my aching body over, I immediately fell asleep. It was a hard sixteen hours of sleep without dreams or nightmares. I had already lived the nightmare. I hoped it was finally over.

Chapter 10
Hardly Getting Over It

Like a stray cat lost in the dark, the new year quietly slipped into Caldwell with hardly a notice. It was without confetti, champagne, or celebration. It was a new day, and perhaps for me, a new start. A mix of sleet and freezing rain fell from a dark afternoon sky as I raced across a slick Route 27 on my way to Frank's Supper Club in a desperate attempt to find Crystal. It had been weeks since Whitey's death, and I hadn't seen her. Nobody had. Since the fateful night at the trailer, I had regularly stopped by her apartment and drove around the county, searching for her. There was no sign of her or the Mustang. I hoped she was still in the area and had not moved back to Florida with her mother and sister. But more importantly, I prayed she was still alive.

The club's mostly empty parking lot was covered with a fresh coating of snow. I hopped out of the car and entered. I stood in the doorway and watched Jack Chub perform a soulful version of Daniel Johnston's sparse, but hopeful ballad *"Love Will Find You in the End."* Four disinterested, back-wood rednecks sat at the bar, disengaged from a world that ignored them, staring into draughts of light beer. A barstool separated each of them. After the song, I was the only one who clapped. Jack acknowledged me with a head nod and started into throaty version of 'Blue

Valentine'. Taking a seat at the bar, I ordered a stout and shot of whiskey.

"Have you seen Crystal Foley?" I asked Sam, the bartender, before knocking back the whiskey.

"Nope," he answered with an affirmative shake of his head.

I nodded as he refilled the shot glass. I threw a twenty-dollar bill on the bar and drained the second shot. I listened to a few songs by Jack as I finished the stout. Before leaving, I walked to the stage and tossed a one-hundred-dollar bill into the empty tip jar. Jack smiled.

"Have you seen Johnny?" he asked.

"No, I haven't."

"If you do, can you tell 'em 'Jack's lookin' for 'em'?"

"I think he's starting over."

"A fresh start's nearly always good, but hard to do, especially here. I know. I've tried."

My next stop was Butterman's then-abandoned house. Still with a key, I cautiously entered. The sprawling house was eerily quiet. It had been locked since Crystal and I found out about his death. By the mess and musty smell of the place, it didn't seem as if anyone had been there. Dirty dishes filled the sink. The trashcan in the kitchen was full and needed to be emptied. Crystal's water glass hadn't moved where she had left it last by the couch when I informed her that her father was dead. There was an ashtray filled with lipstick-stained cigarette butts. Many of Crystal's personal items remained- a sweater, a partial pack of cigarettes, a faded t-shirt, lip gloss, assorted chocolates, and a knit winter hat. I reached for the hat and held it close to my face. The clean, fresh scent of citrus and coconut left behind from the shampoo, soaps, and oils she preferred immediately reminded me of the first night she took me for a ride in her new Mustang to the Supper Club. Holding the knit hat to my face, I had to find out what had happened to her. I couldn't leave town without knowing.

A muted sun had just set as darkness covered the dreary New Year's Day landscape. In a longshot attempt to locate Crystal, I drove to her apartment one final time. There was still no sign of the Mustang. A fresh, undisturbed inch of snow covered the empty driveway and sidewalk that led to the front door. I pulled into the driveway, parked the car, shut off the engine, and waited. I studied the darkened apartment for nearly an hour, not taking my eyes off the place. I eventually thought that I had seen the curtain from a first-floor window move. I hurriedly got out of the car and rushed to the entrance.

"Crystal!" I called, knocking on the front door. "Crystal!"

The place was quiet; nothing stirred, and no one answered.

"Crystal!" I called again, pounding on the door. "Please! We need to talk!"

I tried turning the front doorknob, but it was locked.

"Crystal!" I called out, aggressively shaking at the locked door.

After a few minutes, I retreated to the car and stared at the apartment. Again, I believed I saw the same curtain in the same window slightly move. But maybe it didn't, I wasn't sure. Maybe I imagined it had. I desperately wanted and needed to see Crystal again to know that she was all right, and at the very least, to say goodbye. I was leaving Caldwell soon and felt helpless not knowing her fate. Before I could pull away, I got out of the car and stood outside the bedroom window, tapping it repeatedly. But the curtain didn't move, and no one came to the window. I returned to the car and again watched the apartment for a short time, before driving away.

The January sky busted open. Large flakes of snow poured and fluttered with a stiff, frosty wind. The frozen landscape was gray, and the mood was darker. Alone, Crystal stood at the doorway of an old shack, carrying a familiar knapsack that hung from her shoulder. Her bright red Mustang looked out of place. It was parked off a mostly unpassable hollow road, outside the rundown shack nestled in a grove of young pines and leafless maple trees. The air was filled with the smell of burning wood. A blueish-white plume of smoke billowed from a crumbling brick chimney attached to the side of the shack. The wind howled through the empty branches of the tall maples that marked the property.

Crystal knocked on the door and waited several minutes. Eventually, the door slowly pushed open. Bundled in a fur hat, stained heavy down coat, and wool socks, Johnny Fogg appeared. He was unshaven, pale, and looked to have lost weight, which was significant as he didn't have much weight to lose.

He stared at Crystal unable to hide his shivering body. She studied him closely.

"You okay?"

"Ain't never been sicker. Can't sleep. I piss myself when I do. Can't eat. If I do, I puke it up or shits myself. Can't get warm. I jus' sits here and stares at the fire, like I'm waitin' to die."

She continued to study him.

"Tryin' to live a clean life," he said, "is hard, whether you want it or not."

"Do you need anything?"

He shook his head as she reached the knapsack to him.

"What's this?" he asked, taking it.

"It's all there."

He pulled out a handful of one-hundred-dollar bills bundled together and stared at the money a moment.

"What am I goin' do with it?"

"Spend it, save it, give it away. I don't care. I don't want anything to do with it."

He stared at her, then gazed back to the money.

"So long, Johnny."

He continued to study the money as she walked to her car and pulled away. Johnny backed into the shack that had been vacant since his father's death many years ago and was greeted by his dog. He petted Rufus a few times, before grabbing a log on the fireplace hearth next to a smoldering fire. He poked the small fire a couple of times with an iron shaft, causing it spark. The dog wandered closer to the fire as he tossed the log in. After warming his shivering hands a moment, he entered the sparse kitchen followed by the dog and filled the dog's bowls with fresh food and water. At the door, he stepped into a pair of worn-out, mud-caked boots and slipped his shaking hands into wool mittens. Reaching for the knapsack, he walked outside.

Slinging the pack of money over his back, he tracked up a trail and over a hill that were covered with a fresh layer of snow for nearly one-half mile. His breath hung heavy in the air as he stopped to take a break, lighting a cigarette with still shaky, unsteady hands. With the cigarette dangling from his mouth, he readjusted the pack on his back and started up a second hill. After another quarter of a mile, he climbed a third hill and approached an empty, blood-stained wheelbarrow that distinctly sat alone, nearly buried in snow in a mostly flat field next to a familiar mine shaft. His father's shack was located on an opposite ridge from the infamous trailer Johnny tried to forget.

Lighting a cigarette, he stepped to the edge of the shaft and stared into the dark void- a void that hid many awful secrets known only to Johnny. Removing his wool hat, he scratched the crown of his head and wiped at the sweat on his forehead. He calmly pulled the pack from his back, unzipped it open, and stared at the money, taking several puffs on the cigarette. After a brief hesitation, he turned the pack upside down and shook it until all of a million dollars disappeared. He then spiked the empty knapsack into the shaft and flicked the cigarette in behind it. Staring into the shaft, he took another step closer to the edge. Not looking away from the black hole, his hands shook more violently. The cold, brisk wind blew against his gaunt, weary face and lifted his thinning hair from his head, tossing it over his eyes. He moved the hair from his eyes, still staring at the empty space. Tears rolled down his cheeks, and his nose started to run. He sobbed out loud and closed his eyes. Breathing heavy, his heart pounded. For many minutes, he fought with all the strength he had an overwhelming urge to take one last, unforgiving step forward.

"Aaaawwwww!" he screamed out, struggling to take a step back from the edge, almost as if paralyzed.

Backing away from the hole, he fell to his knees in the snow and wept, pounding the frozen ground. For he knew, that wouldn't be last time he would have to fight with the little strength left in his soul to save himself.

I stood at the pharmacy counter having just filled my last prescription at the drug store. My forehead and nose looked better. I had told everyone the bumps and bruises were from a fall on the ice. Evelyn seemed upset about my leaving Caldwell. She didn't say a word to me that morning. Archie rambled on as usual. He was more concerned about the Caldwell County high football team not making the state playoffs for the thirtieth straight time that year. Mr. Morris snoozed in the waiting area. As the replacement pharmacist approached, I removed my Super-Rite smock and handed it to Tammy. She was still distraught about Butterman's death. It had been difficult listening to the crazy and outlandish theories involving Butterman and his murder being discussed and debated by the regular customers in the store, knowing what had really happened.

Tammy and I hadn't talked much the last few days that I worked. I had offered my resignation to Super-Rite soon after the incident at the trailer. Because of the unusual circumstances concerning the store with Butterman's death, the corporate office reluctantly let me out of my contract early. Fortunately, they also had been able to hire a new pharmacist to replace me, allowing me to leave the store as soon as I wanted. I glanced around the pharmacy feeling a little sad to be leaving but curious about what would be next. Tammy reached her arms out and hugged me.

"We wish you'd reconsider," she said, letting go of me. "We still could use one more pharmacist."

"I need to join the real world again."

"Why don't you move into Mr. Butterman's place?"

"I wish it was that easy."

"Please stop and visit if you're ever passin' through."

"Who passes through here?"

She smiled. I nodded and looked around, before shaking the new pharmacist's hand and stepping out of the drug store for the final time. It was a chilly but sunny day. Town was bustling. The downtown streets were crowded, mostly because it was the beginning of the month and the locals had money to burn as the social security and welfare checks were out. I didn't have any idea of what I would do next, or more importantly, where I would go. But I did know, at least I thought, I needed out of Caldwell.

As I stood in the entrance of the drug store, I glanced around town. I only had lived and worked there a short time, but oddly it felt like home, even more so than Pittsburgh. I would miss the place. I gazed briefly at the savings and loan. Aaron's attempted robbery there, or Whitey's set-up of Aaron, happened only a few weeks earlier. The folks in the area appeared to have quickly forgotten about it. Scores of people entered and exited the bank with hearty salutations and friendly greetings for one another without seemingly a care in the world. But not me. When I thought of that day, I had a better appreciation of the brevity of life. I was lucky to be alive.

I then glanced to the motel and thought of Crystal. I would never forget the first time I saw her or our first trip to the Supper Club. I thought of her laughing smile when we fished and swam in the river, the night in the field under the stars. I missed our late nights together- the feel of her warm skin under me, in my hands. And I could never forget the moment she informed me that I was to be a father. The thought of not seeing Crystal again left me with a sick feeling and an emptiness I couldn't describe. But it was most likely for the best that I was leaving Caldwell alone. I had a clean slate- a chance for a new start, and I was a much different than when I arrived several months earlier.

I stepped away from the drug store and walked to my car in the parking lot. My initial plan was to drive south, someplace warm, a beach maybe, and take a needed vacation. I hadn't fully processed everything that I experienced and even survived through while in West Virginia. I even thought of going back to Pittsburgh, moving into my grandmother's home, and re-charging my batteries, as they say, before making any real decisions. Before I could go anywhere, I needed to make one last stop at Butterman's house to retrieve the last of my belongings.

As I approached the driveway to the house, I slowed the car. Crystal's red Mustang was parked close against the garage door. I hesitated a moment before pulling in behind it. I sat inside my car with it running for many minutes, staring at the house. Finally, I got out and climbed the stairs in front. I tried the door. It was unlocked. I took a deep breath and pushed it open. All the lights were off. Crystal sat on the floor in the living room next to the fireplace. A blazing fire roared, illuminating the room. We didn't say a word for several minutes.

"When I saw your car," I finally spoke, "I almost didn't come in."

"Are you going back to Pittsburgh?"

We studied each other. I didn't move from the open doorway.

"I don't think I've ever be the same," I confessed. "I'm hardly getting over it."

I entered. We didn't take our eyes from each other. I sat on the couch across from her.

"I thought you might be dead. Where've you been?"

"Can you be a pharmacist anywhere?"

"I'd have to get a license in the state where I ended up."

"Would that be hard?"

"Who'd you kill behind my back in the trailer?"

"It was self-defense," she quickly said.

"Who was it?"

"Dorsey."

"Dorsey?"

"He was Whitey's back-up. Dorsey would come kill us all if something went wrong. He was distracted when he found you tied to a chair."

"So, I was bait?"

"You're alive. And I knew if Dorsey was still around, we were in trouble. He knew about everything."

"I've been waiting for the sheriff to visit."

"Don't worry. He's as crooked as all the others. He doesn't need anyone snooping around here. He conveniently shuttled Aaron from prison to a rehab hospital a long way from here."

"And the Dorsey brothers?"

"Will never be found."

"Were you the one who got rid of their bodies and the mess?"

"Yes."

"And the drugs and guns?"

"Gone."

"What about all that money?"

"Still, so many questions."

"Where's the money?"

"I gave it away."

"All of it?"

"All of it."

I slid off the couch and joined her on the floor.

"What about your fiancée?" she asked, not taking her eyes from mine.

"The ring's at the pawn shop."

We stared a moment, not saying a word. She turned and peered into the fire.

"You don't have to be anywhere, do you?"

"Not immediately," I said.

"We can stay here, at least until spring. There's plenty of food and wood for the fireplace. And the Chicken Man will be open if we get bored."

She glanced back to me.

"This feels like home."

"What's up with the baby?"

"You're off the hook."

I didn't initially respond. She turned away and stared into the fire.

"You all right?"

"I'd like to try again," she said, not much louder than a whisper.

I gently rubbed her back as she tried to quickly wipe at her glistening eyes without me noticing.

"What happens after spring?" I asked.

"Does it matter if we have each other?"

She turned and faced me. I edged my body closer. Her teary eyes sparkled in the dancing orange glow of the burning fire.

"I won't leave Caldwell without you," she said, reaching out her hand.

"I'd follow you to hell at this point," I said, taking her hand in mine.

"You already have."

She tried to pull her hand away, but I wouldn't let her.

"I won't let go this time."

And I didn't. I held her hand through the night and into the next morning as she fell asleep in my arms under a blanket on the floor. We kept the fire burning for days, not leaving the house. I tried not to think about what would happen next. Spring was out of sight and far away. As I pulled her body closer to mine, my future was more uncertain than ever- my life temporarily placed on hold. But I didn't care. Never had I been so free. And we both were finally home.

THE END.

About the Author

Jim Antonini resides in Morgantown, WV. Excerpts of this book placed as a quarterfinalist in the 2013 Writers on the Storm Competition, a quarterfinalist in the 2013 Scriptapalooza Screenplay Competition, and a semi-finalist in the 2013 Screenplay Festival Competition.

Cover artwork by Chris Antonini.

CPSIA information can be obtained
at www.ICGtesting.com
Printed in the USA
BVHW071148080720
583260BV00001B/15

9 780578 671215